Copyright © 2021 by Rae B. Lake

All rights reserved.

No part of this book may be reproduced in any form or by any electronic or mechanical means, including information storage and retrieval systems, without written permission from the author, except for the use of brief quotations in a book review.

SVEN'S MARK

JURIC CRIME FAMILY
BOOK ONE

RAE B. LAKE

ACKNOWLEDGMENTS

To my Goodfella! LOL, we both know I have an unhealthy obsession with that movie. Thank you so much for putting up with my ticks and eccentricities. Your acceptance and support makes all this so much easier.

To my mini bosses- One day you both will grow up and rule the world. I have no doubt that you will be the best that you can be and momma can't wait to see what life has in store for you.

To my friends, family and readers! ARE YOU READY!!! Step into the Juric family. This is the first full length novel in my mafia series. I hope you love it! I know I had so much fun writing it!

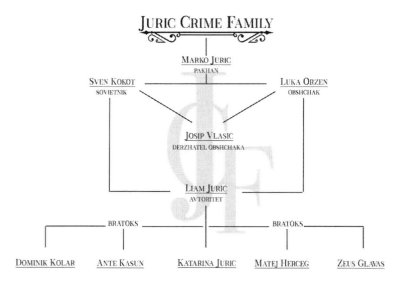

Juric Crime Family

Marko Juric — Pakhan

Sven Kokot — Sovietnik

Luka Orzen — Obshchak

Josip Vlasic — Derzhatel Obshchaka

Liam Juric — Avtoritet

Bratoks: **Dominik Kolar**, **Ante Kasun**, **Katarina Juric**

Bratoks: **Matej Herceg**, **Zeus Glavas**

Allied Families
Vavra Crime Family, DeLuca Clan, Sever Crime Family

1

Sven

I close my eyes as blood splatters my face.

Fucking bastard soiling my good damn suit. I pull out a handkerchief from my inner pocket and wipe the offensive liquid off my face.

"What did you tell them? Drago?"

"*Ništa*! I swear I told them nothing, you have to believe me!" He cries. This man is a waste of space and I would have to talk to Dominik about who he lets onto his team. There was a recent robbery attempt at one of our underground poker games and the only one that hadn't been thoroughly vetted is this fuck right here. That's okay. That's where I come in. I would get the answers out of him and make sure that whoever had made the fuck up would pay for the transgression against the family.

You would think that a small slip like letting a poker game get robbed wasn't that big of a deal, but it was. It was disrespect and no one disrespects Marko Juric or the Juric Family. My family.

"I'm going to ask you one more time, what did you tell them?"

"*Niš-*"

Before he could even get the entire word out of his mouth, I am bringing the small mallet across his face. His bottom lip explodes as if someone had lit a small stick of dynamite in his shit spewing orifice. He slumps down in the chair that he is secured to and blood trickles out of his mouth.

"Drago, you know what it means to be part of this family, do you not?"

He mumbles, trying to speak. I grab hold of his cheeks and squeeze them together, feeling the jagged pieces of his teeth trying to push their way through the thin buccal tissue. He groans loudly and fat tears roll down his face.

"Go out with some pride, you are doomed either way. Show me that you are worthy of calling yourself an associate of the family. If not, I will make sure that your death is long and painful. Tell me what you told them, Drago."

The man in the chair closes his eyes and nods his head. He takes a long shuddering breath before he opens up his swelling eyes and stares me directly in the eyes. "I only told them that there would be a large pot. That the poker games have a large supply of people that don't know what the fuck they're doing playing cards. I never thought that they would show up and try to steal from us. Never. I would never do something like that! *Obećavam, Molim.* I swear to you Sven. *Molim.*"

I believe him. There aren't very many people that would go up against me or pretty much anyone else in the

Juric family, it was fucking suicide. Unfortunately for Drago, ignorance doesn't absolve him of his sins.

"*Vjerujem ti,* honestly, I believe everything you've said. Thank you." I smile at him. When I see him take a breath in relief, I pull out my glock and shoot him four times in the face. Demolishing anything that would be considered a recognizable part of his face. There would be no open casket for him. Go against the family, you get put down like a dog.

Blood had splattered on me again. I fucking hate that part of killing. It is always so fucking messy.

"Franjo, make sure you get this all cleaned up. I don't want to come back here and find anything that reminds me of Drago. You understand?" I order one of the guards.

"Da, I'll handle it."

I nod at him once. I know that he will. Franjo may be just a low-level soldier, but he has always been committed to our cause. Loyal.

I pull my arms out of my suit jacket to lay it folded over my forearm. Casually I check the mirror to make sure that none of the blood remains visible. This might be Vegas but walking outside with huge amounts of blood on your person is still frowned upon. I'd rather not bring myself any unwanted attention. I take one of the many elevators up and it leaves me in the back hall of a small massage parlor. The Košnica or the Hive as the Americans call it, is basically an entirely underground large mansion. A system of two floors complete with bedrooms, conference rooms, and even a medium sized event space. Dozens of elevators that all lead out to different and seemingly innocent businesses—massage parlors, bars, drive up chapels. It's a maze that only my family knows about. You would be surprised at how easy it is to let people build under your land when you knew that you were going to get paid handsomely.

The Juric Family has Košnicas up and down the west coast, basically like having a small country under your feet. Our hands were in many different pots. We had to make sure that whatever we did, we would be able to do it without worrying about police or enemies finding us.

"Mr. Sven, have a nice evening." Xian, the owner of the parlor bows slightly and wishes me well. She gets paid well to keep our secret.

"You as well." I smile slightly before walking out into the surprisingly cool night. The weather doesn't faze me though, being from Croatia meant the cold had already been embedded in my soul.

I walk into the long line of tourists and do my best not to come into contact with any of them. Moving easily through the crowd passing sex workers, desolate gamblers, and wide-eyed tourists with every stride. I've been in America for many years now, but I don't think I will ever get over how they completely abuse the gifts that they are given. The freedoms, the sacrifices, the protection, all of it the furthest thing from their mind. It was sickening and honestly disrespectful.

I stroll into the self-serve parking lot, one that the family owns, and is always full on this side of the strip, and head toward my black E class BMW. It's big, sleek and screams power. I don't waste time with the attendant and he knows better than to come over to me if I have no need for him. I'm perfectly fucking capable of turning the key myself. I'm out on the congested back roads for all of five minutes before my cellphone begins to ring.

Luka.

Luka is Marko Juric's left hand man, the leader of security for all the Juric crime family, and my adopted brother. I'm certain he wouldn't be calling me if there wasn't something amiss.

I slide the answer indicator on the dashboard and a deep voice rumbles through my speakers.

"Sven?"

"Da? Something wrong?" I want to get straight to the point, there is no need for niceties.

"No, nothing wrong, but your presence has been requested. We have unexpected visitors. Marko says you need to be here."

I swear I hear him smiling through the speaker, but I don't have time to ask him anything else. The line goes dead before I can figure out what is going on. It's not unusual for Marko to request my attention at a moment's notice. He is my leader, boss, Pakhan, the man I've pledged my loyalty and servitude to, and the man that adopted me. If he told me to feed my arm to a tiger I would without question.

We didn't have any visitors set to come in, so whoever it is must be high up in command for them to get an audience with Marko.

I turn my car towards the large estate hidden deep in the rocky hills of Nevada. It would take me a good hour to get there from here. Only keeping Marko waiting isn't something that I'm going to do.

2

Sven

I pull up to the large cul-de-sac and park my car behind what I assume is Luka's. He's flashier than I, whereas I get my belongings to blend in, he buys a canary yellow Porsche. A dare for anyone to try him.

The front door opens before I can make it up the marble stairs, "*Gospodine* Kokot, kako ste?"

"Dobro, *hvala*." I put my hand out to David who has been the butler here since Mr. Juric had transitioned over to the states. "I trust all is well tonight?"

"Absolutely sir. It is a joyous night I am told." He steps aside so that I may make my way inside.

The heels of my shoes click against the dark grey marble floor. I barely take time to look up at the art lining the walls. All of it expensive, unique and probably stolen.

There are guards littered all around the large house, but a cluster of them are gathering in front of the main room where we would be meeting. Three of them I know, the other three I didn't. If I wasn't on edge before, being confronted with unfamiliar guests is enough to have my anxiety rising.

It's my job to know what is going on within my family. I should know who these people are, but I have no idea. Something's clearly off. I don't let my uncertainty about the situation stop me though. I move forward and the crowd parts to let me into the meeting room.

Marko is sitting at the end of the table with a large spread of food in front of him. Josip, Luka and Liam are all there with him as well. If all the heads are being called in, then whoever the visitor is must be important.

"Ahh, finally ... I thought you would never make it." Marko picks up a piece of bread and dips it into a thick brown broth before biting a piece off. "Come sit down. We have wonderful news."

I take a chance and glance at Josip—the records keeper for us. He knows everything about the family and all of our business ventures. Even some things I'm sure many of us would like to be kept hidden.

"I'm sorry for the delay. I was taking care of our little problem with Drago."

Marko nods his head, "And what did you find?"

"Nothing that we didn't already know, the problem was handled. I'm sure Luka will not have any further issues at our card games from that bunch."

"I haven't heard anything since that one incident. I believe the hint has been taken." Luka laughs and picks up his tumbler to toss back whatever liquor he was nursing.

"Good. Good. Just what I want to hear." Marko pushes his plate away and then folds his hands on the table.

Time for business then.

"As you can see, *Prijatelj,* my family is completely intact."

I look down at the other end of the table where our guest is sitting. A man I hadn't seen in at least half a decade, Ivan Sever, the head of the Sever crime family.

"Da, so it seems. You must forgive me, after all that has happened in the last few years, it's difficult for me to trust anyone on their word alone. You are correct. The truce between us has always been strong, but with this match I'm sure that it will only prove stronger. A real testament of loyalty and trust." Ivan raises a shot glass up towards Marko, in a flurry, a few of the hired help rush to the table and poor shots for the rest of us. We all raise our shot glasses before we down the clear burning liquor as a form of respect for our leader and our guests.

I clench my jaw trying desperately to remember my place. I was used to having all the information available, but now I'm sitting at this table completely clueless as to what is going on.

I did hear the words match. I assume a marriage has been arranged. This is something that happens all the time in our way of life. We marry not for love, but for strength, power, and allies.

I push my small glass to the center of the table. I don't want to be out of place, but I'm at a complete loss as to why I would need to be here and what match we are celebrating. If Ivan Sever was still the head of his family, it makes sense that he would want to ensure the truces he'd set up years ago are still strong. If that was all that I was here for than I could go, except Marko was not dismissing me. There must be something else.

"Mr. Juric excuse the interruption, but it seems I've missed a key element of this conversation."

"Indeed, and the most important part!" Marko claps his hands in front of himself and turns his fake smile on me.

"Ivan here has completely overhauled his entire crew. He had many snakes to kill. I assured him that our alliance is as strong as ever and we would be ever so grateful to have a powerful family back in the field with us. A strong ally."

"Agreed, this is all good to hear."

"But wait ... there's more." Luka says from under his breath, only myself and Josip hear it though. The small crack in Josip's cool expression leads me to believe that there is something I'm not going to like about it. Like everyone is in on a huge joke and I'm still trying to figure it out.

"Furthermore, in order to re-solidify our bond as allies so to speak, I believe a match must be made between our two families. As Marko does not have any biological sons as of yet, the responsibility to connect our families falls to the men he holds in the highest regard, his adopted sons." Ivan says, his Croatian accent thick and causing his words to run into each other.

"Indeed, and there are no men I trust more than the men in this room right now." I turn my eyes back to Marko, the joke's sitting like a big fucking elephant in the middle of the table in front me.

They can't be saying what the fuck I think they are saying.

My eyes jump over to Liam, Marko's brother. "*Čestitam*! I'm sure your union will be a fruitful one."

No! Fuck no!

"Marko!" I turn back to him with a million and one reasons why I know this is a bad fucking idea. He's marrying me off! Women are only good for very few fucking things. More times than not they screw with the flow of events. If I were to serve this family in the best way possible, I need to be free of all responsibilities that may cause me to hesitate. A fucking wife would definitely be a hindrance. I don't understand how the hell he can't see that. "Can we speak about this in private?" I say between gritted teeth.

"Ah, seems as if your man here is unhappy with the arrangement that you have taken your time to set up." Ivan taunts. I turn and see him staring at Marko. If I continue on the path that I was on it would be seen as a sign of weakness. Ivan is testing to see how much strength Marko has. All of that starts with the men he holds in his highest regard. If one of us is quick to cross him there is no telling how many of those who are further away will do the same.

I softly swipe my thumb against my fingertips, a meditation trick I had learned ages ago back in the motherland. This was not the fucking time to lose my cool. Although there really was never a good time to do that. I didn't want Ivan to see the anger brewing deep inside me.

"No, I'm sure whoever Mr. Juric has chosen for me is an excellent match. I only wish to discuss the mere logistics of it all." I turn my face back to Ivan, "I'd be honored to have your daughter wear my mark."

Ivan smirks before he tosses his napkin down on his plate, "That pleases us all then. It's not my daughter you will be marrying though. It's my niece, Ema."

Ema? Who the hell is that? I rack my brain for any information that I may have on his niece. Though I vaguely remember a few incidents where a niece was mentioned, she's not a real major player. In fact, I was sure that her father, Filip Sever had been excommunicated from the family. Why was he trying to marry off this niece now?

"Ema. Right. I know of her." I smile and focus back on the table. Somehow, I had to get out of this. I didn't want to marry anyone. Not now, not ever. Some members of other families are quick to marry and lock up what they believed would be a perfect match, but I know that there is no perfect match for me. A woman would just hold me back.

"Well, Marko, the food and the company have been wonderful. But I must be going to bed now. The journey was long." Ivan stands from his seat. "Again, Čestitam!"

Congratulations, there was nothing congratulatory about this situation. I feel like someone had just wrapped a ball and chain around my neck.

"Ah, yes of course let me set you up for the night, I would hate to have you try and find a hotel now. There is plenty of space here." Marko stands and walks over to his company completely disregarding that I'm about to lose my shit.

I WAIT in the main room drinking more alcohol than I have had in a while.

"You might want to take it easy. I'm not sure your bride is going to appreciate marrying a lush." Luka jokes as he walks up behind me.

"*Jebote!*" I slam my glass down onto the small table and clench my other hand's fist. "What the hell is this? Why all of a sudden is Marko concerned with Ivan Sever?"

"Well, you know he was one of the main leaders when it came down to the militias over in Albania. Sure, they paid him and his men, but he has grown stronger in the time that he has been away. Now he has new soldiers, his table is completely his own bloodline. He's a strong ally."

"Strong ally or not, marrying someone right now is the dumbest idea I have ever fucking heard of. I mean why didn't he think of one of the Bratoks? Why would he choose me for this shit?" the tension building behind my eyes is becoming unbearable. I couldn't see any good coming out of this.

"Ah, don't let it get to you, we are all going to get hitched at one point or another. But you know how it goes with these matches. You only need to keep her around for a year." Luka slaps me on the back and pours himself another drink.

A year, that was the respectable amount of time to be married to someone in our life before I could divorce. Of course, I would have to pay her out and she could still make my life a misery later on down the line. Though as long as I didn't have children with her, there was nothing that would really hold me to her.

"A year is far too long. Well at least I won't have to deal with this for a few months. I can get what I need to do all set up and then worry about my blushing bride." I tried to let the waves of annoyance fall away, but when I look back up to Luka, he is staring at me with a hesitant smile on his face.

"What?"

"Well, I guess you really haven't heard the logistics of it all yet. You're set to be married on Sunday."

My mouth drops open and I wait for him to tell me that he is just joking. Sunday is only one day away! Does he mean Sunday next month? Surely this is a fucking joke.

"Yeah, she will be here tomorrow, but I don't think you will have time to visit with her until your wedding. Apparently, it'll be a small celebration with a few people to come. All for show, you know how it goes."

I did know how it went since I was usually the one that set up these arrangements. I was the one that dug into a family or an associate and figured out which of their children would be the best match to further our cause. I knew that a marriage could be put on hold for years, while some marriages happened in a matter of hours. None of this was news to me. What was news to me is that I'm the one at the wrong end of this one.

"No, absolutely not." I turn away from Luka and race out of the door in the direction of the stairs. The guards try to stop me. It's well past the time that Marko usually sees visitors, but this isn't something that could wait. I only had a day.

They put their hands out to stop me.

"Get the hell out of my way." When they don't move, I feel the tenuous tether on my temper snap, "*Sada!*" I roar and they jump out of the way immediately. I take the stairs two at a time until I am standing at what is the door of Mr. Juric's main suite. I run my thumb along my fingers for a second before I knock on the door.

"*Da?*" He answers.

"Mr. Juric, it's Sven, may I have a moment of your time please? It's urgent."

I wait for a few seconds, but don't dare to knock on the door again. Marko doesn't have to move fast for anyone. I might be mad, but I'm not stupid enough to think that would change for me.

The door swings open and Marko glares at me with those piercing gold eyes. He sucks his teeth and opens the door wider so that I may come inside.

"Do you know what time it is? I was already fast asleep."

"I understand. I apologize, but Luka has revealed some rather troubling news that I need a bit of clarity on."

"Oh?" Marko tightens the belt around his waist and sits down in one of the plush burgundy chairs in his massive suite. "What news is that?"

"The news that I am to be married on Sunday. Is that accurate?"

"Yes."

The matter-of-fact way he speaks has me biting my tongue to keep my respect.

"Marko, with all due respect, this seems to be a bit sudden. You've never declared that I was going to be pushed into marrying anyone. Why now ..."

Marko's expression turns deadly, and I know in that instant I have stepped too fucking far.

"Who are you to tell me how I should run my family? If I say you are to marry a fucking goat that is what you do."

"Marko this is bullshit!"

I saw the hand coming before I even finished the sentence. I could have easily moved out of the way or counterattacked, but my head would be off my body before I even had a chance to get married if I did. Marko jumps out of his chair and slaps me hard against my face. A father reprimanding a son.

It pisses me off, but I know I can't retaliate. There's something so fucking degrading about a grown man smacking another grown man that it just eats you down to your damn soul.

"Sven, you overstep. Your loyalty has never been called to question. Do you want me to start now?"

He's not looking for me to answer.

"Besides, I thought this was the perfect way for you to

make amends for that fuck up with Bryn. That could have ended much worse for us."

I look away, now understanding what's going on. This is my punishment for the incorrect information I'd given to one of our hitmen a few months back.

Dagger is one of the best hitmen in the world and loyal to the Juric family. When he had come to me checking that his newest mark was fair game, he took my word for it. The problem is I didn't know that Ilia Vavra had a hidden illegitimate child. He'd claimed her one-time years ago, but after that we didn't hear much about her. She was all grown up in that picture completely unrecognizable. I'd told Dagger she was fair game, and he went to kill her. Turns out that someone in the Vavra family wanted to destroy the truce that Marko Juric and Ilia Vavra had written up years earlier. It was my information that almost started a war.

I'm damn good at what I do, but I'm not omniscient.

"I see. As you wish Marko. I'll make the family proud."

He smiles at me and grips my shoulder hard. For an older man he is incredibly strong.

"Good, now be on your way." He turns dismissing me.

I nod once and turn to walk out of his room. There is nothing more I can say tonight. I have to marry this woman if I want to prove to Marko that I am truly loyal to the family. I'd walk through hot coals for miles if that is what it took to get my name back into good standing with him. I'm sure getting married wouldn't really be that bad. I could handle this shit with my eyes closed.

3

Sven

The wedding is tomorrow, and I feel like my life is over. Decorations and guests are already at Marko's estate. I had to go back to my home to pick up a suit for me to wear and my ID.

When I make it back to Marko's estate on Sunday the amount of people running about is suffocating. There is enough security here to protect a small country. A few Bratoks, and associates from both families will be joining in on the festivities.

None of them here, because they are happy for the joining of the families. No, they are here to validate the union. Witnesses.

There is a small room that I use here when I am digging into a problem. The computers are state of the art and I use them to figure out who is trying to kill us or where we can exploit someone in their time of need. Today I need to use it to figure out who is my wife to be.

I type her name in the search engine and of course nothing comes up that would be of interest to me. I dive deeper into more hidden channels and find out information that I already know. This girl is the daughter of Filip Sever who works in Alaska as a fisherman. She has a quaint life there and has had nothing to do with the family after Filip decided he wouldn't go along with a directive from his brother. I don't understand what is so important that it would require these two to be brought back into the family.

I focus more on the woman, going through photo after photo of her. She is beautiful, there is no denying that, but she looks like she's a bit vulgar. Chugging beer, middle fingers in photos, and even passed out on the side of the road. Not someone I would ever take a second glance at, yet here I am being forced to marry her.

A deep growl rumbles in my chest when I catch a photo of her nude, only feathers and sequins covering her body. She can't do shit like that, not if she is going to be mine. What is hidden beneath her clothing is only something that I should be seeing not the fucking world. How the fuck was I going to get this woman to heel? Rather, when was I going to find the time to do it.

There are photos of her smiling, dancing, and even passed out, but nothing showing that she is already with someone else. Maybe that would be a blessing. Maybe she was single, and I wouldn't have to kill a boyfriend in order for her to completely submit to me.

There is one photo of her that stops me in my tracks. It's a black and white photo of her holding on to an older man. I assume it's her father Filip, and she is smiling. It's breathtaking. Her wavy hair frames her face, the smile on her face is slightly crooked as one side goes up higher than the other. Her eyes squint when she smiles but I can still see the twinkle in them. She is enchanting.

"Wow, it looks like you lucked out with that one." At some point Liam had walked in while I was staring at the photo. Liam Juric is Marko's older brother, but he isn't as hard as Marko. Don't get me wrong, he is the Brigadier, but even if he runs all the players in the family, he is nothing when it comes to his brother.

"I wouldn't call this luck. I just need to know what I'm getting myself into before tomorrow."

"Son, I promise you that you will not find out who that woman is through photos and what others have posted on social media. You'll make her yours and then you will know everything you need to know."

I wish it were that easy. I wish that she could just meet me and would instantaneously submit to me. Except something about these photos lets me know that I'm not going to get my wish.

Liam puts some papers down where I can see them. Another problem for me to work on. He doesn't say anything else, just leaves me there to figure out who my wife to be is. Though I'm no closer to knowing her than I was a day ago when I barely knew she existed.

4

Sven

It's my wedding day.

My fucking wedding day.

I'd rather someone shove nails through my cock if it meant I wouldn't have to do this. I know that there's no getting out of this, so I resign myself to just getting this shit over with as fast as possible. In, out and then in a year I can let her go.

365 days and counting.

Really it wasn't as bad of a punishment as I could have gotten. Marko could have killed me for the mistake I'd made with Dagger and Bryn. He didn't though, I should be grateful.

"Mr. Kokot. We are ready for you." One of the housekeepers says through the closed door.

"Ok, I'll be there in a minute." I bark through the door. I'm working. This woman is already holding me back and we haven't even said I do yet.

Over the past few weeks there have been quite a few hits on some of our smaller locations. Restaurants, convenient stores, car washes, places that don't really bring in much money, but places that we are committed to protect. All the hits have been the same and whoever is doing it seems to be getting more and more brave with each hit. Luckily, no one has died as of yet. Except things are escalating. If we can't figure out what is going on quickly and handle it, it may look like we can't follow through on our word. Definitely not something we want associated with our family.

Another knock on the door breaks my attention.

"*Odlazite!*" I yell through the door. "Go away!" I repeat it in English just in case it's one of the workers that does not speak Croatian.

I hear a quick shuffle of feet and go back to the paperwork in front of me. I'm not seeing a fucking connection. These attacks are happening all the way up and down the west coast and as far inland as Texas. The only thing that connects them is that all the places hit are places that we have a foot hold in.

Another knock at the door. "For fuck's sake! What?" I scream out. Why can't they leave me the hell alone?

The door bursts open and Ivan Sever himself is at the doorway. "Are you intending to leave my niece waiting at the altar? Because I will have your fucking head on a spit right now if you plan on embarrassing me in that way." He growls at me.

What, leaving her at the altar? I still had twenty minutes before the ceremony is due to start. I look down at my watch.

"*K Vragu!*" I jump up and push the papers out of the way. I was supposed to be at the altar thirty minutes ago. "I apologize, I'm coming now." I straighten my tie and jacket as Ivan's eyes still bore into me.

"Don't keep me waiting any longer." He spits out.

My eyes snap in his direction and though I'm doing my very best to remain respectful. This man is not my leader. I may want this to go well for Marko, but Ivan Sever can eat a fucking dick. "I assure you that everything will go as planned. But you standing here in my presence will do nothing except delay the festivities. We can stand here and stare each other down if you would prefer or we can get this underway. Your choice Mr. Sever."

He opens his mouth to respond, but just waved his hands in the air to dismiss it before walking out the door. A few seconds later I'm walking down into the large backyard. The landscape further out is arid, full of rocky brown cliffs, but around the large home Marko has a beautiful green landscape. I cringe to think about how much it costs to upkeep an oasis such as this.

I make my way to the front of the makeshift aisle and stand on the side that is indicated for the groom. There are at most two dozen people here that are not workers or security. None of which I feel incredibly close with.

The typical bridal march starts, and everyone seated stand to attention. A woman in a beautiful fitted white gown starts down the aisle towards me.

Hatred.

I hate her before I even get a good look at her. She is being walked down the aisle by her uncle. I look over to the bride's side of the aisle, but don't see her father there. Why would he not want to walk his daughter down the aisle? Unless this isn't the union that he really wants for her. I don't blame him.

I can't tell for sure, but it looks as if Ivan is more dragging Ema than actually walking her. She is resisting. I see him roll his eyes and then reach into his pocket. Seconds later she whimpers and clutches at her neck. Her fingers grazing the diamond encrusted choker that she is wearing. As the wedding march comes to an end, she is standing in front of me. I grab for her hand out of Ivan's grasp, and she rips it away.

I glance over to the side, though I don't need to look to know that everyone is staring at us. Not to see how beautiful she is, but to see how I handle her. I grab her hand again, but this time when she tries to move away, I press my thumb hard into the soft space between her thumb and forefinger. With the pressure her mouth parts in a gasp and she stands up straight.

Tears stream down her face and she breathes hard. I would ease up my hold on her, but I can't afford allowing her to act a fool right now.

She can stay as far away from me as she wants once this is all over, but not right now.

The priest goes through his entire speech. One I suddenly wish was a lot shorter. When it comes to the vows and the promising of one another her tears pick up substantially.

The priest starts with her. Making her promise to obey me in richer and poorer, sickness and health, till death do us part.

I was thinking more like one year until we part.

"Do you Ema, take Sven to be your husband?"

She doesn't answer and then she cries out. Her hand goes to her throat and I can see the redness of her delicate skin around where her necklace lies.

I turn my head to see a sinister smile on Ivan's face and

a small device in his hand. Something is attached to that choker she has around her neck.

I stare at Ivan. He lets go of whatever button he is holding, and Ema takes in a deep breath.

"*Požuri!*" I snarl at both Ema and the priest. They both need to hurry this shit up.

"I do." Her voice comes out in a squeak. Weak and soft as her tears wipe the makeup clear off her face.

"Do you Sven, take Ema to be your wife"?" The priest asks right away.

"I do." I glare at the priest; he is purposefully taking his sweet fucking time. I may not want a fucking wife, but if she is to be mine, I'm not going to let anyone do whatever they fucking please to her.

"By the power vested in me I now pronounce you husband and wife."

Before the priest could get all the words out of his mouth I reach forward and hook my hand beneath the choker to pop it off her neck. I toss it to the floor not bothering to look over to where Ivan is sitting. He knows it's for him.

Ema's eyebrows furrow slightly, but she doesn't move any closer to me.

"You may kiss the bride." The priest says and I move in. She turns her head away from me.

She's been my wife for seconds and already she is infuriating the fuck out of me.

I grab her cheeks and squeeze before I turn her face back to me. I press my lips to hers even though I can feel her trying to push away. I'm not usually one to take a woman by force, but I will do what I need to do in order to get this shit over with.

I don't dare put my tongue in her mouth, I'm sure she would bite it off if I tried.

There is a round of applause as I pull away from her and the photographer takes a picture of us. Neither one of us is smiling, we are barely holding on to each other. We look like a couple destined for divorce.

I can only fucking hope.

5

Sven

I have to drag her down the aisle as the guests clap politely and wish us well from either side of the aisle. The second that we are inside and out of the view of our guests it seems like she becomes more ferocious.

"*Miči se s mene, zvijeri!*" she yanks at my hand, "Did you hear me? I said get off!"

I don't respond to her; I don't have time for this shit. She is going to learn right now that I'm not someone to fucking play with. I tug her into the next room and slam the door behind us. We are in private for the first time since I have put my eyes on her.

"Let me go!" She screams and swings her free hand towards my face. She connects only once, but continues to swing at me.

"Stop! Now!" I fight to catch her other hand, but not before she stomps her heeled foot down on my toes.

"*Jebote!*" I let her go and instinctually reach down to my throbbing toes.

"Fuck you, let me go!" She screeches and pushes me as she tries to run out of the room.

I don't remember the last time I put out this much fucking effort for anything. I lunge for her and grab a hold of her dress. The soft fabric tears every time she tries to pull away. I grasp it tightly and pull her back. I wrap my arms around her small waist and pull her close against my body. She wiggles around and tries to elbow me repeatedly. After the second time she connects with my side I see red.

"Damn it!" I fling her back onto the bed. She falls down hard, her head whipping forward and her breath whooshing out of her mouth in a rush. I take that as my chance to subdue her. I rush to the bed and straddle her. My full body weight on top of her, one of my hands fighting to restrain both of her wrists.

"Stop this right the fuck now."

"No! Fuck you! Let me out of here." She bucks against me even more, but gets nowhere. She is a fireball, but she is a small thing. Much smaller than I would have assumed from the photos that I've seen of her.

"Such vulgar language, that is highly disappointing."

"Well, be prepared for a lifetime of fucking disappointments. Now get the hell off of me!"

"You're not going anywhere, you're my wife now. You'll do as I say. I say you fucking stop this shit right now!" I snarl down into her face.

"I say you go to hell!" She sucks up and then spits directly into my face.

The vile liquid slides down from my eyebrow and into my eye before it rolls off to the side of my face. Before I can calm myself down, I pull my hand back and smack her hard against her face. She whimpers and leans to the side, her face buried into the crook of her arm. Her cheek that was once a pale white colored by a bit of blush is now a dull fire red.

"Ema." I call her name, but she doesn't look up. She just keeps her eyes averted. "Ema, look at me." I breathe through my nose trying to get a grip on myself again. Still, she doesn't look.

"Ema!" I grab her face hard and turn it in my direction. Her hate filled eyes meet mine as tears rush down the sides of her face and into her ears. Her lipstick is smudged. Her eyes are dark from the mascara that is smeared all around. She's a mess, but for the next year at least she will be my mess. "You may not want to be here. You may not want any of what is happening. But it's fucking happening. Get over it and get your shit together. I will not be embarrassed or be made to look weak. Do you understand?"

She simply glares at me, but doesn't say a word.

"*Odgovori mi!*" I shake her slightly to get her to respond.

"I will never get over this. I will never accept it. You'll be a widow before long, because you are going to have to kill me to keep me here." her voice shakes due to the tears that she has shed, but her words are clear. This isn't going to be an easy union. She's going to fight me every step of the way.

"So be it then." I raise myself off of her and stare down at her ripped up dress before my eyes meet her dark brown ones. "I will warn you though, there is more security here than all of the state combined. You have no allies here. No one will rescue you. No one will free you and no one here respects you. If you insist on running, they will only hunt you down like a wild animal and bring you right back to me. Now I have an event to attend and will not leave my family waiting. You will not leave this room." I order her and turn before she can respond.

"What? You can't just leave me in here!" She screams, but I slam the door in her face and hold it shut.

I turn towards one of the guards. "Find me the key."

Ema pulls and kicks at the door screaming obscenities, but I don't let go.

"Sven." Luka comes up brandishing a key. Finally, my arms were getting tired even though it doesn't seem like she was getting tired of trying to get out. I lock the door and slide the key in my pocket before I look to the guards that are standing near the area. "You will not let her out. I don't care how much she screams or fucking begs, you will not open this fucking door. Do you understand?"

"*Da.*" They all respond. Two guards leave their posts and come to stand in front of the door that my bride is behind.

I rub the back of my neck and turn towards Luka so we can head down to my wedding reception. I'm assuming that most of the guests have gotten started without me and are already drunk, we Croatians know how to have a good time.

Luka is staring at me wide eyed, not even the smallest smirk on his face.

"What?" I ask already annoyed by everything that is going on around me.

"You look like hell, you may want to clean yourself up before we make our rounds."

When I look down to my suit, I can see that my shirt is untucked, my tie is crooked, and I've lost a cufflink. "*Sranje!*" I rush to the nearest bathroom to do just as Luka suggested.

I almost laugh at my reflection when I finally catch a glimpse of myself. That woman did a fucking number on me. My hair is a mess and there is a slight scratch on my face and neck, not to mention the spit that is still on my face. I grab one of the decorative towels from the holder and wet it so I can wash my face. Following that I make my hair more presentable and straighten my clothing. By the time I'm finished one would have never thought that I was just fighting with my new wife. Besides the slight scratch on my face and neck everything looks like it was in its correct place. Just how I fucking liked it.

I step out of the bathroom and Luka is waiting for me. "Fuck me, I never want this shit to happen to me." he shakes his head and walks ahead of me. If I shoot him in the back of the head, I wonder how many people would mind.

The ballroom that Marko had allowed to be used for the reception is already buzzing when I walk in.

"Ah, Sven! *Čestitam*! Where is that lovely wife of yours?" Dominik asks, he runs all of our gambling and money laundering operations.

"She's not feeling very well and needed to take a rest. I assured her I would keep the crowd away." I reply doing my best to keep up with appearances.

"I understand. Well, I'm sure you can take good care of her tonight when you claim her as your own. That may be the only reason I ever want to get married. Several times." he laughs and sticks his hand out for me to shake. So many of those that work with Mr. Juric find marriage to be nothing more than getting your very own sex slave. Most of the time that is just what it is. A pussy that you are stuck with for the rest of your life. I didn't need that. I could get pussy any time I want.

I shake his hand and move on to the next person.

Josip. "Well Sven looks like you got yourself a handful." He points to my face.

"Josip, you have no idea. Did you read over the paperwork? Did you see the deal that made Marko want me to marry into this family? I understand that they are up and coming in our world, but I don't understand why so quickly and why now." If I were anyone else, I know Josip would have stopped me from talking before I even got the question out of my mouth, but he let me continue. As the record keeper for the family Josip knew everything. I would go as far to say that he knew even more than me when it came to deals made.

"You know there is always something underneath it all. It's not something you need to concern yourself with. All you need to know is that you have to make sure she doesn't die. You can keep her in your closet chained to a pole for all they care, but she has to stay alive. I'll let Mr. Juric fill you in on the rest." He puts his hand out for me to shake. "I know it's not necessarily the best time for you, but congratulations anyway."

"*Hvala.*" I reply before he moves away.

"Sven, well this is quite the surprise." Kaja and his woman Sabina are in front of me now to offer their congratulations.

"You and me both." I smile at him and he hands me a shot glass filled with clear liquid—vodka I assume.

"*Živjeli.*" He says and raises the small glass. I down mine quickly, reveling in the harsh burn as it slides down my throat.

"Thanks."

"So where is your bride?" Sabina asks, her eyes scanning the crowd.

"She's not the happiest person in the world right now, she's taking a nap." I make another excuse.

"That's too bad, I would have loved to meet her. She was a vision." Sabina replies respectfully. I'm sure she wants to know more about my lovely bride, but she knows better than to press it. Kaja is only a Vor, a made man, but he found a good one when he made Sabina his woman. Too bad they can't all be like that.

"Hopefully some other time." I smile and kiss her cheek before moving on to the next person waiting for my attention.

"Mr. Juric, thank you for letting me have my ceremony here. As always your home is gorgeous." I say, putting my hand out first in a sign of respect.

"Ah Sven, cut the shit. I know you're not happy right now." He laughs slightly. He may be a cold-blooded killer, but he had calmed down over the years. Not so quick to just chop someone's head off.

"I'll do what I need to in order to prove my loyalty to the family. You know that."

"Of course, I do. It's why I chose you for her. Ivan told me how wild that girl is, how horrible of a match she would make for anyone. If there is anyone that can tame that wildcat, I know it is you." He shrugs and brings a cup he is holding in his hand up to his mouth. From the outside it would seem like we are just talking about the weather or the latest football game. Instead, we are talking about how well I'll be able to train and discipline this girl —my wife.

"Mr. Juric, I'll accept the challenge, but I can't guarantee that it will go how we want it to. We've been united for all of an hour and already I've had to strike her. It's not something I revel in doing."

"Ahh, earn her respect and the rest will follow. It's easier to do that with a firm hand than an empty sack." He takes another swig of his drink.

Marko Juric is old school, where beating women was not just acceptable, but the norm. It's not my way or at least it wasn't. I rub my hand against my pants slightly and can still feel the tingle on my fingertips from the smack against her face.

"I'll do my best."

"You will succeed. I know it. I would hate for something to happen to her within your first year, it would completely nullify the truce I have with Ivan. We don't want that, do we? No, I know you will succeed." He smiles again and finishes his drink before he moves around me to speak with someone else.

Reading between the lines, I had no choice, but to make this shit work. If something happened to Ema during our first year it would cause a rift between him and Ivan. It would for sure mean my death and hers. No, I would just have to stick it the fuck out.

"Congratulations." A man stands in front of me. Someone I don't know.

"Thank you." I reply and shake his outstretched hand.

"I'm Alex, a close associate of Mr. Sever, both Ivan and Filip. Your wife and I have developed quite a friendship over the years."

Whereas I was once looking over his shoulder not really paying attention to him, this last line has me completely focused on him. What kind of fucking friendship did he have with what is mine and why the fuck is he telling me about it? That is unless he wants me to respond. When I see the slight smile curl up on his lips, I know that he is goading me.

"I'm happy that you were able to make it on such short notice. Unfortunately, I doubt Ema will have much time for friends now. With her being my wife and all. I'm sure you understand." I take a step in his direction, closing in on the gap between us. I wasn't about to let him make me look like a fool. Whatever type of relationship they had before today is dead and gone.

"Easy ... Sven, is it?" He questions and I have to stop myself from punching my fist through his face. He is testing my fucking patience right now.

"Mr. Kokot." My voice is hard.

"Yes well, it was never anything more than friendship. I wish you both nothing but the best." He takes a step back and bows his head down slightly.

My eyes follow him as he moves away from me and over to the bar. It's not until another large man is in my space that I focus on what's in front of me. I was getting tired of playing the excited and happy husband.

"I'm surprised you kept her in line as well as you did during the ceremony. Though I'm sure this helped." Ivan Sever stands in front of me and in his hand is the collar that I'd ripped off Ema's neck.

"What is that?"

"Her dog collar." He replies quickly.

"Dog collar?" I'm fluent in English, but it is my second language. Maybe this isn't what I'm thinking it is.

"Yeah, you know, pas, dog. Woof woof." Ivan chuckles and presses the collar in my hand with a small remote.

I swallow my disgust. Before I shove the collar in my pocket, I flip it over in my hand. There are several wired discs adhered to the back of the jewels.

"Ah yes, for discipline. Electricity does wonders keeping her in place."

He was electrocuting her as she stood there in front of me. I knew that something was going on, but I didn't know it was that. Fucking prick. I had to get away from him and fast before I said something that I would regret later. "Thank you for the advice. I really must be moving on." I step back away from him and see there is another line with the rest of the people in attendance waiting for me. It would be completely tactless if I blew them off and just left. Despite that, at this point I think it might be better for me to leave before saying something that I couldn't take back or rectify. I start on my way toward the small crowd, a fake smile plastered on my face, but Kaja diverts me instead. He grabs my arm and pulls me in the opposite direction.

"What the fuck! *Sto radis*!" What the hell is he thinking grabbing me like this?

"Sven, I'm not sure if you ordered your bride to go, but she's making her way without you." Kaja looks out the window directly in front of me and uses his chin to point in that direction. When I look up, I can see a long white train of a wedding gown. Ema had escaped and is trying to get away.

"Sranje!" I take a step, but realize that I can't make a scene. "Kaja, do me a favor, let the rest of the guests know that I've gone to be with my wife. Consummate the marriage or whatever you want to say, but I'm going." I mutter under my breath so no one can hear me, but him. If I'm lucky those that are here will be so drunk that they won't even notice me gone.

He nods his head once slightly. I know that I can count on him. I turn and walk quickly out of the main room not even bothering to turn when one of the guests tries to get my attention. I have a wife to catch.

6

Ema

The last twenty-four hours have been the worst of my life. I went from my calm, normal everyday life to my father telling me that I would have to go with him and my uncle to marry a man I didn't know. I thought it was a joke, but when my uncle physically dragged me onto that plane and strapped me down to the seat, I knew it wasn't. I didn't understand how my father could let him do something like this, but there had to be a reason.

"Tata, you can't make me do this!" I cry as my father stands by the door, his eyes diverted to the ground.

"Ema, if there was another way, I promise you that I would have done it. It's either this or they kill all of us. Think of your mother, your little sisters. I got out of this world, because I was sure that I could keep you all safe. But my name alone is just a target on each of your backs. We can't do this on our own. This has to happen." He takes a step towards me, but I back away.

"I hate you. You hear me? *Mrzim* te!" I scream at my father and he cringes away. I fist my hands and pound at his chest and arms.

"Ema, stop it!" He finally grabs me and holds onto my arms. I fall into his chest already completely exhausted, and I sob.

"Please, don't leave me. I'm scared. I'm so scared, Tata." He cries into my hair. "I know. You're strong. Pure fire runs in your veins. I promise you that you will get through this."

"Let's go, we don't have all day for this bullshit. Wipe your fucking face Filip. Pussy." My uncle Ivan tugs on my arm and pulls me away from my father. I barely know this man, but I know that I've never hated someone as much as I hate Ivan Sever.

I turn back towards my father as Ivan tugs me harder. "Don't stay, I don't want you to stay. I'll be home soon!"

My father drops his head back down and pulls his hands up to his face. In all my years on this earth I have never seen my father break down like this. Truly there was no more that he could do for me right now. I would have to get out of this on my own. I know one thing for sure, I would never be the doting doormat of a wife that they think they are going to get by forcing me into this union.

"Would you stop wriggling around. You're testing my last fucking nerve." Ivan grunts as he yanks me back into his side.

"I'm never going to fucking stop ... you think I'm going to let you force me to marry someone? I won't do it!" I try to pull away again, but this time he just pushes me through a door. It opens as my body falls into it and I crash onto the cold stone floor, three other women are in the room.

"I don't think you understand, I'm not a weakling of a man like your father." He stands over me as I turn over on the floor.

"My father is more of a man than you will ever be." I snap at him.

"Sounds like someone needs to learn some fucking manners!" He pulls his foot back and kicks my leg hard. He pulls back again and repeats the process. I try to crawl away, but he only catches and drags me back. He lands blow after blow. My body curls in on itself as I try to endure the assault.

"Ahh!" My cries echo in the room and I look over to the women in the room. Their expression is blank, obviously this is normal to them.

My back vibrates in agony.

"Please!" I put my hand out to stop the assault.

"That's what I like to hear. Beg. Beg me like the worthless cunt you are." He kicks me again for good measure, then bends down to wrap something around my neck.

I put my hand on my neck and confusion blooms in my mind. It feels like it's jeweled, possibly a diamond collar. I haven't seen it, but it feels very heavy.

"What's this?" I ask even though I think I know what it is.

"It's your leash, behave or I'll having you pissing in your pretty dress."

I tug at the collar on my neck. What the hell did he mean by leash? I tug again, but it doesn't come off easily.

"Ahh, you think I'm playing?" Ivan puts his hand in his pocket and pulls out a small remote. He presses something and instantly it feels like a freight train is running through my brain. White hot electricity licks at my head and pulses down my spine before rocketing towards my fingertips. Singing my nerves with every passing second.

My entire body contracts hard and arches up as the choker continues to electrocute me. Finally, when he releases the button my body relaxes. For something so small this choker packed a hell of a punch. I lay there on the floor for a few moments trying to catch my breath. Everything hurt from the beating he gave me minutes earlier to the lingering shocks from the collar.

This isn't a fight I'm going to win. If I thought he would have some restraint I would keep fighting. Except deep down I know that my uncle would have no problem ending my life and then retaliate by going after my family saying that I had failed at my task.

"My darling niece, now that you know what is in store for you, are you going to play nice?"

I don't say a word, just glare at him.

"My brother really messed up raising you, didn't he?" Ivan grabs me by the arm, making sure to secure the remote in a pocket away from me. He pushes me in the direction of the women in the room.

They all approach me at once and systematically began primping me. They use rags and basins full of warm water to wipe down my skin before they lather me up in some sweet cloying scented oil. When I turn around, Ivan's sitting in the corner his eyes glued to his phone.

At least I can be thankful for that. I think I would have lost my shit if he were staring at me with lust filled eyes while I dressed. He may be an asshole, but we are still blood relatives.

After my skin was properly taken care of, they began to dress me in tight silk underclothes. They tug and fasten strings, every movement causing the pain in my body to peak. Did they have to be so fucking rough?

When I look in the mirror again, I'm clad in a breast to hip corset and they have already started on makeup. They dab concealer and foundation on any bruises that have already begun to form from the beating that I'd just taken. They work quickly applying more to my face so flawlessly I would have thought I was a doll instead of the captive woman that I know I am.

"You're very beautiful, maybe I should have saved you for a more worthy match." Ivan says from behind me.

I turn my head for a second and snarl at him. I don't want him to think that I'm beautiful. Moreover, I don't want to be thought of as a fucking chess piece, a pawn to be moved and sold for his betterment.

The women hovering around me turn my head back to the front so that they can complete the look.

I have to bite my cheek so I don't gasp in wonder. I have never looked this good in my life. If this wasn't such a fucked up situation, I would have thanked them and twirled around.

One of the women left for a second and returns with a large garment bag. I guess it must be the wedding dress.

Part of me wishes that it would be the most hideous thing I have ever seen. Only something tells me that just like their choice in makeup and undergarments this dress is going to be gorgeous and fit me perfectly.

When they pull my dress out of the bag and hang it on the hook, I want to cry. It was absolutely breathtaking, something out of one of my dreams only this time it's a nightmare.

The dress is long, and white, but those are the only typical qualities about it. The fabric seems to be silk, with elaborate drapery from the breast down to the hip. Rhinestones adorn the bodice in a diagonal pattern from the left breast where it's bunched up all the way down to the hem of the long flowing train. On the right side, the pattern spreads out making it look like sparkling raindrops. The neckline is drastically cut in a straight line that I'm sure will press down on my breast. The train is long, at least five feet if I had to measure it. It's gorgeous, but it's the dress I will wear when I marry my captor.

"Done, sir." One of the women says before the three of them turn again and walk away.

"Hmm, well your groom should be down any second. Have a seat." Ivan points to one of the chairs on the other side of the room. The windows look big enough for me to sneak out, but with him sitting right there I can't chance it.

After twenty minutes passes, I can see Ivan getting more and more stressed out. Maybe I was going to get stood up at the altar. A small kernel of hope blossoms in my gut. I might be the first woman in history to actively pray to be left at the altar.

"Kvragu!" He curses and pushes out of the chair. He opens the door and I see him talking to one of the guards posted in the hall. I don't know everything that was said, but the last thing that I heard my uncle say was for him to not let me out of his sight.

A tall thin man with honey blond hair steps into the room and stares at me as if he took my uncle's command literally. I can see pity in his eyes. They are soft and inviting. Even his arms look like they were made for hugs. It's quite possible that not everyone is as crazy as my uncle if I had some help this would be a lot easier.

"Do you speak English?" It's been a few minutes and no

one has come back yet. It felt like if I didn't try to make a run for it now that it may not be possible again.

"Yes, I speak English." The man replies.

"Listen, I know what Ivan told you. Please, I don't want to do this. Is there any way that you can help me?"

"Help you?" The man repeats my words as if they were foreign to his ears.

"Yes, I need to get out of here. I can't do this. Please.""

He chuckles, "You're so lucky that your last name is Sever. I would be forced to rip your tongue out just for insinuating that I would do anything to help a gash such as yourself. Sit down and shut the fuck up." He speaks, but the tone of his voice doesn't change at all. There is no anger, just a calm sweet voice.

I sit down and keep my mouth shut, but try to look away as he continues to glare at me. Now instead of his eyes looking like they are warm and inviting. They look unstable and luring. This one is scarier than my uncle. Another ten minutes passes and still nothing.

My eyes begin to droop as the adrenaline that was once coursing through my veins begins to ebb away.

My heart jumps in surprise when the door is thrown open and my uncle is standing there with a smirk on his face.

"It's time, let's get this show on the road."

Tears prick the back of my eyelids and I do my best not to cry. "I will not fucking do this. How can you force me to do something like this?" I scream at my uncle. His hand presses the remote in his pants and a quick zing of electricity flashes through me. It causes me to lose my breath, but not enough to knock me down.

"First of all, you will do what the fuck I tell you to do. You will suck, fuck, and marry whoever I put in front of you. Don't think for one second that just because you are my niece that I see you as anything more than a tool that can do something for me. This is it. This is what you can do for me, so let's get a fucking move on." He charges over to me and grabs my arm again. He pulls me quickly out of the room. The plain white high heeled pumps that the women gave me weren't built for running so I stumble a few times.

"Wait, I can't move that fast." I hiss out to him, but it does nothing to get him to slow down. He just scoffs and continues to pull me in the direction that he wants me to go.

The telltale wedding march song begins to play as the both of us stop in front of a large ornate door. Those first musical notes strike a chord in my soul, reminding me that I've waited my entire life to hear it. Never like this though. Not being forced to be with someone I didn't know and didn't love.

"Don't make a fool out of me. If you say anything besides what you are supposed to say, not only will I electrocute you until you no longer have any fucking brain cells. But I will go back to fucking Alaska, find your sisters and sell them off to the lowest fucking bidder. Make sure they are only used for breeding." Ivan whispers in my ear before the doors opened wide and the entire congregation turns in my direction.

I'm not familiar with this house, but whoever owns it has a great sense of style. I think we are in some desert state, maybe California or Nevada. Everything has a brown tint to it except the landscape of his property, all of it false lush greenery. There are only about a dozen or so guests in the crowd, but security is dotted everywhere. There is nowhere for me to run even if I had wanted to.

Not to mention that beyond the edge of the property it turned into steep hills and ragged rocks along with just desert. If I took my chances running into a desert I would die for sure.

Ivan tugs me along as my eyes locked for a second on the man standing at the altar waiting for me. I pull back against my uncle's grasp. I was wrong about the man stationed to watch me earlier, he wasn't scary. This man is. His hair is brown, not too long, but not too short. The sides are tapered down. His facial hair is perfectly trimmed and looks as if it's a style that a model would wear. He's tall and appears to have a nice build, but it's his eyes that scare me the most. They are piercing, deep and fucking evil. If they suddenly flashed the fire of the devil I wouldn't be surprised. I don't think I have ever seen anyone with such clear hatred in their eyes. I can't do this. However, I know that if I don't that they are going to go after my family. Somehow, there has to be another way.

"Please, please please." I beg in a whisper to my uncle. He only smirks, tugging me even harder and my feet stumble slightly. His other hand moves around and in a second there is an intense pulse crawling around my neck, electricity squeezes at the sensitive area. Instinctively my hand goes up to my neck and I focus, fixing my feet so that I can walk right. I don't want to die like this in front of all these people writhing on the floor as my uncle electrocutes me to death.

Ivan hands me over to the man at the altar. The bastard has the nerve to try and hold my hand. I try to pull away, but instead of letting me go he tightens his grip on my hand to an almost unbearable level. He presses on the webbing between my thumb and pointer finger. I swear it feels as if it is about to pop off with the amount of force he's applying. Tears have already begun streaming down my face and this added pain just forces more to come. I can't focus on what the priest is saying, but there is a point where he stops talking. I cry out in pain as electricity slams into my neck again. I must be required to do something. Is this the part where I say I do?

"I do." I mutter out.

The man in front of me, the priest calls him Sven. He stares at me; his eyes go to my choker and then swing over to Ivan who is sitting in the front row smiling at us. Sven turns his gaze to the priest.

"*Požuri!*" he mutters.

Hurry?

Why is he in such a rush? What does he have planned for after this? I shudder at the thought.

The priest rushes through the rest of the service. To my surprise the second that he says the famous line declaring me Sven's wife, my husband reaches up. He grasps the collar around my neck and rips it off, tossing it in Ivan's direction. If I wasn't so shocked at the sudden movement I would have clapped in relief. What the hell was he playing at? It's obvious that he isn't just going to let me go from the death grip he has on my hand. Why would he take it off?

Turning, together we walk down the aisle. Again I try to pull out of his grasp, but he doesn't let go.

He pulls us into a room inside the house away from the eyes of security and guests.

"*Miči se s mene, zvijeri!*" I yank my arm again. "Did you hear me? I said get off." I repeat it for him in English. I'd only heard him say the one word in Croatian before, but I didn't know for sure if that was his mother tongue or not.

He doesn't respond to me and it just pisses me off

further. Everyone has been pushing me. Shuffling me about to go along with whatever they want. I can't fucking stand it.

"Let me go!" I scream and swing my free arm around. I wasn't expecting to land a shot on him and the fact that his eyes open wide in surprise means that he wasn't expecting it either. I feel like a shark in water that smells blood. I pull my hand back and continue to swing hoping to get another hit on him. He does his best to get a grip of my swinging arms, but I end up landing a few more hits.

"Stop! Now!" He roars at me and manages to catch my hand. I wasn't going to give up that easy. I slam my foot down on his and he lets me go. The suddenness of it jars me, but I rapidly focus. I dash towards the door, but in this dress I'm not as fast as I usually am. He catches me quickly, tearing my dress a few times, and tosses me down on the bed. Still, I continue to fight, I elbow and kick doing everything possible to get him to release me again. He jumps on the bed to sit directly on top of me and not just slightly, but with his full body weight. Soaking wet I'm about a hundred and thirty-five pounds. Not a stick, but nowhere near big enough to handle this man sitting on top of me.

I almost laugh out loud when he tells me that I'm his wife and that I have to do what he says. I wonder just what fucking century he thought we were in, because I don't know any real marriage that works like that.

With my body and my hands pinned down I do the only thing I can do to fight back. I hock up a phlegm ball and spit it directly into his face. The rage triples in his eyes and I have no way to brace against the blow I see coming. He let's go of one of my hands and slaps me hard across my face. The sting is humbling. He only smacks me. The force behind it lets me know that he could do so much worse. I'm fighting a losing battle.

"Ema!" He screams in my face, but I'd turned away. I don't want him to see how defeated I am.

"Ema." he calls out again, but this time he grabs my cheeks and forces my face in his direction. I have no choice but to look at him. I'm so fucking confused by what I see when I look at him. He is the one keeping me captive. He is the one that is forcing me to do this, but he is visibly trying to calm himself down and looks remorseful. I tuck that bit of information deep into my mind. Maybe I can use it later to get him to let me go.

He tells me that he won't be made to look weak, that he won't be embarrassed, not by me. None of his tirade said anything about him wanting to keep me forever, or that he can't wait to get his hands on me. Already he is better than my uncle.

I breathe a sigh of relief when he climbs off me and heads toward the door. He was going to leave me here.

Wait, he was going to leave me here!

"What? You can't just leave me in here!" I rush behind him, but I'm too late. He slams the door. I tug on it a few good times and feel the door moving, but it seems like there is someone holding it shut. I kick and scream, demanding that he let me out, but he doesn't answer me. No one answers me. When I hear the resounding click of a lock, I know for sure that he has locked me in the room. With anyone that might help me outside enjoying a party that is meant to be in celebration of my recent nuptials. This is not how I expected my wedding to be—forced to walk down the aisle with my uncle, married to a man who is no better than a prison guard and locked in a room like a caged animal during my reception. Not even close to the wedding my dreams were made of.

I bang on the door for a few minutes after the lock had turned, but just like before no one answers me. I can hear music and people laughing at the reception going on. Their laughter pulls at emotions deep inside of me that I've been trying to keep a lid on. I fall straight down and began to cry. It felt like I was stuck in the fucking twilight zone. How could no one see that I needed help? Why wasn't anyone coming to fucking rescue me? I want to go home. I want my mother. I want my family. I just want to go home. I have to get home. No matter what I must get back to my sisters. The tears squeeze at my throat. I'm in hysterics and know I need to get a grip on myself.

"Ok, Ema. Get your shit together. No one is coming to rescue you. You have to get out of this on your own. Let's go." I reprimand myself before sucking in a few deep breaths and look around the room. It's rather large with plenty of plush furniture and artwork. Finding something that is hard enough to be used to defend myself isn't a problem. The problem is even if I found hundreds of weapons there is only one of me and a lot of them. There is no way that I would be able to beat them all off.

I turn around in a circle trying to see if there is anything else I could do. A window.

I rush over to it and take a glimpse out. There are two guards walking back and forth, but they stay long periods of time at the ends of the property. When I look at the actual window, I see that there are some wires attached to it, but only on the bottom panel. The top panel seems to be completely free. It would be a bit of a drop from the top window, but maybe I can make a rope to get down quickly. I'm the daughter of a fucking fisherman, if there is one thing I know, its ropes and knots. I could use some of the linens from the bed to make a rope strong enough to hold my weight as I scale down the side of the large building. It would just take time. I'm hoping Sven would be gone long enough to give me the time I needed to do everything.

15 minutes, that was how long it took for me to fashion a rope. I tie it onto the ornate chandelier and hoist myself up. It looks to be about 10 feet off the ground from the bottom pane of the window. From the top pane it was about 13 feet, not something I wanted to jump.

I use chairs and ottomans gathered from around the room to climb up to the top of the window. After some difficult tugging I manage to get the top portion of the window to slide down. I wait until the guards pass again before quickly shuffling out of the small opening. My dress doing everything in its power to keep me inside the room. The chandelier groans as it holds up my body weight and tilts at an angle towards the window.

I don't let the bottom of the rope fall to the ground since I don't want to alert the guards to what is happening behind their backs. I scurry down the rope letting it unfurl little by little as I make my way down the side of the house. The guards are standing at the furthest corner of the property laughing and joking around. Not paying any attention at all to the house or what I'm doing. Thank God for that.

I almost jump in excitement when my feet touch the ground, but I don't have the time. I let go of the rope and take off as fast as I can, my heels kicked off somewhere in the room behind me long forgotten. The dirt digs into the soles of my feet, but I don't dwell on it. I race off towards the hills. I'm not familiar with the terrain, reaching a steep cliff I have no choice but to change direction and run the opposite way. I can see the clear glass wall of the prison I was just in and pray that no one notices me running through the arid terrain. There are a few scattered trees and some brush around, but nothing that would completely hide me.

"Fuck! Fuck!" I stop for a second to catch my breath. Looking on either side of me, I try to see if I would be able to find a neighbor or someone that might help me. I see nothing but dirt and rocky cliffs.

There is nothing as far as my eyes can see. "Shit!" I stomp my foot once, but focus on a direction and just take off. Maybe I can find some where to hide and then later tonight rush back past the house when they can't see me.

In the distance I hear an engine roar to life.

"No, no," I whisper in a panic and push my legs to go faster. They know that I'm gone. The desperation to find somewhere to hide is overtaking me. I start to climb down a dangerous cliff face. My dress and bare feet not allowing me to move faster than a fucking turtle.

Tears burn the back of my eyelids when I hear the engine come to a stop somewhere above me.

"What the fuck are you doing?" Sven bellows, and when I look up, he is leaning over the edge of the cliff looking down at me.

"Just let me leave. Please!" I scream out. I reach my foot out again, but the next foot hold is too far away. My hand slips slightly as I try to stretch further.

"Stop! Fucking stop! You're going to fall!" Sven screams again.

My fingers shake as I continue to try to keep my grip. I look to the side and realize there is nowhere for me to go but up. Either way I stretch it's too far. I try to keep going down, but when I set my foot onto a rock it cuts into the soft flesh.

"Ahh!" I screech out in pain as I pull my foot back and work to get back on the previous foothold.

"Stop being a fucking idiot." Sven leans down and puts his hand out for me to grab.

"No, I won't go back." I say, but even as I do, I know that if I don't go up with him the only other place for me to go is straight down to my death. I don't know how I didn't realize how fucking high I was before. Even if I didn't die my legs would break for sure on impact.

"Ema, there is nowhere for you to go. You're going to fucking kill yourself. Believe me it's not worth this. Come on."

When I look back up to him, I expect to see anger. It's there, but along with it is panic. The same way that he had looked earlier when he was standing at the altar with me and Ivan was electrocuting me. Like he didn't like the fact that I was hurting. "Come on. Reach up."

Fuck.

I pull myself back up with a deep grunt and try to reach up to where he is, but I only move up enough to graze his fingertips. Oh fuck, I'm really going to fall.

"I can't. I can't fucking do it. It's too far."

"Bullshit. You can do it. Try again." Sven orders and stretches down to me a bit further.

My arms shake hard, and I try to pull myself up again. Instead of going up though the previous hand hold crumbles and I fall further down. I scream loud and grasp desperately for anything to hold onto.

"Ahh, help. Please. Oh God, I'm going to fall. " I cry and the tears blind me momentarily as I clutch to the side of this steep cliff.

"Ema! Shit!" Sven curses above me. "Ema, look at me!"

I can't move, if I move I'm going to fall. I can't look.

"Ema!" He roars and bangs his hand down on the edge of the cliff, causing some of the dirt and rocks to fall down towards my head. "Look at me!"

I blink a few times and pull my head back slowly so that I can see him.

"You can do this. I know you can. There is a hand hold right there. Do you see it?" He points to an area right next to me and I chance to look over there. I do, it's not far. Still just the thought of moving from the small safe space I'd managed to carve out for myself is enough of a reason to make me feel like I'm drowning in anxiety. What if it gives way? I'll fall.

"It'll break off."

"It might, then we will find another. If you stay there you will fall for sure, at least this one is going to give you a chance. Come on, fucking reach for it."

I nod my head once. I knew he was right, my arms already felt like someone had lit them on fire. I reach out and get a good grip on the rock jutting out from the side of the cliff. It seems sturdy enough and I move some of my weight over there.

"*Dobro*, now look right under you. There is another one for your foot."

My eyes follow where his finger is pointing and just like before there is another piece of rock. I raise my leg and place my foot on the rock. Thankfully, it was smoother than the last one I tried and sturdy too. I can see another foothold not far away and transfer my weight to begin the slow climb up.

"Yes, just like that Ema." Sven encourages me from

above. He has to move over to stay directly above me, because the path he put me on is slightly diagonal.

Finally, after what feels like an eternity, I feel his hand wrap around my wrist and a strong tug lifts me clear off the side of the cliff face.

He pulls me to safety, dragging me quickly from the edge.

"Thank you. Thank you so much." I blurb out and try to turn over to my front. My hands will not lift me up.

"Ema, if I knew that your death wouldn't be looked on as my failure, I would have let you fall."

I raise my eyes only slightly to peer at him, surely he's just being sarcastic.

He brushes his clothing off and walks back towards his car.

"Hurry the hell up and get in the car." He doesn't turn around to see if he can help me. He doesn't soften his voice either. This man fucking hates me.

I roll back around to lay on the ground, my tears falling down my face as I stare up at the beautiful sky. I'm not going to die since he isn't going to let me. This is my life—a captive of a man who can barely stand to look at me.

7

Sven

It takes her a few minutes to get in the car, but it's all for the best. If she had gotten in the car right away, she would have seen how badly I was shaking. If she had grabbed on to the wrong rock, she would have tumbled to her death. I'm not used to saving people. Killing people yes, all the time. Only to actively need to keep someone alive, someone who is so set on getting themselves killed is just not something that I am used to doing.

"What the hell is wrong with your leg?"

When she got up, she'd limped over to the car slowly and even putting her leg into my car is enough to have her hissing out in pain.

"Nothing." She grumbles out.

"Do you have to make everything so fucking difficult?" I sigh and pinch the bridge of my nose.

"I was just running through the fucking desert and hurt my leg, for fuck's sake."

I open my mouth to say something, but then think against it. Fuck it, if she doesn't want me to know what the fuck is wrong with her leg than I just won't fucking know. She's alive that is all that matters right now.

"Where did you think you were going to fucking go? It's the fucking desert."

"I was trying to get away from you, but I thought that was evident." She snaps back at me and turns to look out the window. It's not very far back to Marko's house, but that's not where I'm going. I can't focus on her when I'm trying to play socialite with everyone there.

When I blow past the house and turn onto the road that will take us to the main highway, she speaks to me again.

"You know you missed the house, right?"

"You know you ask a lot of questions, right?" I spit back at her. "The wedding is over, I'm not really in the mood to party. Are you?" I glare at her for a second before I turn back to the road.

"No, fuck that."

I cringe, "Do you have to curse all the time?"

She gasps and then turns in my direction, "Hell fucking yes, I have to fucking curse all the fucking goddamn time, you can eat a bunch of hot rotten shit if you think I won't. You know that old saying curse like a sailor, well that shit is me. You don't like it. Fucking divorce me."

I tighten my grip on the steering wheel. She is testing the shit out of me. Pushing to see just how far she can go and so far, I haven't had the chance to push back.

"Oh, wait that's right I guess you can't fucking divorce me. You'd look weak. Pussy-" She continues to berate me. I'm not built to take that shit from anyone, let alone someone who's basically dependent on me to survive. My hand flies off the steering wheel and I grab a huge chunk of her hair and yank back.

"Ahh!" She screams and tries to pry my fingers loose.

"Who the fuck do you think you are talking to?" I shake her head once and she grips my wrist trying to buffer the blow. "I don't know what you are used to, but you will have some fucking respect when you talk to me. I have no damn problem showing you just how fucked you are in this situation, don't fucking test me Ema. If you're not going to have some fucking respect than keep your fucking mouth shut. Now apologize."

Her eyes nearly pop out of her head when I tell her to apologize.

"No." She grunts out,

I look again towards the street making sure that I'm not going to crash. Lucky for me the road is clear, a straight away. I pull her hair even harder, and she cries out in pain. I have to stop myself from flinging her face forward into the dashboard. The last thing that I want is to mess up the leather in my car.

"You're about to be a bald woman, fucking apologize." I grunt out again.

"Sorry. I'm sorry." She holds out for as long as she can before she finally gives in.

"Good, now keep your mouth shut. There is nothing else that you need to say to me." I let go of her hair and her head pops back to the seat as she rubs her hand over her sore scalp.

I don't need her to talk. I just need her to be my wife.

WE PULL up to the side of my home. It used to be my place

of sanctuary, but now that Ema is here, it feels like my own personal hell.

"We're here." I say without looking over to her.

"You live here?"

"Is there a problem?" I bark back at her, my fists already balled up in tension. I relax a little bit when I see that instead of being snarky or disrespectful, she is looking up at my house in wonder. Though my home is not as grand as Marko Juric's it is just as secluded. Instead of the stone that Marko used in his home I chose thick wood. I didn't particularly care for the desert or the extreme heat. Deep inside I miss the snow and the lush greenery of my mother country. The wood makes me feel a little more at home. It's a two-story home with 6 bedrooms, a study, a large kitchen, and a dining room. There is a sitting room along with a small, enclosed deck. I had a hot tub put in and a large pond like pool in the backyard. There are surveillance cameras looking outside the property, but not inside. My business didn't need to be documented. My home didn't match the area, but I didn't care, it was home to me. When she doesn't say anything else, I turn and walk towards the door. I do have a housekeeper, Olive, but she doesn't usually stay around on the weekends. I'm surprised when she opens the door.

"Are you working tonight?" I ask her before I take another step.

"If you need me I will." Olive nods, "Sir?" She says and looks over to Ema who must be coming in behind me.

"This is Ema, my wife. She'll be living here. Make sure she gets out of that filthy dress and set her up in my bedroom. I have a few things that need to be handled before I head to sleep. Understood?" It's the only explanation I give and the only one I will ever give. Olive doesn't need to know anything more than what I've already told her. She doesn't usually ask questions either. I keep on going not bothering to check if Ema is behind me. There is nowhere for her to run. Not only do I live at the very edge of this small community, but there is nothing here, only sand and rocks around my home. I had bought the next two lots so no one would be able to build there. I didn't use it, just liked to keep my life private. Even if she does decide to run, I'll just have to get back in my car and chase her down again.

I open the door to my study, books and computer screens take up the majority of the walls. Though I also have a large L shaped desk along with an enclosed fireplace and sitting area. The thickly padded chair directly in front of the fireplace is my favorite space. I just fall into the overstuffed chair and exhale. Today has worn me down and I still have work to do though. I send a text message to Kaja to have him bring me the paperwork that I'd left back at the wedding. I would need to get to the bottom of that soon.

After about an hour or so, I'm lost in a sea of emails and surveillance videos. This is my relaxation—work, getting the drop on our enemies before they can get one over on us. I'm usually incredibly thorough in all of my work which is why when an error was discovered in the situation with Bryn and Dagger it was hard for most people to believe. I won't be letting something like that ever happen again. I switch over to the next email right before there is a knock at my door.

"Yes?" I answer calmly

"Mr. Kokot ... I'm sorry. I know you are working right now, but the girl, I mean, Mrs. Kokot," she corrects herself, unsure of what to actually call her, "is refusing to go into your room or change out of her wedding dress. She is laying on the ground by the door."

I roll my eyes and push out of my chair. There goes my peace. "Fine, I'll deal with it." I dig into the drawer of my desk and pull out a few things I'm sure I'm going to need before the night is over. I stuff them into my pocket and make my way to my bedroom door past the timid Olive.

I take a few steps out of my study and can see the dirty white dress in a pile on the floor. Ema, both filthy and tired still inside of it.

"Didn't you hear me tell you to go into the room?" I say calmly as I approach her.

"Did I tell you I want to go into your room?" She argues.

Nope, not going to do this shit. I lunge at her and grab hold of her dress dragging her across the floor.

"No! Stop it!" She screams and tries to kick me. Except the dress is so big that she kicks nothing but tulle and silk.

I get her into my room, doing my best to stay away from her swinging arms and feet.

"I hate you! Let me go!" She screams again, but her cries fall on deaf ears. I grab her roughly by her waist flipping her around so that she is face down before I lift her off the bed. She fights to get off the bed, but I'd figured she would do something like that. I take the cuffs I had shoved in my pocket earlier and attach one side to her small wrist and the other to the headboard of my bed. "You want to fight like a dog, then live like one. I tried to make this as fucking easy as possible, but you want it hard. I can do that for you."

"What the fuck is this shit?" She curses again. I flick the back of my hand lightly, against her mouth. Not to injure her just to shock. She sucks her lips in surprise. I grab hold of her chin and wipe my thumb against her plump bottom lip.

"I told you in the car that you needed to watch your fucking mouth. Keep it up and I'll slice out your tongue. Is that what you want?"

She just shakes her head no. I nod and get off the bed.

"Sven," She calls out to me before I can get to the door. I ignore her. "Sven!" She screams out again.

"What?" I turn, my anger ramping up again.

"You can't just leave me tied up here."

"I can, and I intend to."

"What if I have to use the bathroom? You can't do this." She shakes her arm and the heavy metal clanks against my headboard.

"I'll make sure Olive brings a bucket here for you. Be nice or it won't come for a while."

I open the door and walk out, but not before I hear her scream something unintelligible at me. I almost feel bad that I'm laughing at her frustration, but at least now she knows a little bit of what I feel.

8

Sven

"Mr. Kokot, Kaja is here for you." Olive says from right outside my door,

I look up from what I'm doing at the computer. It's well past ten at night. "Thank you, I'll be right out. Have him wait in the sitting area, please."

Olive nods once and goes to do what I ask. She's a good worker, never makes a fuss. I make a few notes about the auction that is set to take place in the next few months over in Ireland. Marko is going to need to either show face or send someone in his place if he intends to stay prevalent in those circles. Auctioning women is not something that I condone, but there are quite a few of the family's associates who have no shame admitting that they buy and sell women at these auctions. It's just a part of the life that I'm in.

Straightening out the sweater and slacks that I had changed into after I got out of that dirty suit.

Kaja is down in the main area, tapping the manilla folder on his thigh waiting for me to come.

"Ah, brother there you are." He says as I walk into the room.

"Thank you for bringing this to me. I forgot to retrieve it on my way out of the reception."

He chuckles softly, "Talk about exciting. Did you make it?"

It had just dawned on me that the last time Kaja saw me, I was racing to my car so I could chase after my wife who was running toward the fucking cliffs. He had no idea if she was alive or not.

"Just barely, the crazy woman was hanging off the side of a cliff, trying to climb down."

"Climb down?" Kaja gasps out.

"Yeah, she nearly fell." I shake my head and fall down on the opposite end of the sitting couch.

"Fuck, I guess that is one way to get the hell out of your marriage."

"You know I can't, right?"

"What do you mean?" Kaja asks leaning forward to set the paperwork on the small coffee table in front of us.

"Kaja, you and I both know that this marriage has to last at least a year for the Sever family to believe that the deal has been satisfied."

"Fuck that, lock her in a room then. We've had prisoners for longer than that."

"That's what I've done." I admit and lean back on the chair closing my eyes. "She's locked up in my bedroom. Like a dog."

Kaja doesn't say a word, just sits there with me until the screaming starts. Every hour or so Ema would scream until she tuckered out.

"Jebote." I growl out a curse, now I have to deal with this crap.

"Well, brother I guess it's about time you get on with your honeymoon." Kaja jokes and stands to leave. If he weren't married already to a woman who I was certain would stab him in his sleep, I would tell him to take Ema.

"I guess so, thank you again for bringing this by for me." I walk him to the door and just as he is leaving, I stop him to find out if anyone else knew what I was going through here.

"Kaja, did Marko say anything when I didn't come back?"

"Not a word. Ivan tried to cause a stink, but Marko shut that down in an instant. This shit is going to be hard and I'm sure Marko knows that. They are going to come checking for her soon though. I hope you can get her in line before that." Kaja shrugs and puts his hand out for me to shake. Everything in the family is always a power play. If your woman walks all over you, you weren't fit to be part of the family. If you went against the word of your leader you weren't fit. If you couldn't invoke compliance, you weren't fit. They may say that this was all a way to make sure that we have good allies, but in reality, it was all to see which one of us was the weakest. This may very well be the first test between the Sever family and the Juric family, but I'm sure it won't be the last.

"I know it. Ok. Go on, I'm sure Sabina is worried about you."

"Sabina is actually worried about her. You remember she came from a rough situation herself. She empathizes with the girl."

I didn't need to hear that shit. There was nothing about

her situation that I could empathize with. She was forced into it the same as I. Ema didn't seem to have a lot of empathy for me either.

"Tell her she'll live."

"I guess that is one promise you can keep."

"The only one." I nod and he walks out to his car. When I close the door, Ema is still screaming at the top of her lungs.

Olive stands in the hallway, her eyes wide and questioning. I can't get mad at her for not going in to deal with the woman, this wasn't in her job description. Ema was my problem.

I push past my housekeeper and barge into my own bedroom. "Shut your damn mouth." I roar at the woman.

"Let me out." Ema replies, her voice is raw and cracking from screaming for so long.

"We've already been over this. I'm not going to let you out. You're not going to leave any time soon. There is no one here that can hear you and those that do are not going to let you out. So shut the hell up!" I demand.

She cringes back at the ferocity of my voice.

"You can't keep me locked up in here like an animal." She continues.

"Yes, I can. You act like one and that is how I'm going to treat you." Once I'm satisfied that she is going to stop screaming I turn to leave.

"Please." Her voice as soft as a whisper, "I promise I won't try and run ... just take the cuffs off me. Please."

"You want a favor now? After all the bullshit you put me through, you actually think I should do something for you to make your time with me easier. I will do no such thing. You can rot here attached to my bed. I'll warn you like I did before, my patience has run out with all the screaming. Keep your mouth shut." I turn and leave before she has the chance to say anything else. This time instead of more screaming when I close the door, I hear crying.

Low sobs that seem to come from deep in her soul. A soul that I would have to break.

Midnight comes and goes by the time I am ready to go to sleep. I figured out a few more things about the auction that is set to take place in Ireland. There is a list of women already on the docket as being available for bidding. The cheapest woman that I saw so far was 2 million US dollars. This was the cheapest. With more than two dozen women coming up for auction and more added to the docket every week that is a crazy amount of profit. Something I'm sure Marko is going to want to know about.

When I get up from my desk, I can barely keep my eyes open. I make sure to secure my computer, locking up all the physical papers on my desk before I stumble out of the room and head in the direction of one of the guest rooms.

I put my hand on the door of one of the three guest rooms, "No, this is my fucking house." in my sleep deprived state I realize that this may be the wrong decision, but I refuse to let her keep me out of my own bedroom.

I turn the doorknob to my bedroom quietly expecting to see her sound asleep, but when she jumps up in surprise I just walk in normally.

"What are you doing?" She croaks out.

"I'm going to sleep." I answer.

"Where? Here?" her voice raises with each word.

"That is my bed."

She shakes her head no, "Then put me somewhere else."

"You are my wife." I reply just as nonchalantly.

"You can't possibly think that I will be sleeping with you." She scoffs in my direction.

The fact that she thinks she has any choice in the matter ruffles my feathers.

"Yes, you will be sleeping with me ... and if at any point in the night I feel like you are intentionally trying to hurt me or ruin my sleep I will make sure you regret it. I don't want you to have an accident." I pull a gun out of my side drawer and lay it against my chest, my hand on the grip as I lay back against my fluffy pillows.

"What the hell are you doing? Ok, you've proven your point. You don't need to sleep with that. I'm not going to do anything."

"I don't trust you and until I do this is how I'm going to have to keep you in line." I settle down into the bed and close my eyes.

"You're crazy, you're absolutely out of your fucking mind." She whispers out. My eyes pop open at her words. As quick as a snake I turn towards her and press the muzzle of my gun flush against her head.

She gasps out loudly and instantly begins to quake in fear. She doesn't say another word though.

"You listening, Ema?" I whisper close enough to her ear so that she can hear me.

She subtly nods her head yes.

"Watch your fucking mouth. I don't like it. I will not tell you again. Do you understand?" She nods again and I pull the gun away from her.

When I lay back down, I hear a muffled cry. I turn to

look at her, but she has her back to me with her face pressed to the pillow. Crying as her heart breaks into a million pieces. The tears I can deal with, cursing I cannot.

9

Sven

I'm up at 6 in the morning, later than I usually am. When I wake Ema is already awake or she never went to sleep from the night before. I pull the covers off and get out of bed making sure to bring the gun still in my hand with me to the bathroom. I wash, brush my teeth and change into something suitable for the day. All the while her eyes track my movements, but she doesn't say a word. That's fine with me. I don't need her to say anything. She can be mute for the rest of her life for all I care.

When I'm finished with my morning routine, I look at her. She's still clad in that filthy dress, the last remnants of her makeup on her face and dirt from the desert caked in her hair.

"Do you want to shower?" I ask.

"I don't want sh-" She catches herself and her eyes drop down to the gun that I now have tucked away in my pants, "I don't want anything from you." She snarls.

"So be it," My will is stronger than hers. She might have been the strongest where she came from, but this is my world. There is no way that I'm going to let her wear me down. I walk out the door and make my way over to my dining area where Olive already has a plate of food waiting for me. Only there is a second plate.

"Sir, your wife? Will she be joining you today?"

"No, Ema has decided to stay in bed today. I have things needing to be done that will require me to leave. You are not to go in the room, I don't care how much she screams. She has her bucket, there is nothing more that she needs. She has said so herself, she wants nothing from me, so I have nothing to give her." I don't feel bad about this in the least. She wants to play hard than I can make this shit really fucking hard.

"But sir, she has to eat." Olive puts her head down not daring to look me in the eyes as she goes against the orders that I had just gave her.

"She will fucking starve!" I yell at her.

"As you wish." Olive nods and scurries away.

I look back one final time towards my room. Olive won't let her out, and there is no way for her to get out of the cuffs. If this is the game she wanted to play than this is what we would play.

I MAKE my way down to the strip and park my car in the semi-full parking lot of the Thirsty Sandy. It's a bar right next to the Stratosphere Hotel and also another entrance into the Košnica.

I nod to the bartender and head to the back. There was no need for me to give the pass phrase, everyone here knew I was welcome. I saunter over to Nik, the guard today, at the stairs.

"Sven, *Kako si?*"

"*Dobri, A ti?*"

"Same shit, different day." He steps back to let me pass.

There were no scheduled meetings today, but all of the rooms were still buzzing with activity. I knew that Marko would be here.

"Zeus? Is that you?"

The tall man with jet black hair turns around in my direction. Zeus deals with all of our political friends. Whether they want to be our friends or not is a different story. He is a whizz when it comes to extortion.

"Ah, Sven. It's been a long time." He reaches out and shakes my hand. It has indeed been a while, about two years since the last time I saw him in the flesh.

"Yes, how are things?" I pull away from him and wait for any updates that I might need to know.

"Nothing out of the ordinary. All projects are running smooth."

"That's good to hear."

"Indeed, though I hear you have good news as well."

"Oh?" I ask completely bewildered as to what he could be referencing.

He laughs and cocks his head to the side, "It was my understanding that you got married yesterday?"

My mood instantly drops at the mention of my wife. The one I'd left handcuffed to my bed, still in her dirty wedding dress with dusty hair.

"Yes, indeed I did." I give him a polite smile before I square my shoulders and look for a way to get out of this conversation.

"Sorry I missed the festivities."

"Nothing to miss. I said I do and so did she, that was the gist of it all. Now if you will excuse me, I have to catch up with Mr. Juric." I give him a stiff nod before brushing past him and towards the left wing of the underground network.

Somehow, that woman even has the ability to jerk me out of my comfort zone when she is miles away. I hate her. My calm is usually unbreakable, but everything about her has me doing things I would rarely do. Being rude to people I would never be rude to, even though I'm number two in the entire Juric crime family I like to keep the lines of communications open with everyone. Now that I have to worry about Ema, I don't want to communicate with anyone. I don't want people to ask about her or know that she's fucking alive. Only 364 more days until I can be through with her.

I knock on the door to the dining room, at least that is what Marko uses it for. A banquet style table sits in the room with food on every available open space.

"Ući." Someone says and I enter. Marko sits at the middle of the table with Ivan Sever, his son Petar Sever, and his brother Filip Sever. Filip also happens to be my father-in-law.

"Ah, if it's not the happy groom." Marko jokes before he picks up a cup and puts it to his mouth to take a drink.

I bite the inside of my mouth to keep my face from showing how I really feel.

"I'm sorry, I didn't realize that you still had company." I nod my head and turn to leave.

"Nonsense, I know you're on your honeymoon, I couldn't expect you to be a host to your in-laws now could I." Marko stares at me. Another test.

"I appreciate that." I walk over to Filip and put my hand out to him. "Nice to make your acquaintance." He doesn't say a word, shakes my hand and looks away.

"I'm happy you are here anyway. We have a few things to discuss with your father-in-law and I know you are going to want to know exactly what is going on." Marko gestures to a seat. I do as I'm told and sit down.

If they were going to talk about Ema, I would lose my mind.

"Now that everyone is here, we can really get down to business. Filip here seems to think the journey from the Russian coast to his place in Alaska will be too dangerous for us to get our cargo across."

Oh, they were talking real business.

"What is the payload?" I ask completely zoning into what was going on.

"Two nuclear war heads to start and then a continuous funnel of guns and ammunition. I think Filip's crab boat is perfect for what we need." Marko continues before he is cut off by Petar.

"It's more than perfect. I don't even understand what the need for a conversation is. We should just get the merchandise hauled."

I train my eyes on the young boy. In his family he actually holds the same position as I, but he is still very young. Ivan is trying to keep as much as he can in the family, but this kid is far too young to understand what goes into this. "We are having this conversation, because dealing in nuclear arms and even small arms is enough to draw serious attention. I wouldn't dare to think you want that kind of heat on your family. I know I don't want it on mine."

Petar, doesn't reply, just stares at me like he wants to slit my throat. I dare him to try.

"The coast guard will catch me. There is no way for me to sneak it past them." Filip speaks up.

"How often do they run checks on your boat?"

He shakes his head and folds his hands on the table like an errant child who has just been caught in a lie, "Not often."

"I understand the risk, but more times than not the best place to hide something is right under their nose." I did my best to put the man's mind at ease.

"What of my crew?"

"Do you think they will go along with the program? If not, we can have them replaced quickly." I offer as a solution.

"No, they won't ask questions. Don't fire them."

Ivan scoffs at the end of the table, "How can we truly trust this man to control a crew enough that they won't snitch? We need to just get rid of them all." Ivan waves his hand in the air and picks up a Danish that is sitting on one of the serving plates in front of him and takes a big bite.

"I disagree, if we just get rid of all the crew it would draw more attention. But at the end of the day the decision is up to you, Mr. Juric." I look towards my boss who sits back in his chair and contemplates the question that I've posed for him.

"I think you're right. If Filip here says that he believes his crew will get things done then I'm sure that they will, besides he knows what will happen if he fucks this up. Isn't that right Filip?"

I turn to my father-in-law and watch as he nods his head once.

Ah, another piece of the puzzle falls into place. This is one of the reasons it was so important for me to wed Ema —to keep her father in line.

"Give me a few days to pull together some information on your crew and I will know for certain if they can be trusted. Also, I'm going to need the exact make and model of your fishing vessel to get some schematics drawn up for storage." Both Marko and Ivan nod their heads in agreement, the only one to question my plan is Filip.

"Why do you need to put storage in? There is a lot of space I don't think we will need that."

"We need to put every effort forward to make sure that the goods we are trying to bring over remain hidden. Leaving it out in the open is a sure way to get it noticed. Think of it as a precaution, if the coast guard does happen to board your boat than they won't easily see it."

"Ok, I understand." Filip leans back in his chair, placated for the moment.

"Pa, to je *divno*, now that we have a plan, Ivan will work on the seller over in Russia. Seems he needs a bit of convincing, but it shouldn't be too long. Sven go on, I know you have other matters to tend to." He shoots me a wink like he was pulling me in on some inside joke that I didn't know about. I'd rather be anywhere else, but home.

"I do." I give them all a quick glance before getting up from the table.

"Sven, may I have a word?" Filip stands from his chair as well.

I wonder if this is the part where he tells me if I don't let Ema go, he is going to kill me. Isn't that what they do in all the movies?

"Of course." I take a few steps and Filip follows.

"I know it's not my place, but how is Ema?" His eyes are downcast, I wasn't expecting this. Most people are fearful of us. They know not to ask us about our personal relationships, but with Filip being the brother of the head of his family I would have thought that he would have a bit more aggression to him. This isn't an enemy or even someone who wants to be an ally to our cause. He is simply a father concerned about his daughter.

"Ema is fine." I answer quickly and to the point.

His eyes finally raise up to mine, "She's not. I promise you she's not fine. I know how this works. I know she's your property now, but she will fight to the death if she feels like she has no way out. That's just how she is, stubborn."

I could agree with that description, "Yes, I agree. She is stubborn. Fortunately, now that she's mine, I'll just have to make sure I break her out of that nasty habit."

Fear flashes in his eyes and I can see his jaw clench with the need to react. I can only assume he thought that I would soften at this admission.

Soft is not in my repertoire.

I rub a hand down my face "Look, I can guarantee that while she is with me, I will keep her safe. Whatever trouble she gets into on her own though, is her own problem."

"I'll take that. Thank you." Filip puts his hand out again for me to shake and I do.

"Oh, Sven, you left so suddenly yesterday I forgot to give you your tools." Marko pushes back from the table, wiping his mouth with a cloth napkin and makes his way towards the side of the room.

"Tools?" I ask a bit miffed at what he is talking about.

"Yes, you do intend to put your mark on your wife, do you not?" He turns to glare at me, waiting on the answer.

My mark.

I have never put my mark on any woman in all my life and I'm honestly not looking forward to doing it now. For all those who are considered part of the Juric family, we have a bit of a tradition of tattooing our signature on our significant others. Mostly to let others know that this one is off limits. If I were to try to take or sleep with a woman who had someone else's mark, it would be the height of disrespect. The problem is that this wasn't done with the typical tattoo gun that you would see in a shop. The tattoo must be placed using the traditional method—a needle and dye. It's the same method that is used in some prison systems all around the world today.

I have heard horror stories about the tattoo becoming infected or one of the family tattooing their signature on their woman's face. It's supposed to be a bonding experience between the newly married couple, but some have chosen to use it as a form of torture. I didn't really want to do it, but knew that I had to. It was the last step in showing ownership. Once my mark was on her, she was truly mine.

"Of course. I'll start it this evening." I walk back over and grab the small brown case that held the dye, new needle, and other tools.

"Make sure you do. We wouldn't want her to be running around without a leash ... so to speak." Ivan cracks, still sitting at the table.

I want to reach over and slam his head down into the table, he was truly getting on my fucking nerves.

Somehow, I hold my composure. "No, we wouldn't want that to happen now do we." I return his smirk before turning my eyes to Marko, "Is that all? I need to get this information together and make my rounds at a few of the casinos."

"Yes, yes. We'll talk later." Marko turns back to the table waving his hand in dismissal.

Quickly, I walk out of the room with the small case of tools I'll need to use to mark Ema, feeling like a 5-ton weight in my hand. I'm not looking forward to this at all.

10

Sven

By the time I finish all my running around it was well into the early hours of the evening. Though I made every excuse possible to prolong my time out of the house by 7 at night I had nothing left to do, but attend to my ball and chain.

The house is quiet when I walk in the door. As I open the door, I see a large bouquet of blood red roses. Odd. Olive jumps up from where she is sitting on the couch reading a book.

"Sir."

"What's this?"

"Wedding present for the bride." She answers automatically. "Though it didn't say who it was from."

I nod my head, it's probably from one of the people at the wedding. It's not unusual to give gifts, but these roses are a strange choice.

I dismiss it and walk further into the area, "Olive, how are things?"

She breathes hard and averts her eyes to the side. "She screamed and cried all day. Sir, I know I have no say in how you ..."

"You don't. I don't pay you to tell me how to conduct my business. If she screamed and cried all day than that is my business. I'll take care of it."

"Mr. Kokot." Olive stood firm, her eyes flaring with anger and determination.

"Fucking hell. What is it?"

"She's your wife. Not a dog. You'll never break her this way. She'll fight you to the end."

This is the second time today that someone has told me that my woman was going to fight me with her every breath. Well she'd be breathless by the time I was through with her. I can't yield to her just because she decides to put up a fight.

"Are you through?" I ask leering at my suddenly boisterous housekeeper.

"Yes, sir." She replies and puts her head down in compliance.

"I'll have dinner in my study." I spit out over my shoulder and make my way to my bedroom. I've been in this suit all day and the Nevada heat is getting to me.

A stench I have never smelled coming from my home smacks me in the face as soon as I open my bedroom door.

"*Koji vrag*?" I put my hand over my nose to buffer the smell. "What the hell is that smell?" I look around the room trying to find the dead animal that must be the cause. I don't see anything, besides my blushing bride. Still clad in her dirty wedding dress. The sheet partially covering one of her arms and legs.

The smell is coming from her. How fucking disgusting.

"You smell horrible." I snarl at her and make my way over to the bed. I can't have this in my space. "You need to wash your ass." I reach under the sheet to the handcuff, but when I touch her wrist, my fingers touch blood.

"Get the hell off me!" She yells as she tries to keep the sheet where she has it placed.

"What the hell did you do?" I yell right back as I snatch the sheet down off her. Her wrist is rubbed raw and there are clear indentations in the headboard where the cuff attaches to it. It looked as if she was trying to saw her way out using the handcuff itself. She had gotten about quarter of an inch into the wood all the way around.

If I would have come home later, she might have been able to weaken the wood enough to where she would have been able to break it. Smart woman.

"Get away from me!" She kicks at me and that smell wafts in the air again. Her brow is beaded with sweat.

"Damn it woman, do you want to sit here in your filth?"

She chuckles at that, "What do you expect me to do? I don't want to be here. I didn't sign up for this!"

"Neither did I." I roar at her.

She cringes back.

I take a deep breath, I wasn't used to all these intense emotions.

"Ema, there is no way out of this besides death. I don't intend on letting you die or get away. I gave my word to your father that you would be safe …"

"My father?" She cuts me off. Her eyes open wide in surprise.

"Yes, I saw your father today. I told him that I would keep you safe, but you seem to want to make that as hard as possible."

"I don't want to depend on you for my safety. I was completely safe back home." Her eyes flit to the side as if she is hiding something.

"I don't doubt it, from what I found out about you. Your father took care to keep you and your family as secluded as possible."

She leans closer to me, "Then let me go. I can go back there, and no one will ever have to know."

"No." I answer.

Her face falls and she leans heavily against the back of the bed. "Then I guess we are just going to be fighting forever."

"You'll lose." I say, pushing a strand of dirty hair out of her face. It's such a shame she's like this, she really is a beautiful woman.

When she doesn't say anything else, I reach over and undo the cuff. She gasps out in pain when I finally get the metal off. Her wrist isn't cut too badly, but it'll need to be cleaned.

"Stand up." I order her and she swings her legs slowly off the edge of the bed. When she puts pressure down on the ground her legs give out and I have to catch her before she falls. Her hands latch on to my forearms and her thighs rub up against me. If she weren't so fucking disobedient this could have gone a different way. I push her slightly so that she is settled on her own feet and not leaning on me.

"Take the dress off." I order again.

"Get out." She says.

Privacy, she is asking for privacy. If she would have done it with even a bit of manners, I might have granted her request.

"Take the fucking dress off." I order, my voice filled with annoyance from having to repeat myself.

"Get the hell out of here!" She screams at me before she plants her hands on my chest and gives me a firm shove. Constantly testing me, relentlessly pushing the very edges of my patience.

I turn to walk toward the door and hear her huff out in surprise. She thinks that she's won this round when actually it's only getting started.

I reach down to the knob and engage the lock. "You're going to learn, and soon, that if you choose to fight against me, you're the one who will always lose." I shrug out of my jacket and toss it into one of my side chairs before I turn in her direction.

I move the knife that I always keep with me to the front of my pants so she can see it. Her body shivers slightly and her eyes water, but she doesn't let a tear fall.

"Now you have two choices. Either you take that filthy dress off on your own or I will take it off for you. Those are you only choices."

"Fuck you." The words shoot from her mouth like daggers.

Red clouds my vision as I rush back to where she is. She swings her arms trying to fight me off, but I'm tired of playing games with her. I grab her by the neck and push her back down on the bed. I would need to burn these fucking sheets she smells so bad.

"You bastard. I hate you! Get your hands off me!" She yells while she continues to beat her fists on every part of my body that she can reach. I reach down and pull out my knife.

She sucks in a deep breath when I press it to the side of her face forcing her head to the side so that I can whisper in her ear.

"You willing to die for that dress?" I growl out from

above her. My hand grips her neck tightly and my other hand presses the edge of the knife against her cheek. Her skin is pale white, and she is stock still. "I gave you your chance. Don't worry, I'll get this off for you." I trail the knife down her face a white trail where the metal forced the blood from beneath her skin in its wake.

"Please." She murmurs weakly as I dip the knife in the delicate space between her breasts.

"Please? Isn't that wonderful, it's nice to see that you do have some manners after all. They won't help you now though." I move my hand from her throat and pull the dress up away from her skin as much as I can before I slip the blade of the knife into the fabric. It slices through the soft material like butter.

She whimpers, but she doesn't move as I continue to cut the dirty dress off of her. Less than a minute later the dress is flayed out like a sheet underneath her, the fabric cut down the center and splayed out on either side of her. Now she lay under me with nothing more than her corset and underwear. Filthy, foul smelling yet breathtakingly gorgeous. I can see the diamond under all this dirt. I may not want to be in this situation, but I can at least marvel at its spoils.

"Turn over."

Her eyes cut to mine and her mouth opens, the defiance already on her tongue.

"Shall I cut this off you too or are you going to do what you're told?"

She snaps her mouth shut and slowly turns around. I put my knife back in the waist of my pants where the sheath is stowed. I softly grasp the strings that keep her bound in this corset. Slowly I undo them hole by hole until she is laying in front of me with nothing on but her white underwear. I'm pleased to realize that most of the funk is coming from the dress and not from her person. I can't help myself when I reach out with my finger and trail the tip down the column of her spine. Here, I should put my mark here. She flinches slightly then relaxes. Goosebumps erupt on her arms and she starts breathing slower.

Peace. Finally, a moment of peace. I back away from her and she turns around on the bed using her arms to cover her chest.

"Come." I order and put my hand out for her. She stands under her own power leaving my hand hanging in the air. I use it to grab her arm and drag her in the direction of the ensuite bathroom.

I hear her gasp when we get in the bathroom, but when I turn to look at her, her face is still a mask of anger.

"Take off your underwear."

She doesn't even bother to fight back, just yanks her panties down and steps out of them. Now she has to separate her arms to keep herself covered.

I push her slightly in the direction of the shower.

My bathroom is one of the few rooms that I took great care in designing. The shower is big enough for half a dozen people and the walls can be programmed to give off a soothing glow in the color of your choosing. There's a space where essential oils can be placed as well waterproof speakers lining the back of the showerhead. All of these features make this shower one of the best places in the house. She steps in, but still refuses to move her hands from her private areas.

Maybe the popular saying, I'll show you mine if you show me yours will work to convince her to lose some of her inhibitions.

I undo my shirt untucking it from my pants.

"What ... No ... What do you think you're doing?" Her eyes widen in surprise.

"You've already shown me that I can't trust you enough to leave you alone. You need to shower, looks like I'm going to have to shower with you." I kick my shoes off and undo my pants.

"Oh God." She squeaks before she jerks her head up to stare at the ceiling. "I promise I won't do anything in here. I can take a shower by myself. I promise."

I pull my socks off and pad over to the shower. "You promise? Now you want to be good?" I ask, my naked body only inches away from hers.

Her head drops down slightly, so she is looking up in my eyes. "Yes, I promise. I'll be a good girl." She says it eagerly before the innuendo of what she had just said dawns on her, and she rolls her eyes.

"Maybe next time, now move your hands." I order her again, but she doesn't.

I take another step back and clench my fists. I hate this. I fucking hate this.

"You want to make this hard? Shall I hold you down and scrub you clean myself. You're dirty. You aren't getting out of here without taking a shower and I'm not leaving you in here by yourself."

I grab her hand and try to pull it away from her chest, but she holds firm. Before I can use more of my strength, she asks me a question that stops me in my tracks.

"Why do you want to hurt me? Is that part of the deal?" Her eyes on mine, her bottom lip trembling either from fear or the cold, and her shoulders are hunched over in defeat.

"What? What are you talking about?"

"You said you didn't want to be in this marriage either, is that why you want to hurt me?"

I let go of her, my hands dropping uselessly at my side.

"I don't want to hurt you, Ema, but I can't let you go." I move further away towards the other side of the shower. "Look, you've showered with people before, right? Sports or maybe grade school?"

She puffs a breath through her nose before shaking her head at me, "Yeah, but those were other women. I haven't bothered to check, but I don't think you fit that description."

As if it were a poke at my ego, I stand up taller, my muscles flexing a little. "No, Ema, I'm all man."

"Then I don't understand what you are getting at here."

"You shower there. I'll shower here. I won't touch you and you can pretend like I'm not even here. That's the best I can offer you."

"You'll still see." She whispers and looks away, a slight blush crawling up her almost ghostly pale skin.

A groan rolls through my chest, I want to see. I'm her husband so why shouldn't I?

"Will I be the first to see you?" I ask.

She closes her eyes and a deep shudder crawls over her, "No." She bites out. The word harsher than I would have expected.

"Look at me." She gazes away disregarding my request. "Look at me." My deep voice bounces off the walls of the vast shower and finally she looks back up to me. I back away until the back of my legs hit the stone bench under the shower head on the opposite side.

After a second her eyes hesitantly leave my face and scan down my body. I wait until she has had her fill. I've never been one to show off, but just like I take pride in my family and my work, I take pride in my body. I exercise vigorously and my body is proof of that. When her eyes finally make their way back up to mine, instead of the shame that was there before now there is a hint of something new. If I were a betting man, I would say it was lust.

"You have nothing to be ashamed of. You have my word that I'll be a gentleman and will not touch you."

A soft smirk inches up one side of her mouth. "Sven, I don't think there is one gentle bone in your body." She turns away from me towards the shower before I can respond to her assumption. She turns the lever and flinches back slightly as the cold water hits her skin. When she gets the water to the right temperature she slithers back under the spray.

I turn to the side always keeping one eye on her and turn the water on for my showerhead. I let the water roll over me washing the bullshit of this day down the drain with it. I catch a slight movement out the corner of my eye. Ema has inched to the side slightly searching for something.

Soap.

"That dark blue bottle is soap, the light blue bottle is shampoo."

"Oh … ok thanks." Her voice is soft; she picks up the dark blue bottle and using only her hand begins to wash herself. Over and over, she lathers up and rinses off. I watch as the water draining off her body turns from a light brown back to clear. Her body is littered with bruises and abrasions. Some of which look painful, she must have been in tremendous pain sleeping in the position that I'd put her in with the cuffs. Maybe I can find a different way to keep her in the bed at night when I sleep? My house was never built to be a prison, but I can do more to make it more secure and still give her a bit of freedom.

"What's this?" her question jars me from my daydream.

"Ambiance." I reply simply.

"Ambiance?" her eyebrows furrow in and her hand reaches out to the in wall electronic display. It was all touch screen.

With one touch she turns off the lights in the bathroom and her eyes quickly jump to mine probably to see what my reaction will be.

"Find whatever you like. I find the blue particularly soothing." I urge her on.

She presses a hand to her mouth, every once in a while, her finger flicking at the screen to see other options.

I pick up the bottle of shampoo and after pouring a small amount in the palm of my hand I leave her to make whatever choice she wants as I wash my hair. I close my eyes and a red hue appears behind my eyelids. She must have turned the opacity way up. When I open my eyes again, I have to blink through the water to process what I'm looking at.

The red light bounces off her skin like a glow, her dark hair is wet and swinging down her back as she rakes her fingers through the strands. Her head's tilted back, eyes closed, mouth slightly open, and her glorious body is facing me.

Her breasts bounce with each movement of her hands in her hair. She has a bruise on one side of her stomach, but my eyes flit over that and focus on the way her waist curves in delicately before flaring out into soft hips.

Her pussy has one strip of hair like an arrow pointing to the hidden treasure between her legs. I knew she was beautiful before. However, as I stand here and stare at her completely bare, I don't think I was prepared for just how gorgeous she really is.

Painfully beautiful and all fucking mine.

My cock stirs to life as I continue to dwell on the fact that mere feet away from me is one of the most gorgeous women I have ever laid my eyes on. I fight against my need to grip my dick even when the ache begins in my balls.

"Mmmm." She moans as she dips her head to one side and scratches at her scalp. The groan from her mouth evokes one from me.

"Fuck."

Her eyes pop open, one eyebrow inching up as she catches sight of my massive hard on. "I don't remember anyone in grade school doing that."

"I'm not in fucking grade school."

"No, you're not." She laughs and the small motion causes her chest to rise.

My feet begin to move before I realize what I'm doing. My cock a magnet and she's the rarest metal, I'm drawn to her.

Her laughing stops and I move closer into her space until her back is pressed hard against the wall. I put one hand over her head and the other on the side caging her in. I wonder what noises she will make when she's bouncing on my dick?

"What are you doing?"

She stares at me, her breathing coming quickly and her tongue snaking out to lick her already wet lips. Nervous.

My eyes follow the way her tongue trails along her lips and I can feel a bead of precum leak out the slit of my cock. I move a bit closer, the very tip of my cock barely brushing against her midsection.

"You promised you wouldn't touch me. You gave me your word." Her voice is breathy, but it's her words that are like a smack to the face.

I did. I gave her my word that I wouldn't touch her. I always keep my word.

I push away from her so suddenly that she stumbles forward slightly at my departure. I turn and walk back to my shower letting the water wash over me a little longer to cool the lust sizzling through my skin before I turn the stream off.

"You have two minutes to come out of this shower, if you don't I will come back in here and pull you out by your hair." I don't wait for her to answer. I know she heard me. I step out of the shower, pick up my clothes and weapon to walk out of the bathroom leaving the door open so I can still see her if I wanted. I have more important shit to be focused on then her. I'd be better off trying to figure out how to conceal a nuclear warhead on a fishing vessel than trying to imagine how my name would sound tumbling from between those plump lips as I pounded orgasm after blissful orgasm out of her body.

Yeah, I'd definitely be better doing work.

11

Sven

I pinch the bridge of my nose as I sit back and listen to excuse after excuse pouring through the phone. Ante is the head of the nuclear arms division of our outfit and so far, he really hasn't had much to do. Now that we are ready to really start diving into procuring some arms of our own it seems to be problem after fucking problem with him.

"*Ja ne marim*. Why should I care about the problems you are facing? You have a job Ante. One Marko trusts you with. If you make him regret that decision you are going to have me to deal with. I expect a favorable update when I speak with you again." I hang up the phone without him replying. Ante is a valuable member of the Juric family, a cousin to Marko, but sometimes the man could be a real ungrateful bastard. Had any other member come to me about not being able to complete a task due to something that wasn't completely insurmountable, I'm sure Marko would be telling me to take him out. There would be no such order with Ante.

Ivan had come through on his end and spoken to the owner of the nukes, he convinced him to let them go to us. I was already working on getting the schematics together for the boat, but Ante was supposed to get the storage of said nuke under control. It's not like we could store the warhead in a fucking closet.

There is a soft knock on the door and my eyes jump up at the sound.

"Sir, will you be taking your breakfast here?"

"Yes, thank you." I avert my eyes back down to the papers on the desk.

"And your lady?" She asks her tone a little sharper than I'm used to. It would seem as if my keeping Ema locked up is rubbing Olive the wrong way. I hope I wouldn't have to discipline her too. All the women in my life were really getting on my nerves.

I let out a sigh and stand from the desk. "Bring both of our meals to the dining table, I'll have her out there in a second."

A small smile brightens her face, I roll my eyes in annoyance.

As I walk over towards my room, I don't hear anything. I quicken my pace. She's like a child, a quiet child is usually getting into trouble. When I open the door, Ema is in the bed just staring at the wall. Not even turned towards the window so she can see out of it, but staring at nothingness. I had handcuffed her to the bed again, but it didn't look like she moved at all since I left her here this morning.

I walk over to where she is, "You need to eat." I reach for the handcuffs and she pulls her hand away.

"I already told you, I don't want anything from you."

"Did you think I was playing around when I said that I wasn't going to let you die?" I grab her wrist again, this time not letting her pull away.

"You can't force me to eat. I don't care what you put in front of me. You want to keep me alive then you're going to have to let me go." She turns her head back to the wall trying to ignore me.

"Fine, you want to make this shit hard. Let's fucking make it hard." I undo her restraints and yank her from the bed. She intentionally lets her legs buckle so she falls down to the floor. Fucking hell. I don't have time for this shit.

"Get up and walk or so help me I will drag you there." My anger peaks at her disobedience. I've sat through conversations where people had guns drawn to my head and not gotten this angry. I grab her arm and pull her up.

"Get off of me! I won't fucking do it!" She screeches at the top of her lungs as she tries to pull away from me. I tug her harder through the hallway not even stopping when she lets her whole body go limp and I'm basically dragging her on the floor.

"Oh!" Olive rushes to the side room and when she sees me dragging Ema behind me, she is shocked at the sight.

"Is breakfast on the table?" I ask, raising my voice over Ema screaming at me.

"Yes sir!" Olive answers right away just as loud.

When we get to the dining room, I pick Ema up like a rag doll and drop her in a chair. Her face is red and splotchy, and her chest is heaving up and down with each breath. She's looking away from me, her arms crossed over her chest as her legs tap up and down in frustration. My eyes drift slightly to the smooth area of her thighs. She is only wearing a long t-shirt after her shower this morning —one of mine.

I shake my head to get some semblance of focus back. I must teach a lesson to my beautiful wife. One she's intent on not learning. Disobedience will not be tolerated.

I reach over and grab the plate that Olive has laid out for her.

There is scrambled eggs, toast, fruit, and link sausages. More than I would usually eat, but I assume she was trying to cater to my wife as well.

"Eat."

"You eat it." Ema snaps at me.

I slam my hand down on the table, both Olive and Ema jump in fear. I glance over to Olive and something she said before stands out in my mind. She said that I'd never break Ema this way.

I exhale and count to five before I pick up the fork, a bit of fruit and hold it out to her mouth. Maybe if I'm softer she'll be more receptive.

"You have to eat." I tell her again and present the cantaloupe for her to take. Her eyes squint and her nostrils flare, but I don't back down. When I press the fork to her mouth gently, she smacks my hand away.

"Mother fucker!" The anger I was struggling so hard to keep down roars to the surface. I grab her by the neck and push her, so her chair is leaning on its back legs "You need to fucking eat. Even if I have to force every fucking piece of this food down your goddamn throat, I will!"

"No! Fuck you!" She kicks and screams.

Her antics are like gasoline to the fucking flame. I growl and get a grip on her flailing arms quickly before I drag her out of the chair and sit down in her place. I drape her upper body over my leg and have to use the other one to hold her legs somewhat in place.

My eyes dart all around the immediate area for something that I can use, anything to get the anger out without killing her. With how I feel right now I might break some bones if I hit her with my hand. I lean forward, pulling the wooden serving spoon out of the fruit dish that Olive had left on the table for us and pull up Ema's shirt.

"What the hell are you doing? Let me go! I fucking hate you!" She screeches and continues to try to wiggle away.

"I told you about that fucking mouth! I told you not to fucking disobey me! You want to act like a damn child having a temper tantrum. This what you want!" I bellow at her and bring the large wooden spoon down on her ass. A bright red mark blossoming on the surface after every blow. I didn't count or hear if she said stop. The more she wiggles and tries to break free, the more I hit her. I hit her until the skin on her beautiful ass was purple and the capillaries had burst in some places, I beat her until she stops trying to get away.

The sounds of her wailing in pain, her breaths hiccupping and wheezing through her. I drop the spoon on the ground in shock. How the fuck did I let myself get that carried away?

When I move my hands away, she rolls off my legs to lay on the floor crying big painful tears.

I can't bear to look at her for very long. It's pitiful and completely unlike me.

Another muffled sob comes from the other side of the room. When I look up, I see Olive at the doorway a hand over her mouth and tears falling from her eyes. In the background I hear the doorbell ring, but Olive doesn't move.

"Olive, things are under control in here. Go find out who is at the door." Olive glares at me for a second before she walks out the kitchen toward the front door.

I want to be mad that she is acting out like this, but truthfully, I'm ashamed. Ashamed that I was so rough with Ema, that I did it in front of the help, and most importantly ashamed that I even let myself get to this point.

I can't let her see it though. I clench my jaw trying to keep the blank mask on my face and reach over with my hand to pick up some eggs with my fingers.

I lean down to where she is lying and she gasps out in anticipation of another blow, "Ema, eat." She turns her head back in my direction, her red eyes examining my face like she was trying to figure out the secrets of eternal life, but she didn't move. "Please." the word burns me from the inside out.

She swallows once before she opens her mouth and I softly place the food in her mouth. She chews it, all the while keeping eye contact with me.

"I knew you would know how to get her in line. That's exactly where she belongs dirty and crying at your feet. Teach her, her place." A voice I wasn't expecting to hear bounces around the room.

My eyes pop up to Ivan Sever as he glares down at his niece crying and in pain at my feet. He has the nerve to smile at her.

"What are you doing here?"

"Ah, no need to talk business yet. I wouldn't mind seeing a show." He chuckles. "Dump her food on the floor, let her eat it off there." He takes a step towards the table and I quickly get in front of him.

"Ivan, I don't know what you are doing in my home, but I find it highly disrespectful that you think you can talk about or to my wife in that manner." I make sure to keep his gaze, so he knows I'm not messing around with him.

"She's my niece. I'm the one who gave her-"

"Yes, you gave her to me. We are now wed which means she is mine and of no more concern for you. I will take care of her how I deem fit. You have no say in the matter." I clutch my hands behind my back, "Now as you can see you have disturbed us during a very private time, what is it that I can do to help you?" I keep my composure.

Why is it that I can keep my cool with him, hell with everyone else, but Ema makes me turn into a rage monster at every turn?

Ivan stands in shock for a second before he speaks. He is the head of his family and no one talks to him like I just did, just as I would never talk to Marko like that. Fortunately for me Ivan Sever is not the head of my fucking family and right now he is trespassing in my home.

"I see my opinion is not as wanted as I may have thought. That's fine." He shoots me a fake smile, "I just came by to follow up on the schematics of the ship. I'm leaving today for Russia, that bastard is going to want to know how we plan on getting it out of the country."

"Is that for him to worry about?" My voice is even, professional.

"I would say so, if it gets caught that side of the border, they will be coming for him."

"I understand. Let me get the draft of the schematics and you will have something to show them."

When I turn, Ema is struggling to get off the floor. I walk over to where she is and bend down to her. She flinches and stays tense as I put my arms under her legs and behind her back to lift her off the floor making sure to keep the short shirt pulled down over her private areas.

"Do you want to go to the bedroom, or do you want to sit out here?"

"Sven, I don't have time for this." Ivan says loudly.

I whip around with my wife in my arms, "Ivan, I'm sure you are a very busy man, but my wife needs to be taken care of. If you have a problem with that you can leave, and I will catch up with you when I have a chance. Otherwise, give me a minute and I will be right with you." I wait for him to say something in return. Except when he doesn't, I turn with Ema in my arms and ask her again where she wants to go.

"The bed." She says her lips in a tight line and her eyebrows tightly knitted together. I walk swiftly with her in my arms and place her gently on my bed. She flinches as her backside touches the cool sheets. I quickly take the weapons out of the side dresser before I walk to the door.

"I'm going to have Olive bring your breakfast in here to you." I stare at her for a second. "You will eat it." I make sure she knows that she isn't off the hook.

"Yes, Sven I'll eat the food."

I nod once and walk out of the bedroom. I leave the handcuffs off. I hope she realizes this little bit of freedom is my way of apologizing for the spoon. It's the closest thing she will get to the real thing.

I close the door behind me and walk back to where Ivan is still waiting. A little bit of humility for the man who thinks he runs the world.

"Now that I have that settled, I'll get you what I have."

"Looks like you don't know what to do with a Sever woman." He scoffs and just stares at me. His eyes peering into mine waiting for a reaction. One I wouldn't give him. He wasn't worth my time.

"Lucky for me she is no longer a Sever woman. What I choose to do with her is my decision alone. She belongs to me."

"Not like I would know. From what I can see she's still on the market."

My heartrate picks up. Is he saying that he is going to nullify the agreement? Have I already failed the task that Marko has given me? "How so? She is safe and alive. That is the only stipulation that I know of."

"Where's her mark Sven? It would be quite the shame if she were to be taken or worse sold off, without your mark there is no way for anyone to prove who she belongs to. From what I can see there is no mark on her." He smiles at me, a sinister expression that makes me want to bury my fist in his face.

"It'll get done. I needed to make sure that her body was well enough to take it. Shortly she will bear my mark." I nod my head once in assurance.

"Oh, I have all the faith in the world Sven. As I'm sure Marko does too, that's the reason he chose you."

I clamp my mouth shut, I know when someone is baiting me and Ivan Sever is looking for a fight. I have enough fight on my hands with my wife and no time or patience for him.

"Follow me. I have the schematics in my office." I turn without waiting for him.

What I have isn't much, but it's enough to hopefully appease his contacts over in Russia. "Da, this should work. I guess, I'll be on my way then." Ivan puts his hand out to shake and part of me wants to reject it, but I know that would be an unneeded sign of disrespect. I don't have to like the man I just have to work with him. It's for the betterment of my family. When we get these weapons, we will be as close to a powerhouse force as there is in the world.

Whatever we would need to do to make sure that we got these nukes I would put up with. I couldn't fail Marko again.

"Safe travels." I nod once after I finish shaking his hand and breathe a sigh of relief when I see him walking out. Finally, a bit of peace.

12

Ema

The pain is so intense. My ass screams in pain with every swat of the spoon. I don't know if I have ever been so humiliated in my life. I'm a grown woman and was getting a spanking like a child. This wasn't just any spanking though, he had picked up a spoon. Every time he brought it down it felt like he was taking a piece of my skin away when he picked it back up. The beating seems to go on forever and when he is done not only am I crying, but so is the housekeeper. I can't stay here. I won't be treated like this.

When he lets me go, I fall to the ground and he stands over me with some food in his hands. My spirit wants me to spit in his face. I will not be broken so easily. My body on the other hand is telling me to do something completely different. Anything, if it means that he won't hit me again.

"Ema, eat." he says softly. I keep my eyes locked on his, there is regret there. His features are soft. "Please."

I nearly have a stroke right there. Did he just say please to me? The same man who had just beat me so hard, I was sure my ass was bleeding, was speaking to me with manners.

I open my mouth and take the first bites of sustenance that I've had in days. I haven't eaten anything since before the wedding. I had only drunk the water that the housekeeper had brought to me and some more from the faucet this morning. If he weren't so close to me, I would have moaned in delight at how good it tasted on my tongue.

"I knew you would know how to get her in line."

Shock rockets through my system as a voice I hadn't expected to hear echoes in the large space that is the dining room. Why is my asshole of an uncle here?

The softness that was just on Sven's face instantly drains away and is replaced by a cold look—a mask of indifference.

"Ah, no need to talk business yet. I wouldn't mind seeing a show. Dump the food on the floor, let her eat it off there." My uncle suggests. I have to hang my head now; haven't I been humiliated enough. When will my suffering fucking end and what have I done in this life or a past one to be subjected to this?

My head shoots back up when Sven steps in between me and my uncle. A protective stance and an attitude to match.

"Ivan, I don't know what you are doing in my home, but I find it highly disrespectful-" I drown the rest of the conversation out as I stare up at Sven's back completely dumbfounded. Was he defending me right now? The way he had snapped the choker off my neck at the wedding is the same thing he was doing now. I don't understand if I'm nothing more than a prisoner to him than why he is consistently going out of his way to protect me from my uncle. What kind of game is this? I try to get off the floor, but my ass and legs burn from the beating.

It's only when Sven turns around and addresses me that I realize they are watching me struggle.

"Do you want to go to the bedroom, or do you want to sit out here?" His expression shifts again when he bends down to where I am. The soft open look in his eyes is back. Ivan tries to draw him away from me by telling him that he doesn't have enough time. Except Sven is set on taking care of me first before he deals with my uncle. All of a sudden, I have become higher on the totem pole than my uncle. Even from where I sit, I can see Ivan tense in anger.

Sven asks me again where I want to go and the last thing I want is to sit out here to look at my uncle and listen to him talk. If I never had to be in the same room as my uncle again, I would be okay with that. "The bed." I say.

I expected him to give me permission to go. I expected him to pick me up by my arm and drag me back the same way he'd dragged me here. What I didn't expect was for him to pick me up in a bridal carry and hold me close to his chest while carrying me carefully back to his room.

Once I was settled, he made a quick round of the room, pulling out a few weapons and stuffing them on either side of the waist of his pants. I wonder how many damn guns he had in here.

The thought of there always being a weapon nearby makes me nervous.

"I'm going to have Olive bring your breakfast in here to you, you will eat it." He stares at me waiting for my answer. Another small change.

"Yes, Sven, I'll eat the food." I didn't want to admit it, but that taste of eggs he gave me was enough to have my stomach cramping like crazy. It would be dumb not to eat the food, with that he nods and leaves the room.

A few seconds later Olive comes in with my plate and sets it up for me near the bed.

She takes a few steps in the direction of the door, but turns back to me. "Are you ok?"

"Why do you care?" The audacity. Now she wants to say something like she cares. Where the hell was all this concern when that man was beating my ass? She was standing there just watching him. No, I didn't want her help now.

"Ma'am ..."

I cut her off immediately, "Oh stop it with the ma'am shit. My name is Ema."

"Sorry, Ema, I don't know what is happening with Sven. I've never seen him behave like this, not with anyone." She whispers.

"I guess I'm just the lucky winner then aren't I." I snap back at her and look away.

"No. I'm sorry this is happening to you. Do you want some advice?"

"Does it look like I need your advice right now?" I swing my eyes back in her direction, my lip curling up slightly in a snarl. If she really wanted to help me so badly, there were many opportunities for her to do it since I'd come here.

"Yes, actually it does."

"Whatever." I cross my arms over my chest and try to ignore her, but she doesn't move away.

"Mr. Kokot doesn't tolerate disrespect, but he is also incredibly loyal. What I've seen of him before this is a hardworking man who just wants to be perfect at everything that he does. You're not getting out. I can tell you that for a fact, but maybe your time here doesn't have to be so horrendous. If you would just stop antagonizing him, poking at his soft spots maybe you'll be able to actually call this place home."

A strange sound bubbles up out of my throat. Laughter, I hadn't heard myself laugh for a while. Did this lady have the nerve to insinuate that I would ever call this place home? That I would ever see this place as anything more than a prison? She must be crazy.

"He kidnapped me and forced me to marry him, and you want me to be sweet to him?" My eyebrows crawl all the way up my forehead at my astonishment.

"What has being a bitch to him gotten you besides a raw ass and an empty bed. You have control over certain things, work with what you have and not what you want, because that's not going to get you anywhere." She bows her head slightly when she finishes, "Of course that is only my humble opinion. Whatever you decide I'm here to serve." With that she turns and walks out of the room leaving me with my food and an annoyed feeling. I know she's right. I know all this fighting is getting me nowhere, but it's not in my nature to just lay back and take it.

No, what she said is bullshit.

I pick up the plate and start shoveling food into my mouth. It's so good. At least I think it is. I'm eating so fast that I can't even say for sure that I've tasted anything. Once I've finished my meal I lay down and wait for Sven to come back or not. I never know when he is going to show up. I run my hand into my freshly washed hair.

"Oh, dumbass!" I berate myself. It only now dawns on me that both of my arms are free. I'm not chained to the bed like I had been. He's not sleeping next to me with a gun in his hand and he is distracted by my Uncle right now. This is the perfect fucking time for me to get out of here and I'm just here laying on the bed like I'm on vacation.

I hop out of bed and rush over to the door. When I put my ear to the wood, I can still hear Sven and my uncle talking. Their meeting would at least give me a few minutes surely. I only have one of his shirts on and nothing else since I don't own anything in this house. I rush over to a chest of drawers and pick out the first thing that I think I could make fit. I settle on a pair of light jogging pants with drawstrings. They are way longer than I need, but I'm not trying to make a fashion statement right now. I don't have to worry about a coat, because it's hot as hell out. My only other issue is my footwear. I didn't even have the heels I wore for the wedding since I left those at the other house. I open another drawer and pull out a few pairs of sports socks. Again, they were too big for me, but that actually worked for what I wanted them for. I try to slip on the first pair, but when I press the sock to my foot a severe pain shot up my leg like electricity.

"Oh fuck!" I put a hand over my mouth, trying to breathe through the pain. I lift up my leg and did my best to look at my foot. It was the same one that I had stabbed with a rock when I was trying to run away on my wedding day.

The actual cut itself wasn't very long, maybe about half an inch and it was already closing up. There is a bit of discharge and the cut itself is red, but what could I expect it was fresh. I take better care when I try to put the sock on the second time. It still hurt, but this time I was able to manage through the pain. I slip on three more pairs of socks and when I went to stand, I could barely feel the floor with all the extra padding from the socks.

"Perfect." I rush back over to the door and put my ear close to listen, just to make sure. They are still talking. I look around the room again for a weapon, but everything is either locked up or Sven already took them with him. That's fine I don't need a weapon, I just need to get the fuck out of here. First, I try the window, but can see there is an alarm on it. I don't want to take a chance and have it go off. Now I need to find some other place that is easy to open.

I open the door to the bedroom and it's only then that I realize I have no idea where I am or how big the house is. I know I'm on the first floor, but I don't know where Sven and my uncle are inside the house. I don't want to accidentally walk by the dining room. Although, when he was carrying me before I thought I had seen a different hallway for me to go down. I slide my back against the wall as quietly as I can, taking care not to put much pressure on my legs or rear. The socks make it easy to not make a sound, but the pain in my ass and foot are making it difficult to concentrate. I stay to the shadows and see the hallway on the opposite side of his bedroom. I quickly, but quietly rush that way until I am standing in a small space directly outside what looks like a sunroom. A door opens in the back part of the house and I hear footsteps making their way in my direction.

"Shit, shit shit!" I mumble to myself before doing the only thing I can think of. I hide. I rush into the sunroom and pull back one of the curtains to wrap myself in it. I only hear one set of footsteps, sounding like they are going straight for the front door. When the door opens and closes, I do my best to peek out from my hiding space without moving the curtain. When I don't see anyone else in the immediate area I move from my hiding spot. The door is only a few paces away from me. If I can get there, I'm free. I may be a few miles away from anyone, but I did see other houses on the way here. There had to be people around that would help me.

I run on my tip toes towards the door. Excitement bubbles up in my chest at the nearness of my freedom. I did it. I finally fucking did it.

I put my hand on the doorknob and turn.

"Ema!" Sven bellows from across the house.

Fuck!

I turn for the briefest of seconds to see that Sven had come back down. I act as if I didn't hear him. I can't stop now that my freedom is so close, I have to make a run for it. I swing the door open no longer caring if he hears me and run with all the strength I had in my body. The property seemed to go on forever. Despite that I will myself not to give up even when the pain in my legs felt as if my muscles were being ripped from the bone and every step sends shock waves of pain through my body from the cut on my foot.

I stumble down a small hill, but pop right back up to keep running.

"Oh please, please … please!" I cry to myself. I can hear him behind me, running and almost right on my tail.

"Get over here!" He roars as he tackles me to the ground. Not lightly either, he tackles me like he is playing professional football.

The air is knocked out of my body, but I still try to get away. I kick out at him.

"Stop!" He yells as he turns me around and pins me down underneath his body. The rage that had disappeared earlier was back in his eyes. The dark swirl of evil present in the way he peers down at me. "Stop it now!" he orders again.

I don't.

"Where the fuck do you think you are going? There is nothing out here. There is no one to fucking help you! When are you going to get that through your fucking mind! For fuck's sake, you're driving me insane." He has a grip on my hands and squeezes so hard I swear I can feel the bones popping out of place.

"Just let me go! I'm never going to stop trying to leave. I want to go home! I need to go home! I don't want to be here. I can't be in this life. I can't!" I scream back at him. The tears clouding my vision and the last bit of energy from the food he let me have bottoming out. My arms fall limp and I cry there laying in the arid dirt.

HSSSSSS

"Fuck, don't move." Sven says from above me. His body now completely frozen above mine. If it weren't from his complete change in tone, I wouldn't have thought anything of it. Except the tension in the air tells me that something is wrong. Something more than what is going on right now. I blink the tears out of my eyes and look up at him. His eyes are locked on something to my left.

HSSSSSSS

I don't move my head, but look over with just my eyes as far as I possibly can. A fucking snake. A big fucking snake is slithering in our direction, the upper half of its body is completely off the ground as it stares at me only a few inches away. It could strike right now and I would be up shit creek.

"Oh shit, move!" I whisper yell at Sven.

"No, if we try to move now it's going to attack us."

I start to tremble slightly, I just can't help it. The sudden surge of adrenaline that is going through my body from fear is causing me to shake.

"Shhh, Ema. I got you. Don't move." Sven says softly. I feel him moving his hand on the other side. Away from the snake and he pulls out the same knife that he had this morning. "Suck in a breath, softly." He whispers. I do what he asks, and he passes the knife between us to his opposite hand.

He is completely stock still, everything frozen except for his arm. The snake lunges once and I squeak out a scream as my body clenches up even harder. In a blink of an eye Sven pushes me back with one hand and brings down the knife in his other hand right as the snake decided to strike. The metal weapon having gone straight through the snake's body about an inch or so away from its head. The back part of its body curls around Sven's hand and the weapon, but its head was stuck in the ground. It was only a few seconds before the animal died. It's diamond shaped head falling limp to the dirt only centimeters away from where I was. This man had just saved my life from a fucking snake.

"Are you ok?" he unravels the snake from around his wrist before he brings his hand up to my face.

"Yeah, I think so ... Yeah." the tremors that I had when I was trying to stay still almost tripled in intensity now that the threat was gone.

He reaches over to pull the knife out of the dead snake and wipes it off in the dirt.

"Next time you'll think twice about just running out into an area you don't know. I promise you there are more things than just me here that you need to be worried about."

"Things worse than you?" I correct his statement.

"No, there is nothing worse than me. You'll remember that too." He gets off me, but instead of just waiting for me to get up, once again he shoves his hands under my legs and behind my back. Gently he raises me to his chest and carries me all the way back to the house.

One minute he's breaking me down and in the next he is holding onto me like I'm a porcelain doll. I don't think I've ever been so confused in my life.

13

Sven

Holding her to my chest as we walk back to the house was the only few seconds of calm that I would have for the rest of the day. Once we were back in the house Ema began fighting again to try and get out. She screams and cries, pulling at me. Nothing that happened outside seemed to stick with her. It didn't seem to matter that my home was the only one out here for at least a mile or that to the back of my property was just miles and miles of dirt and rocks. It was insignificant that poisonous animals were out there that could hurt her. None of that mattered to her, so now we're back to square one. Back to me having to shackle her to the bed. I leave her there kicking and screaming until she passes out. Having her around is more than just a nuisance, its physically draining.

A few hours later I hear her moving around. I know I need to reprimand her now that she's awake from her nap. She can't keep this up, it's going to get both of us killed.

I steel myself, almost willing my anger not to get the best of me. With her it feels as if it only takes a small spark to set me off. When I open the door, I see she is sitting up in the bed, her head is hanging down and the arm that is attached to the cuff is bent in an awkward position.

"Ema, we need to talk. You can't keep doing this shit."

"Fuck you."

My body tenses.

"I told you about your damn mouth. I won't-" She cuts me off before I can finish what I'm saying.

"You won't tolerate it. I don't give a fuck. Fuck you, fuck your stupid house, fuck your sexy face, fuck it all." Her head lolls to the side slowly.

I dart over to where she is, expecting her to strike out with her feet or even her free arm. Usually she's as quick as a whip, but this time she's off by a few seconds. Her arm goes up as I'm already there in front of her. I grab her hair and snarl down at her.

"You must think this is the worst I can do to you. I've been more than lenient with you. They told me to lock you in a closet and throw you the scraps from my table. Let's start with that shall we?"

I wait for the screaming, for the fighting. Instead, she laughs. Not just a chuckle, but a deep hearty laugh. Her eyes are still slightly closed, and she sways side to side.

"Ema?"

"Hmmm?"

"Ema, open your eyes and look at me." When she doesn't, I move my hand from her hair. When I pull my hand away it's wet with sweat.

"What the fuck." I wipe my hand down the front of my pants. "Ema, open your goddamn eyes!" I bark at her. She opens them comically wide. I can see her pupils are dilated, making her grey eyes look black.

"Shit, what did you take? Ema, do you hear me? Did you take anything?" I don't know how she could have since she's been tied up all day. There are no drugs here. "Ema!"

She's not giving me anything though. I don't know what is wrong with her, but I know that something is.

"Olive!" I roar loud. When she doesn't come right away, I scream again and again.

Finally, my housekeeper burst through the door with nothing but her pajamas on.

"Oh, my goodness. What's going on?"

"I don't know. Did you give her any medication?"

"No, not at all."

"She's sweating and incoherent." A million possibilities fly through my mind. The only thing that sticks out among all the chaos is those words.

Not her words.

"Have you checked her for fever? Is she ill?"

Fever? I put my hand to her head, but it doesn't feel very hot to me. "I can't tell go get me a thermometer, now. " I order her, and Olive runs quickly out the room. I quickly undo Ema's restraint, sit down on the bed and pull her to me. She whimpers in pain and in her incoherent state she clutches to me.

"Sven? Where are you? Stay Sven." She mumbles as she nuzzles closer to me. Stay? Just hours ago, she was trying to get away. I know she's not lucid and I shouldn't take what she is saying to heart. What shocks me more is the fact that I want to. I want her to want me to stay. I want her to need me. I'm tired of fighting with this woman who is as stuck in this situation with me. I want some peace.

"*Bejbe.* It's ok. I'm here. Shh." I soothe her the best way I know how as I wait for Olive to come back with the thermometer. I rock her and stroke her hair until it seems as if she's calming down.

"Here it is." Olive hustles back in the room out of breath with a temporal thermometer in her hand.

I activate it and press it to Ema's head.

104.9

"Holy shit!"

"You need to get that fever down." Olive says forcefully, but I'm already getting up with Ema and rushing towards the bathroom.

"Olive, call Kaja and have him send the doctor over here. Now. Tell him it's a family emergency and I want the doctor here within the next 20 minutes." She nods her head and takes off for the phone. "My frustrating woman, what's happening? What's happened to you?" I whisper out loud as I turn the cold water on all the shower heads. I pull my wallet and phone out of my pockets before kicking my shoes off. The frigid spray shocks her right out of her deep slumber and she screams, trying to get away.

"Stop! Ema ... Ema listen to me."

"Let me out! Let me go!" She fights trying to escape the cold water.

"Ema!" I grab her face the best I can and force her to focus on me. "Don't fight me."

"No more. I don't want to fight you anymore." Her eyes drift closed again.

"Ema, stay awake. Come on, stay awake." I shake her again and her eyes open up.

"Ok."

I laugh slightly and pull her closer to me. "That was probably the first time you didn't argue with me."

"What's happening?" She looks around the shower. She must be coming to.

"Ema, you have a very high fever. When did you get ill? Why didn't you say anything?"

"I didn't realize. Why would it matter anyway? I'm just a prisoner." She leans her head back into the spray of the water.

"No, you're not my prisoner. You're my wife. We may not have gotten together under the most traditional of circumstances, but it doesn't have to be like this." I snap my mouth shut at my admission. I pray she isn't lucid enough to remember. The last thing I want is for her to hold it over my head later.

"You care?"

"I can. I don't need to be this monster you are turning me into. I want you to be safe and content. Your happiness included."

"Be nicer then." She yawns and lays her head against my shoulder. Her forehead cooler thanks to the water from the shower. I feel her body go limp as she falls back to sleep. I stay in that shower for a long while just trying to get a grip on these thoughts running through my head.

"Mr. Kokot." Olive is at the bathroom door.

"Yes?"

"The doctor is here?"

"Thank fuck." I stand up with Ema's limp body in my arms, a trail of water following us as I walk out of the bathroom.

Kaja and Dr. Tomik are already in the room.

"Jesus, what happened to her?" Kaja came over to help me get her on the bed.

"I don't know, she tried to run yesterday. I left her in the room for a few hours when I came back she was like this. She wasn't sick yesterday." I think back on everything that I had noticed over the past few days and sickness wasn't one of them.

"I'll have to take some blood. She's obviously fighting off an infection, but until that comes back I won't know. I can give her some broad-spectrum antibiotics. Do you know if she is allergic to anything?"

"No."

"No, you don't know, or she isn't?"

"No, she isn't" I bark out. Why isn't he moving faster? What the fuck is the point of all these questions?

"Ok, and you say she hasn't been sick before tonight? No cuts, no new underlying conditions."

"No, no."

"What of your mark, maybe that's the culprit?" Kaja asks.

"No, I haven't marked her yet." I watch his eyebrows shoot up, but he doesn't say anything.

"Wait a minute." I thought back over the last few days. I vaguely remember her complaining of her leg hurting her. She has quite a few scrapes and bruises from all the times she'd tried to escape. "She has some cuts on her side and back. She was complaining also of her leg hurting her, but she had recently tried to climb a mountain. It didn't go well for her."

"That's an understatement." Kaja says under her breath.

"Ok, that's a start. See if you can find a wound that looks infected. Red, raised, hot to the touch, puss. Things like that." The doctor sets up an IV with a bag of clear fluid.

"What's that?"

"The fever will have dehydrated her. Fluids, Saline. Quickly, get these wet clothes off."

"Right." I begin to peel the oversized clothes off her body when I notice Kaja is still in the room, though his head's down. "Get the hell out."

He puts his head up and turns toward the door.

"Kaja, bring my duffle bag out of the car. I'm going to need a few more things. Please." The doctor looks up at Kaja to make sure he hasn't offended him. Kaja may not be a high-ranking member of the family, but he is still a Vor. He should be treated with respect at all times.

"On it." Kaja leaves the room and heads down for the bag the doctor needs.

I quickly peel the rest of her clothing off. Both the doctor and I start looking for any cuts or wounds with strange discoloration. We found quite a few, but nothing that looks like an infection.

"Did you check her leg?" the doctor asks from where he is by her head, checking her scalp.

I start at her hip and search for anything. Besides a few scrapes nothing looks bad. In fact, most of her injuries look like they were pretty much healed. I get to her ankle and when I put pressure on it, she pulls away slightly, a light moan leaving her mouth.

"What's that?" Dr. Tomik turns to me.

"Nothing, I don't see-" I lift her foot and right in the center of the sole is a small cut, but it's dark red and seeping at the sides. "Fuck, I think it's this."

Dr. Tomik moves from what he is doing to come to where I am. "Ah, yes. This is it. That's definitely infected. I'll start her on some focal antibiotics and get this cleaned up."

"Ok now that we know what it is, when will she get better?"

"Mr. Kokot, I'll do everything that I can, but there is no

guarantee that she will get better right away. Depends on how well her body fights off the infection."

Dread starts to inch its way up my throat. "I mean she can't die right? That can't happen?"

"Yes, there is a possibility that she will pass, but it's not the norm in cases like this."

I stop listening the minute he said it was a possibility. I can't have failed her so completely. She was forced into this life, put in my care, and it was my job to make sure that she was ok. Even if she frustrated the hell out of me, I should have been more diligent in her care and not just locked her in the room. I should have caught this sooner.

"Mr. Kokot? Did you hear me?"

"No, repeat." I snap out.

"I said that she will need to be given this antibiotic for ten days, I'll set her up for the night then come back again in the morning to reassess."

"Yes, thank you."

I stand back as he continues his work. Kaja comes back and drops off the rest of the materials that the doctor needs.

"Sven, you want to get a drink?"

"No, I have to stay with her."

"There is nothing more for you to do here. I'm just finishing up the final adjustments and then will just leave her to rest." The doctor looks over his shoulder for a second before he focuses his attention back to Ema.

"Ok, I guess I could use one."

Every step I take towards the study the more I begin to realize just how tired I am.

"You look like hell." Kaja says as I drop into my chair.

"In case you haven't noticed my wife is ill."

"Ah, yes, the same wife you didn't want. I mean no

offense, but I was quite surprised you even called for the doctor to begin with." Kaja pours us both a tumbler of Vodka.

"What? Why would I not?" I snatch the glass from his hand.

"Sven, you were so against the idea of having a wife. I didn't expect you to be so concerned about her care. I mean if she did die from natural circumstances that wouldn't be held against you. You would be free if you just let her pass away."

Just thinking about what he was saying gets me fuming. "Would you let your wife just die?"

"No, but I love Sabina. Even when she frustrates the hell out of me. When she got on every last nerve that I had, I knew she was different than the rest. Strong enough to handle what we do, yet independent enough to put me in my place should I need it. I'm starting to think maybe Ema is the same for you."

I scoff and sit back in my chair, "I don't love that woman. I can't get her to obey shit, she's just bullheaded and frustrating."

Kaja laughed, "I bet she is, the best ones are the ones that make you work. They don't come easy, and after seeing how hard she is making you work ... I think she may just be exactly what you need."

14

Ema

My mouth is so damn dry when I wake up. My body aches all over like I've just run a fucking marathon, but I don't feel as bad as I did the last time I woke up. The last time I'd opened my eyes I was in the shower with Sven. I was held in his arms like he never wanted to let me go. He was holding me how I figured a man should hold their wife. The last man that had held me made my stomach clench with disgust. I hadn't wanted it. I've tried to move on from it, I mean I was seventeen when he took what he wanted. Despite that no one had ever made me feel so at ease that I could focus on anything besides what had happened to me before.

I'm young and of course I have urges, but I've never pushed myself past that edge. I'd never felt as safe as I did that very second I woke up and saw the way that Sven was looking at me. Felt the way that he was holding me, and knew even if he had to lock me in the bathroom to do it, he was going to keep me safe. I don't remember a lot of what was going on, but I do remember him telling me that it didn't have to be like this. I'd been so focused on the fact that I was forced to marry him that it didn't even occur to me that this might be a good match.

When he was holding me in the shower, he'd said it didn't have to be this way. Maybe it didn't.

I stretch out, waking my body up. My foot is bandaged. I wonder if that is the cause of all this. The cut was small last time I had checked it. Though I will admit that I hadn't been taking care of it the best way that I should have.

The door opens and Sven walks in.

"Good morning." My voice is hoarse, but loud enough for him to hear me.

"Ema!" He drops what he has in his hands and comes over to me. "How are you feeling? Your foot?"

"Better. Much better."

"Good." He sits down next to me on the bed. "You caused quite the ruckus around here."

I bristle immediately. "Sorry I had to almost die for a second." I suck my teeth and look away from him. So much for thinking that I could like him.

"Whose fault is that?" He stands up over me, his fists balled and his face flushing, "You keep fucking running away. There is nowhere for you to go. Every time you make an escape attempt, I end up having to save you, pulling your ass out of some fucked up situation. Then on top of all of that you keep your injuries to yourself. If you would have told me about your foot, I would have taken care of it. This didn't have to happen."

"Leave the shackle off." I say calmly.

His eyebrows cinch in confusion, "What?"

"You want things to get better. We have to learn to trust

one another. You're right. There is nowhere for me to go. Nothing that I can do for the time being. So, a compromise. Leave the cuff off and you have my word that I won't try to run away." I'm telling the truth, but my subconscious screams at me, there are people back home that depend on me. My sisters need my protection. Is my telling him that I won't run just me giving up on them. I can't leave them without protection, yet I can't get away from here. I'm stuck.

He shakes his head at me clearly not believing what I'm saying. "What do you expect me to do, watch you every day. I have things that need to be done. Work. I'm already behind on everything, because I keep having to babysit you."

"I'm a grown woman. I don't need babysitting. All I'm asking, as your wife, is for you to leave the cuff off."

He stares at me for a few seconds before he speaks again, "Fine. I'll leave the cuff off. But if I find out that you attempt to leave again. I swear I will have a custom one made so that you'll never be able to get out of this room again."

"I said I won't, you have to trust me."

He pulls a small pouch out of his back pocket and hooks it up to the IV stand that is by the bed.

"What's that?"

"Antibiotics. You need to be on them for the next ten days."

"Ugh, ten days like this? Can't I just take them by mouth like normal?"

"The doctor said you need to take them this way." He continues changing out the bag.

"I hate it, can we just ask? Please?"

His eyes drop down to mine and he sighs out in defeat.

"Fine, I'll see if it's possible."

"Thank you."

He shuffles from foot to foot, looking uncomfortable. I'd take that over angry any day.

After he checked that everything was still working, he turns to leave.

"What are you doing today?" I ask before he can reach the door.

"I have to get a few profiles together of everyone that is going to be working on that deal we have with your uncle. They'll be here any day now to pick up the specs and other information." He turns fully in my direction, "Why?" his glare somehow making me blush. Why should I be embarrassed? It was only me and him in the house. Olive came regularly, but she busied herself with her chores only checking on me when she needed to. I had already been here for a few days. I was lonely.

"Maybe you want to sit in here with me. Talk?"

"You want to ... talk?"

"Yes, I figure we should get to know each other a little better. Maybe help us to not want to kill each other at every turn?"

He nods and takes a few steps closer, "I agree, not wanting to gag and bind you might be good for both of us."

I gasp slightly, "You want to gag me? Then how would I scream? I know you love it when I do that." I laugh at my own joke until I see his face.

"Yes, I'd love to hear you scream." He smiles and shoots me a wink.

I smile wider and look away from him. "Pervert."

"Only with you it seems."

"Lucky me."

"Maybe one day we'll find out just how lucky we both are."

I don't respond, but I clench my thighs closer together at the thought. What would it feel like to be with Sven? Even though I know I shouldn't, he's keeping me here against my will, but I have to admit a part of me hopes it won't be long until I find out.

∼

THREE DAYS OF PLAYING NICE, that was all we could muster.

I have so much on my mind and though I try to talk to him, it's not like he's the easiest man to talk to. Not only that but I'm so worried about my sisters. They're all I can think about and it's putting me on edge. It's not his fault, but right now everything is pissing me off. Even the fact that he had Olive make a stew without asking me if that is what I wanted to eat.

"I don't want this." I push the bowl of stew out from in front of me.

"You need to eat it, you need more protein."

"I don't want protein, I want chocolate or cake or ice cream." I cross my arms over my chest.

"What the hell are you, three? Eat food like an adult."

I lean forward in my chair. "That is the problem, I'm an adult. I should be able to make my own decisions about what I eat! What I wear! What I do! I swear it feels like you have my entire life planned out and I don't even get to see what's on the to-do list!" My voice raises to a high-pitched level.

"Ema, I don't have time for this. We have stew for dinner. Just eat it."

"No!"

After two days on the IV the doctor said that I could take the rest of the course of medication by mouth. I felt fine, the wound was still tender, but loads better than what it was. I would think that with my improving condition, Sven would back off a bit, but it seems like it's the absolute opposite. It feels like he is controlling every aspect of my life. I won't be surprised if he asks me for a piss sample next.

I know this argument is childish, but right now it's the only thing I feel like I have control over. For fuck's sake, the man still has me wearing his clothes.

"Ema, I don't have the patience for this." He leans forward in his chair and pushes the bowl back in front of me.

"I don't care what you have the patience for, I'm not going to eat it." I push it away again.

"Fucking fine!" He yells, stands and tosses my food across the table. "You don't want to eat. Then don't fucking eat!"

I wait for him to hit me or punish me, but he doesn't. He stares at me for a second before he huffs and leaves his bowl of food on the table next to me walking out of the dining area.

I roll my neck and get up to do my best at cleaning up the area. Olive shouldn't have to wake up to this. Thoughts of everything that could be happening back home right now, run rampant in my head. What if he's hurting them? Does my mom have to work more? Why didn't I do more to stop him?

By the time I finished cleaning the stew off the floor, I had worked myself up into a ball of tension. I go upstairs and get in the big empty bed, hopefully a good night's rest will be what I need to relax. I pray it is.

15

Sven

My home is supposed to be my peace yet here she is fucking it up. I sit in my favorite chair in the study staring at the unlit fireplace with a glass of vodka in my hand. I've never met anyone who could wind me up as tightly as Ema and it seems like everything is a fight. Dinner? She was pissed that I fed her. After blowing up like that I need something to take the edge off. I knew this was going to be a test, I just didn't think that it was going to be this fucking difficult.

"No! Please stop! Get away!"

Fear blossoms in my chest as I hear Ema screaming out. I'm here in the study, so it must mean that there is someone else hurting her. Someone is hurting my woman.

I push myself out of the chair and run in the direction of my room. Pulling my gun out of the waist of my pants, I fight to slow down my motions. The last thing I want is for whoever is in there with her to get surprised and hurt her more. What if they are holding a gun or knife to her? They could kill her. A growl tries to push its way up out of my chest, but I push it back down. I have to stay present for this.

I push open the door and see her flailing, her hands swinging wildly as she screams and begs for someone to stop. Thing is, there is no one here. It's just her and whatever demons she is battling in her head.

"*Jebote!*" I curse out and put my gun back into my pants. I quickly walk over to where she is, my heart still beating like crazy out of my chest, but not from thinking she is going to be hurt. No, it's because of the fear I can see plastered on her face even as she sleeps.

"Ema!" I sit on the bed next to her and catch her free arm swinging around, but she still doesn't wake up. I press a hand to her forehead, but there is no fever that I can feel. I shake her shoulders slightly. Her eyes bloodshot and wet from tears open, she doesn't see me though. Instead, she is looking right through me.

"Ema!" I shake her again.

This time she blinks a few times as more tears fall from her eyes before she sucks in a huge breath and her entire body shudders.

"Oh my God. Oh God." Her body crumples as she looks around and sees that she is still in the room and not in whatever nightmare she just had. Surprisingly instead of just falling back to the bed she wraps her arms around me and clutches to me like I'm her lifeline. I hold her back, happy that even if it's only in her time of need she comes to me for a little comfort.

"Hey, what's going on. Are you ok?"

"You have to let me go. Please you have to let me go." She sobs and her head falls down in despair. Her pleas tug at something deep in me that I didn't even realize I could feel.

"Ema, don't start this now you know that I can't. I've already explained this to you. I can't let you go. You have to stay here with me. Is that what you were dreaming about?"

She sobs harder as she croaks out a "No."

"Then what is it? What were you dreaming about that has you so afraid?"

"He's going to come for Mari. Now that I'm not there I just know he is going to come for Mari. I've been trying so hard to get away from you so I can get back to her. She's too young, but that's how he likes them. I was only able to stave him off, because I was always there. Dad is working and mom doesn't believe me. I ... I can't be here." She looks up into my eyes, her words come out fast from her panic and I can tell that she is telling the truth. The sparkle of the tears that are still there does nothing to hide the sincerity in her eyes.

From what I know about her through my research, I believe this Mari she is talking about is her little sister—fourteen years old.

"Mari, your sister? Who is coming for her? How do you know?" I ask trying to get as much information as I can.

"You don't believe me either." Her voice a whisper as she scoots back from me and wipes her eyes.

"No, don't do that." I move closer, closing the space between us. "I just need some information. I believe you. Just tell me what's going on."

"What for, there is nothing that you can do about it. No one has ever been able to do anything about it." Her voice is low and she looks away.

"You don't know much about me. There is very little

that I can't do. Tell me what is going on. Let me help you." My voice is tense. I don't know what or who had hurt her, but I have a burning need to make them hurt worse than they could ever hurt her. No one should ever make her cry like that.

"Fine." She blows out a hard breath and wraps her arms around her legs as she pulls them up to her chest. "In the little town that we live in up in Alaska there aren't very many people, in fact most of the people that come in are either vendors or fishermen. My father can spend months out on the sea fishing and while it does bring in a nice amount, he has to kick back at least half to the family as tribute. My mother still has to go out and do little odd jobs here and there. There is a man in town, Bryson Mixer, he used to watch me and my sisters while my mother went off to work. He was nice at first … let us run around in the backyard, taught me how to drive, gave me my first drink, but then as I hit about fifteen he started to take more of an interest in me. Telling me how beautiful I was, how I was going to make some man very happy when I grew up. How he just wanted to make sure that I was as prepared as I could be when I got married." She continues, but the goosebumps on my arms had already raised. I've heard this story before not the same players, but the same script. I stay quiet as she keeps going.

"He would give me sips of beer, but around fifteen he really started to let me drink, he would give me shots and whiskey. When I got drunk, he would kiss and touch me. I would tell him to stop, but he never did. Always telling me that I liked it because my heart was beating fast or because my nipples would get hard. He got me so drunk one day I couldn't even stand. I shouldn't have drunk that much, but I'd had a fight with my mother. It felt good to have someone who acted like they understood me and treated me like a grown up. He took me in the back room telling me that I needed to get some rest before I threw up. I went to lay down and ... when I woke up, he was raping me. He took my virginity and told me that everyone in town already knew that I was a fast girl. He told me that if I ever told anyone anything that he would just go for one of my sisters. Still, it didn't stop me. The very next day when my mother got home, I told her what had happened and she told me that I was lying. That I had too much to drink, and that old Mr. Mixer had done nothing to me but help me to bed. In fact, I got in trouble all because I was drinking. She punished me for two weeks. That was when I was seventeen. Since then though I convinced my mother that I was mature enough to watch the girls on my own when she would have to work and that we didn't need to go back over to Mr. Mixer's house. Anytime I would complain about having to watch the girls she would say that I didn't have to since Bryson would watch them for her, but I never let him. When he would come over to visit, I would see how he looked at me. I noticed how he was starting to look at Mari. I told her to never be alone with him, but without me there I can't keep him away. He's going to do the same thing to her that he did to me and no one there is going to stop it." She finishes her story and fresh tears stream down her face in panic and desperation.

"Do you know where he lives?" The cogs in my head already turning. She wasn't my wife back then, but she is now. I've always been protective of people in my family. Just the fact that this piece of shit is still walking around free and clear fills me with such an insanely protective purpose that I think I may fly over to Alaska and kill him myself.

"Not the exact address, I just knew how to get there. His place is on one of the backroads. Look don't worry about it. This is my problem. I just hope Mari listens to what I told her. She is a stubborn girl like me, I have no doubt that she will fight him off." Ema closes her eyes and nods her head. Trying her best to console herself and convince herself that everything is going to be fine.

I grab her chin and her eyes pop open. She doesn't have to convince herself that everything is going to be fine, I'm going to make sure it is. "Everything is fine now. Calm down." I loosen my grip on her chin and softly drag my fingers to her neck. "Lay down and wait for me to come back. Don't go to sleep, you understand?"

Her eyebrows pinch and her lips press together as she nods her head yes.

I get up, rushing to get to my office so that I can open up my laptop and do some research. It was almost too easy for me to find this man. It wasn't even like he was hiding. All I had to do was punch in his name and the town in which he lives. Several news articles pop up about the good he has done with the youth in the community. Fucking pedophile piece of shit. I save a clear photo of his face as well as his address and make my way back into the room to Ema.

I sit on the bed next to her and pull up the photo that I'd saved from my search. "Is this the man?" I show her the photo and she cringes away from it like even the act of looking at him causes her pain.

"Yes, how did you get that?" She asks. I almost laugh at the question, there is very little information on this planet that I'm not able to get. Especially in this day and age when everything is run by technology. It's almost too easy sometimes.

"I have my ways." It was the only answer that she would need for the moment. I had other things I needed to do, but this particular problem demanded to be handled as soon as possible. Thankfully, I knew one hitman that would be perfect for the job.

I pluck out my phone and dial Dagger's number. After I had helped him with everything that he needed to do to get his woman back from her tyrant of a father, he is always around when I need him to take someone out. Dagger is probably the best hitman in the entire Juric family. I've never met anyone as thorough as him. Yes, he would do just fine. It didn't even matter that it was nearly two in the morning, Dagger picked up his phone by the third ring.

"Sven?"

Da, listen I need something handled. Right away."

"Time frame?" He asks, need specifics on how long he had to take out the target.

"Twenty-four hours."

"Connection?" He has to know if this job or this target had any links to the family. He would need to go through special channels if they did.

"No."

"Preferences?" He wants to know if there was any special way that I wanted him to complete the job.

"Painful."

"Done, send over the specs. I'll return with confirmation."

I hang up the phone and log into the dark web. From there I send him the man's photo and the location along with any other demographic information that I might have.

"Ok, it's fixed."

"What? What's fixed?" She asks looking at me like I have lost my mind. Her head tilts to the side with eyes squinted.

"Mr. Mixer will be dead in the next twenty-four hours."

Her mouth drops open and a quick breath comes out of her mouth. Her lips open and close a few times before she is able to speak again. "What do you mean? How? You can't just do that."

Now it's my turn to look at her in surprise, "Were you lying?"

"No!" She says quickly, her eyes locking onto mine. "I told you the truth, but you can't just go around killing people."

"Why not? Should he just go around raping little girls? Do you think he should get a pass for doing something like that to you?"

Her eyes close slightly and her bottom lip trembles, "No, of course not. He should pay."

"Then he will. He will pay with his life and he will never be able to hurt Mari or anyone else. He won't be able to hurt you ever again."

She put a hand up to her mouth as another bout of tears fill her eyes. She sobs, the sound breaking my heart much more than I would like to admit.

"Does this upset you?"

She takes a second to inhale and get herself together, "No, I mean it's sudden and intense, but I'm not upset about it. I don't want anyone to get into trouble except him though. I just never thought it would be as easy as that. Just a phone call and done." She shrugs.

"There is so much that I can make easy. All you have to do is ask and it'll be done."

"I'm seeing that." Her voice is low and there is an easy

smile on her face. In this moment I think she may have forgotten that she hates my guts, a lull to the fighting. It makes me feel good to have been able to help her when no one else could.

There is one thing that is on my mind though and I hope that it doesn't put her in a foul mood. Though I think it might give me the answer I had been searching for when we were in the shower together.

"Can I ask you a question?" I wait for her answer as I don't want to push.

"Sure."

"When we were in the shower together and I asked you if I were the only one who had ever seen you. You told me no, but there was force to it, shame? Was Bryson the only one besides me to see you naked?"

She looks away from me, but nods her head. I left it at that. It's no wonder she had such a hard time letting me see her. The only other time she had been that vulnerable, someone raped her.

"Ok, go back to sleep. I'll let you know when it's done." I raise myself off the bed getting ready to go back to the study.

"Will you be long?" Her voice is soft and she is already pulling the covers up over her body.

I have to stop and process what she is asking me. She wants to know if I'll be away from her for a while. It makes sense that she is still rattled from the intensity of the nightmare that she had. I can't deny that it's uplifting to hear that she actually wants me to be with her even if it is to protect her from a dream.

"No. I think I'll go to bed now." There are a few things that I need to get done, but I can do them in the morning. Surprisingly she is asking for me to stay in her own way and I don't want to deny her. I mean it may never happen again.

I walk over to my side of the bed and take off my clothes leaving only my undershirt and boxers on. I get under the blanket with her and can feel her body still slightly trembling. I've only slept in the same bed with a few women and the need to cuddle has never been something that appealed to me. I don't even know why I feel the need to do so now. My initial thought is so that I can keep her in bed. If my arms are wrapped around her, then I don't have to worry about her trying to run away. I'd feel her trying to move. I'm satisfied with that reason. I turn towards her in the bed and very slowly slide my arms around her waist. She stills for a second before she relaxes and settles. When she moves back and my grip tightens around her, I know that my reasoning behind holding her is not about keeping her from escaping, but more from wanting her to be closer.

16

Sven

My cock stirs to life and I press myself hard against the body in front of me—a soft body. A soft body that is moaning and whimpering as I grind against her.

A soft body moaning in my bed.

My eyes pop open, who the fuck is in my bed?

When I wake up completely, I can see Ema's dark hair splayed all around herself and on the pillow. Her chest is still rising slowly, and her mouth is parted slightly as she moans and rubs herself back against me.

"Dammit." I groan and have to stop myself from pulling her tighter against me. I know what I'm doing. Though we might have been on good terms last night if she wakes up this morning and feels me dry humping her, she isn't going to be happy about it in the least. I push myself away from her and the slight whimper that comes out of her mouth as she rolls onto her back has me cursing my self-control.

It's still very early in the morning, barely 5 am, but I have my weekly meeting set up for 6 with Josip. He has the names of crew members over in Alaska that would be willing to get the job done on Filip's fishing vessel as quick as possible. Josip's going to check in for the week and debrief me on any deals that need my attention.

I quickly jump in the shower, a little upset that Ema isn't in here with me. Now that I've had a chance to see what she looks like under the spray of that shower it's really no fun without her.

I dry off and get dressed. When I'm ready to meet Josip, Ema is still sound asleep. I would allow it. She had a rough night.

There is a knock on my bedroom door, and I rush over to open it for Olive. I don't want her to wake Ema.

I put a finger to my mouth indicating that she should be quiet. Her eyes squint as her mouth presses into a tight line before she looks over my shoulder and sees Ema in the bed asleep. Her eyes widen and the tenseness in her face relaxes as she nods her head.

"Josip?" I whisper. She nods again before turning and walking away.

I close the door to my room. I have left her sleeping in the room untethered and part of me wants to trust her enough to believe that she won't try to run away, but I don't. The last time I tried to give her some leeway while I was in a meeting she ran off into the desert and I had to kill a fucking Sidewinder snake. Not something I would look forward to doing again.

There was a candle holder that looked to be the shape that I would need in order to successfully lock her in the room. I hook it onto the doorknob and turn the body of the candle holder so that it was pressing on the wall. If she tries to open the door it would stop it from being pulled back. If I was going to keep this up, I would need to get a lock for the outside of my bedroom door.

When I'm satisfied that she is secure in the room I make my way to the study where I know Josip is waiting for me. That is the norm for our meetings and Josip is a man of habit.

"Ah, I was beginning to think you'd slept in." He jokes when I walk into the study, three minutes past the time we are usually due to start.

"No, just making sure my assets are secure." I reply.

His mouth drops into an O for a second before he nods his head as if he understands, "Your lovely wife still giving you problems?"

"Not problems, just that we are still getting to know each other." I say not wanting to divulge too much.

"I see, well I hope you work them out soon." Josip pulls out one of the chairs near my desk. He sits down, laying his tablet and phone on the dark mahogany wood.

I tilt my head to the side and walk around to my chair. There is something in between the lines of what he just said, "Why is that?"

"I was in a meeting with Marko yesterday and an interesting call came through, I'm assuming it was from Ivan Sever."

I clench my jaw and keep my face blank. On the inside though I was already screaming in frustration.

"I don't know all the details to what was said. But they were talking a lot about your mark and how your wife doesn't have it. Ivan seems to think that you are not upholding your promise to make her your wife."

"*Sranje*! I married her, he was there."

"Yes, so was I, but that is all formality and you know it

as well as I. That mark is the real sign to everyone that the match has been made. Until she has your mark, she's not really your wife at least not in the eyes of the family." Josip shrugs his shoulder. "If they asked me right now, I'd have to agree with Ivan in saying you have not held up your side of the bargain. From the look on Marko's face, he seems to feel the same."

Fuck! Fuck, fuck fuck! Disappointing Marko is not something that I ever wanted to do. Not only since I strive to be the best that I can be for the family, but because in all intents and purposes I view that man as my father, even if isn't by birth. He is only fifteen years older than me, but he'd groomed me from the very beginning. Molded me into the man that I am today. I know he loves me, I mean he adopted me. However, I also know that he will kill me in an instant if I go against him. I'm going to have to get my mark on Ema and quick.

"I see, well my plan is to get her inked as soon as possible though it is none of Ivan's concern and I told him such."

Josip scoffs and puts in his password to open his tablet, "Probably why he is making such a big deal out of it. You have a way of rubbing that man the wrong way."

I don't have a response to that. It's true that Ivan hasn't been one of my favorite people in the world and I would have to learn how to be more cordial with him. Staying allies within the various crime families is hard work and it could be one tiny slight that causes the whole truce to break apart.

"What of the crew?" I dive right into business and Josip doesn't miss a beat. We sit there for the next forty-five minutes going over everything he has for me. The crew is ready to work on the boat right away as soon as I get the final schematics over to them. I would have to finish those up tonight. There are still a few issues that need to be addressed, from the problems Dominik is having with counterfeit marked bills, to the long stay of one of Matej's kidnap victims. Nothing that really needs to be addressed immediately. I would get working on it soon enough. As we close out the meeting, I still hadn't heard Ema try to open the door and the alarm hadn't gone off from her trying to go out of the window. Hopefully she was still asleep and wouldn't realize that I'd locked her in. If I could keep some peace today I would.

Josip stands and promises to send me the rest of the information that I would need to start fixing the problems within the family.

A ping on my phone alerts me of a message. Glancing at my screen I see that it's Dagger letting me know that he is on his way to the location, no doubt already in the air. He is located in Washington so getting up to Alaska shouldn't take him anytime at all.

"Sven, I have a favor to ask of you. Nothing really for you to do, but if you catch wind of any information ..." Josip raises his chin and looks me in the eyes, but his hands give him away. He is nervous. Josip rarely asks for anything and when he does it's for the family. A personal favor. I was intrigued before he could even tell me what it was.

"Go on."

"There are rumors that Lyrica Grady, a friend of Sloane Deluca is missing and in the hands of a white supremacy group. I haven't been able to find out any information. But if anything crosses your path, I'd appreciate a heads up." He stands there and waits for what I have to say.

I should have known and almost shake my head in

discouragement. The Deluca Clan and the Juric Family have had a long-standing truce. Honestly, we don't really have any reason to mix so we are all on friendly terms. The issue is that Josip is sweet on Orabella DeLuca. A woman that he can't have. The warning was sent loud and clear years ago when her father had caught them behind closed doors closer than they should have been. Luckily, they weren't doing anything, but all ties were supposed to have been severed. The fact that Josip was looking into finding a Deluca when the request had not come from the higher ups themselves or straight from Marko could only mean one thing. He was doing some shit he shouldn't.

"I will do what I can."

He exhales, releasing all the stress that he was keeping bottled up for that brief moment in time. He turns to walk away, but before his hand reaches the knob I say.

"Tread carefully." I don't need to explain or give him any more information. He turns his head to the side so he can see me through his peripheral and nods once. Josip realizes that I know he is getting himself into some shit. We don't have to talk about it, but we both know.

17

Sven

The door closes and I grab my own tablet plus a few other things that I think will help me complete these schematics. It's not the first time that I've had to design something for Marko, but it was the first time I would have to do it with a fishing boat. The dimensions were tricky.

When I make it back upstairs, the candlestick has moved. I exhale and brace myself for the fight I'm sure is about to come. I pull the makeshift door stopper away from the knob and slowly open the door. I had left my weapons in the room and she could be holding a gun just waiting for me to come back in.

When I peer in, she is sitting on the bed, hair wet, and a towel wrapped around her body. A scowl on her face as she wiggles her foot in anger.

"I didn't know you were awake." I say as I make my way into the room.

"How would you know? You were off walking around while I was caged in here like a fucking animal."

My body jerks in her direction, I can't stand it when she curses. At me especially. "You must enjoy the punishments, is that what this is? Do you enjoy it?"

Her leg stops shaking and she turns to me quickly, "No. Of course, I don't."

"Then watch your damn mouth. You would think something as simple as stop cursing would be something that you would be able to manage. Instead, it seems like you are intent on pushing me every day with all the fibers of your being." My voice is thick with grit and anger.

"You're right."

My shoulders drop and all the anger that I was about to unleash escapes through my mouth with the next breath I exhale.

I'm right? Did she say that? I must be hearing things.

"What?" I ask just for verification, because she has never been this open to seeing anything my way since she has been here.

"You're right, this is a shit ..." She cringes, "Sorry, I mean this is a bad position for anyone to be in. Neither one of us wants to be in this marriage, but the least I can do is respect how you want to be talked to. It's a battle I don't need to fight."

Did I just win? I look around slightly not knowing what to do with myself. I had spent the last few days fighting this woman tooth and nail on everything. From her mouth to what she wears to even washing her ass and all of a sudden, she was telling me she didn't want to fight.

"That's ... well that's relieving." I can't help, but chuckle.

"I don't know what you want me to wear." She says

clutching at the towel that is still wrapped around her body.

I walk over to my dresser and pull out a fresh pair of jogging pants and a shirt for her to wear along with some socks. She stands with her back to me and quickly puts the clothes on.

Memories of her firm ass rubbing against me as I woke up this morning spring back to the front of my mind. The bruises on her body are starting to turn an ugly yellow color, but at least they are all starting to heal up. They take nothing away from her figure. Curves I'm chomping at the bit to get a piece of. I'm not used to being in the company of women for long periods of time, Olive being the only exception. I need her to keep working as my maid, so I have never even attempted anything with her. Ema is not someone who works for me, this woman bares my name, my ring, and very soon my mark. I'm usually the master of my entire body, but remaining celibate with someone as delicious as Ema sharing my bed with me is proving to be difficult.

When she turns back in my direction clad in my oversized clothes, I have to shake those thoughts out of my head and pray that she doesn't realize how hard I am for her right now.

"Would you care to join me for a working breakfast?" I ask trying to keep the civility between us.

"Sure, I wouldn't mind having some breakfast." She crosses her arms over her chest and walks in my direction, a small limp as she does.

"How's your leg?"

"It's just a little sore. Nothing to worry about."

I accept her explanation, but file it away in the back of my mind. If she is still complaining of it later, I will make a call to the doctor. The very last thing I need is for her to get sick again.

She walks to the dining room and Olive has already placed two plates on the table one at the head and one to the right of it. I sit at the head and Ema sits beside me. Her knee brushing up against mine under the table.

"Sorry." She blushes slightly and tries to move away. I can't stand the embarrassment, there is nothing for her to be worried about. I hook my leg behind her chair and pull it as close to me as possible. If I put my hand under the table, I would easily touch her leg.

"We're married, we should learn to be close to each other." I say as I pick up my fork and start to eat the omelet that Olive has prepared for us. Ema does the same.

"Mr. Kokot, would you like me to take …" Olive walks out of the kitchen and into the dining room a sudden shock on her face when she sees Ema sitting at the table. "I didn't hear anything, I thought you were upstairs. Sorry for the interruption." Olive backs out of the dining room. Though I don't miss the smile on her face when she sees Ema eating on her own accord and not on the floor crying or screaming.

After a few moments of Ema eating what she wants she starts to push the food around. The scraping of the fork against the plate irking my nerves.

"Something on your mind?" I ask, grabbing her wrist to stop her from continuing to make that noise.

She looks up at me and then back down to her plate. The blush crawling back up her face, but this time its accompanied with a clenched jaw. Frustration. "Yesterday, you said there wasn't much that you couldn't do."

I put my fork down and give her my complete attention. She had a request. "That's correct."

She taps her foot quickly before she lets out a hard sigh and looks up to me, "Look I don't like having to ask people for things. In my experience, you never get anything for free."

"Ema, I'm here to keep you safe and make sure that your needs are met. If you need something and it's in my power to get it then you will have it. There is no pretense or need to pay it back. If you were to divorce me right now, in the eyes of the law, you would get half of everything I own anyway." I say it in an effort to appease her.

She relaxes a little bit, before she continues on to what she wants. "You have made it abundantly clear that you intend on keeping me here for a long while."

"Absolutely." I reply quickly.

She rolls her eyes, but continues, "How do you expect me to live? I don't even have underwear. You keep saying you don't want me to act like an animal. But besides me being locked in a room, you don't even give me the basic necessities. I need clothes, a toothbrush, toiletries, something to keep my attention, I need ..."

"Agreed." I say before she can get any more excited than what she already is.

"Agreed?"

"Yes, we will go out today and get you whatever you need."

"Really?" She sits back in her chair surprised.

"Yes. You were dragged into this with nothing and there is no reason that you should stay like that. You need your own things." I nod and pick up my fork, hopefully this conversation is over.

"Let me guess you will be accompanying me?"

"Even into the dressing rooms." I smile at her and she rolls her eyes.

An outing, this could be dangerous. Not that I expect anyone to do anything to her especially with Dagger taking care of the problem in Alaska. Still if something were to happen to her, it would be hard to press a complaint if she didn't have my mark.

Now it was my turn to ask for something difficult, except my request would be permanent and painful.

"Ema, there are certain duties that you and I are expected to fulfill. Duties that we have been slacking on and the families are starting to take notice." I explain.

"Duties like what?" She grabs for her juice and takes a quick swallow.

"For one, you don't bare my mark. I believe your family has a similar tradition when it comes to validating a marriage."

Her face pales, even her pink lips pick up a greyish hue. "Your mark?"

"Our marriage is not valid until you have it. Once you do no one would be able to bother you no matter if you were with me or not." I quickly explain suddenly wanting her to be ok with it. I didn't want her to look so distraught just by the thought of it.

"You're going to brand me?" She whispers.

My mind races as I go over the information that I have about her family's marriage practices. They also had a mark, but theirs was a bit more primitive. It was their family crest and the husband's initials, but it was placed with a branding iron.

"A brand yes, but not in the way you are thinking. For us, our mark is a tattoo. To be precise, my signature tattooed on you."

"Tattoo?" Her body relaxes slightly, apparently a tattoo was less scary than a brand.

"Yes. Ivan noticed that you didn't have one the other day. It's not going over well." I admit to her.

"It'll hurt?"

"Yes, it's a long process, but some say it's meditative."

"Why is it long? I thought you said it was only your signature. That should be one two three, no?"

"It would be with more advanced equipment, but we still use the old method. All done by hand with an individual needle."

"Where will you put it?"

"Where would you like it?"

"Do I have a choice?" She raises her chin, her eyes full of annoyance. Even though I can see that she is having a hard time with it, she is taking this much better than I would have thought

"Yes, if you are going to be amenable to this and I don't have to tie you down. I'll let you choose the location. Anywhere from your ankle to your neck. Be mindful that someone might demand to see this at a moment's notice."

She swirls her drink around in her cup for a few seconds. "Right here." She stands and pulls down her pants slightly pressing to the bottom of her flat stomach. A few inches above her trimmed mound, but low enough that underwear could still hide it.

I focus in on the space that she is showing me. I raise my hand and let my finger trail over the flesh. My mind imagines my name sprawled in my handwriting permanently etched in her skin. Only visible to me yet still speaking loudly to the world that she belongs to me. It excites me much more than I think it should. The possessiveness that I feel for her even though I know I will be letting her go after the year is over triples inside my chest. She'll be mine—signed and delivered.

A soft gasp leaves her mouth, and my eyes jump to hers. Her eyes are alert and entirely focused on my hand. If I had thought that I saw even the smallest amount of fear I would move away. She's already been through enough when it came to someone forcing themselves on her body. Instead, the slight tremble of her body and the soft panting lets me know she likes it. Maybe I'm getting ahead of myself, but it seems like she is having just as hard of a time as I am keeping myself away from her.

She shakes her head, and her eyes fall on the papers that I have on the table with the schematics of how I'm going to hide the nukes.

"What are you doing?" Her eyebrows furrow in and her head angles to the side as she drops the shirt back down. I remove my hand and turn my attention back to the papers. Papers that she shouldn't actually be looking at, but what can it hurt.

"I have to give this to the crew who is going to modify your father's vessel."

"No, the hell you are not!" She basically screams at me.

My head whips in her direction, I give an inch and she takes a fucking yard. "Woman, I've already told you about your damn mouth."

She puts her hands up to calm me, "Sorry that was aggressive, I just didn't expect you to say something like that. I mean it though, you can't alter the boat like that."

"Why is that? It's the perfect dimensions to conceal the multiple warheads."

"I'm assuming you expect this to happen on one of my father's fishing trips?"

"Well yes, that would be the best time, because it's my understanding that its normal for fishing vessels to go that far up for a catch." I ease up a bit as it seems like she is trying to get at something that has nothing to do with her disrespecting me.

"It is, but that will be a full load. If you put this here, you will capsize the boat. You'll kill my father and the crew, not to mention lose whatever you are trying to get back here from the Bering Sea."

I squint my eyes at her, that didn't make sense, but this was the daughter of a long time fisherman. Maybe she knew something I didn't.

"Sit, explain this to me."

She quickly does and for the first time since she got here it feels like we are making some type of progress. I can get used to this.

18

Sven

I hate her.

I hate her and everything that she is doing to me. I don't think I have ever been tortured so thoroughly. When I show her the message from Dagger about the target being taken out, I thought she would be nicer to me, hell even show a little bit of appreciation. Except this feels more like she is taking joy in my agony.

"What about this one?" She asks as she turns around in front of me with the millionth sweater.

"It's fine." I reply without looking at her. When I told her that I was going to be the one to go shopping with her I assumed she would pick up a few packs of underwear, some jeans, a dress or two and that would be it. We've been at this for 8 hours and parts of my brain feel like its dribbling out of my ears.

"You were the one that said you wanted to go shopping

with me. I'm more than perfectly capable of shopping on my own."

"You are also known for trying to make a run for it when you are left on your own as well." I reply gruffly.

"If I weren't here against my will maybe you wouldn't have to worry about that."

"Yeah," I look pointedly at the numerous bags already piled in the corner, "You look like you are having a horrible time." I shake my head and go back to my phone.

I can feel her staring daggers at me, but I don't need to look up. I hear her walking back into the dressing room, probably to try on another sweater that looks exactly the same as the first million.

She must have spent at least 3000 dollars on just clothes alone. It's not the money that I was concerned about, I have more than enough for anything that she would want to buy. It's the indecision. She picks one thing up and puts it back to pick up another. Only to go back to the first one and compare it to the second. Then she finds a third one that looks nothing like the first two and decides that's not good enough. I feel like I'm in my own personal level of Hell.

"Does this make the experience a little better for you?" She says from where she is standing in front of me, a snarky smile on her face.

I look up from my phone for a second and my jaw nearly drops to the floor. She is standing barefoot in a short dark blue dress. It's a satin material and it hugs every single one of her curves that I want to touch. Curves I want to taste. Curves that belong to me. Curves that she is showing the entire fucking store.

"Get the fuck back in there and put some clothes on." I growl out at her. The smile that was on her face drops off and she burns crimson before she turns to walk back into the small dressing room. I take a few breaths to calm myself down and follow behind her. I look around and there is no one watching. Besides if there was, they wouldn't stop me anyway.

I pull the curtain to her dressing room open, and she jumps up in surprise. She spins in my direction, her hand holding the top of the dress to her chest. She was in the middle of peeling herself out of it.

"What ... what are you doing in here?" She stutters.

"What am I doing in here? What are you doing?" I lean closer to her and she backs up until she is against the wall. "What are you doing coming out there in a dress like that? What are you doing showing everyone in the store what's mine?"

"Yours?" she bristles, "I'm my own woman. My body is mine."

"Yes, it belongs to you and you belong to me. I've spent the past few days forcing myself to keep my hands off of you. Not wanting to cloud what we are both here to do, but you seem to want to push my restraint."

"Well, you know what they say, sometimes it's good to let loose." Her voice is soft.

"Let loose, you don't want that." I say and press my hands to the wall on either side of her head.

"You don't know what I want." Her voice is barely audible as she stands there breathing fast and staring at me.

"I know exactly what you want. There will never be another who knows what you want better than me. The question is do you deserve it."

She gasps and goes to push me away except I quickly block her assault. Sliding my hands to the sides of her face

I slam our mouths together. The moan that leaves her mouth has me clawing to get inside of her. One hand roams down her side before it settles on her ass, the smooth material of the satin dress making her skin feel like the surface of a cool pond. The sensation barely squelching the burning fire inside me.

Our tongues swipe and war with each other. As aggressive as we are together, the passion that has been secretly building is beginning to bubble over. She nips at my lips and I press my pelvis into her trying to get some relief for my cock. I'm rock hard and ready to just impale her where she stands, wearing nothing but this dress.

She rips her mouth away from mine clearly thinking she is in control of what is happening here. While there is still ecstasy to be felt I will make her feel it. Using my hand, I keep her head pushed to the side as I lick and suck at her neck. She moans louder and her hands clutch my arms harder. She's rocking her hips against me now, desperate for some relief herself.

"Fuck I can't stand you." She moans out pulling me closer to her and I pull back denying her more friction.

"What did I tell you about that fucking mouth?" I whisper in her ear. "Maybe I need to put something in it for you to remember."

"Shhhhii ... Shoot. Come back." She tugs harder on me and I let her this time. Our mouths find each other again. The sounds of our lips kissing and moans of our need echoing in the air.

The sound of feet coming in our direction catch my attention a mere second before the drape is pulled back, "Hey! You two aren't supposed to-"

"Get the fuck out" I turn and roar at the man. Who the hell did he think he was?

He jumps back so scared that he stumbles and falls on his ass. Before he scrambles to his feet and runs back to wherever he came from.

"You're so angry." Ema laughs at me softly.

"Only when it comes to you." I compose myself and move away from her. "Let's buy what you need from here and be on our way before they call the cops on me."

"Ok." She nods and continues to peel herself out of that dress.

"Buy that dress ... in every fucking color they have." I turn and walk out of the dressing room to the sound of her cackling in laughter.

19

Sven

Finally, after another hour the shopping was done, and we could get back to the house. The strip was alive as always and though we were still a bit away the air's charged with the excitement of the nightlife.

When she strains her eyes to see the lights on the horizon, only then does it dawn on me that she might not even realize where we are. She was pulled from her home, onto a private jet, into a car, and then into Marko Juric's house to marry me. I had really never let her out and there were no TVs in my house except for the guest room I leave for Zeus.

"Have you ever seen Las Vegas?"

Her eyes lit up in wonder, "On the TV." She shrugs again before turning her attention back to the lights.

"You want to go?"

"Can we?" She reaches out and grabs my wrist tightly already pulling me to the car. Her excitement almost makes me crack a smile. I know that I should just go back home. I have shit to do, shit that has already been on hold for the past almost ten hours, because of the shopping spree she needed to take. I would appease her though. Besides the fact that I really was beginning to love seeing her face change as she reacted to certain things, she had saved my ass completely in regard to the fishing vessel. She'd explained it to me easily. Although I had taken into consideration what the ship could hold and the weight it had to stay above in order to float, I designed the hiding space right at the stern of the ship. Not only was the wheelhouse also located at the stern, but apparently the Bering sea was treacherous. A boat being that unlevel would mean that it was less likely to be able to ride the waves and would capsize. If the pots as she called it iced over that would also be added weight. Apparently, the entire boat is likely to freeze over up there and with all the added weight in just one section, the crabbing vessel would never make it back to port. With her help I created brand new schematics that would even out the weight more while making sure that there was still enough room in the tanks for the crabs. Even if the coast guard did board them, they would see that they were just fisherman. It was a genius plan, and one I wouldn't have come up with simply because I didn't know the small details.

 I could show her my appreciation with a tour of the strip. I'd lived here for so long that I've become immune to it, but I'm sure that it must look amazing to her.

 The entire drive there she smiles and asks inane questions.

 "How do they keep the sand out?"

 "How many Elvis impersonators do they really need?"

 "Do they really bury people in the desert?"

I only had a definitive answer to one of those questions and it was yes.

She stops asking so many questions after that.

She wanted to get out to see the people zip-lining. I willed her not to even ask to try it, because there is no way I was going to let her do that shit. I was getting edgy just thinking about it.

Once she had her fill of that, I parked my car in one of the valet lots that the family owns and we went for a short walk.

She turns around every few minutes to take in what was behind her like she hadn't just walked through it. Something like that would have usually drained every last bit of patience I had. Only seeing her smile when I'd spent the last few days with her snarling and screaming made me appreciate the little things.

She spun back around suddenly and her face fell slightly.

"Alex?" She calls out and a man turns toward her.

Alex? Yes, I remember him. He was at our wedding, said that he had a friendship with Ema.

"Oh, what a small place, what are you doing here?" He asks as he comes closer to us and kisses her on the cheek. My hand twitches toward the gun concealed by my shirt before he reaches his hand out to shake mine. I shake it instead of pulling my gun out.

"Just taking in the sights. What are you doing here? I thought for sure that you would be back home by now." She questions.

"Well, you know I have several clients out here. I'm constantly between here, California and back home. I'm thinking about helping a few folks up in Washington with some investment monies. Though I don't have anything up there yet."

"Wow that is so great." Ema says and pats him on the arm. Now I regret not keeping the cuffs on her. Maybe then she wouldn't be able to fucking touch him.

"Yeah, thanks. I'm making the big bucks now." He says. His chest puffing out slightly. Peacocking.

"I heard, it won't be long until you join the billionaires club." Ema nods.

"That's the plan, you know I was always very ambitious."

"Yeah, you're going to get it." Ema nods again.

He hasn't stopped staring at her since Ema called his name. Not just the normal eye contact you would expect from someone who is talking to you, but the eye contact of a lover.

The anger is back, I roll my neck to the side and try to release some of the tension. When he puts his hand on her arm and uses his thumb to caress her shoulder, I nearly shove his fucking head through the window of a car we are standing next to. Instead, I push myself between the two of them surprising them both with my suddenness.

"Like I said at our wedding, Ema is a married woman now, not much time to catch up. My apologies." I glare at him for half a second before I grab Ema's hand and pull her in the opposite direction back to where we'd parked the car.

"Hey, what is your problem?" Ema tries to snatch her arm away from me, but I don't let her go.

Instead, I pick up the pace back to the car. A fight is brewing between us. I can feel it and I don't want to be out in the open when it happens.

"We're going home now!" I bark and pull her harder

behind me. She hisses out in pain and the small limp that she had seconds ago gets a bit worse. I must be aggravating it. Too fucking bad. If she wasn't trying to get away, I wouldn't have to pull so hard.

"Get off of me!" She shouts and uses her free hand to beat against my arm. "I didn't even get to say bye! What is your problem?"

I pull her into the parking lot and wait for the valet to bring my car to the front.

She screams and pulls at me, but I ignore her. I don't have time for this shit. I shouldn't have brought her here.

"Let me go!" She looks around and sees the people walking around, "Help! Someone help!" She screams loud. The people walking in the lot turn to look at her and then look to me.

"Get on." I say and they keep moving. The Juric family owns this parking lot so the only people in it are loyal to the family. I am only under Marko Juric himself so there is no one here that would lift a finger against me. I could be holding a gun to her head and no one would do a damn thing.

She continues to pull and scream, clawing and slapping at my hand to get me off. The valet finally pulls up with my car and I push her into the front driver's seat. She kicks her feet up, but I quickly catch them and push them apart so that I can fit on top of her.

My anger explodes through my body. I put a hand over her mouth and nose cutting off her air supply, but also shutting her up.

"I fucking told you that I wouldn't be embarrassed. You think because I show you a speck of kindness that it means I won't go back to making your life a fucking hell. I only need to keep you alive. Your happiness and what you want to do can mean nothing to me."

Panic begins to bloom in her eyes as I still haven't let her take a breath. She claws at my hand.

"You test me constantly, one day soon you're not going to like what you get in return." I let her mouth go and she gasps in a deep breath before she shudders and starts to cry.

"Get the fuck over there." I point to the passenger side. She doesn't move or if she does it's not fast enough. "*Sada*! Move now!" She squeals in fear as she jumps up to crawl over the console and into the passenger seat.

Tension radiates all through my body, I force myself to get in the car and drive off.

I grip the steering wheel and peel out of the parking lot letting everything I have in me pour into the car. The problem is it's not enough. The further away I get from Alex the more I want to go back and rip his fucking hand off.

I swerve in and out of traffic, for a town that never sleeps they sure do move slow as fuck.

I lay on the horn and swerve again to get in front of a small smart car.

"Sven!" Ema screams and I see her put her hand out to the dashboard as if she is bracing for a crash. I nearly roll my eyes at the ridiculousness of it. I'm not going to fucking crash.

When I successfully pull around the car she lets go.

"Slow down." She says, but I'm tired of hearing her talk.

I maintain the speed that I'm at when she squeals again as someone blows their horn at us.

Her hand comes down on my thigh and she squeezes,

"Sven!" I turn in her direction for a brief second, "You're scaring me. Please, I'm scared. Please slow down." Her voice cracks.

I roar in frustration, but I let my foot come up from the gas slightly. She lets go of my leg when the car slows to a reasonable pace.

The drive to the house is quiet, but electric with tension. Angry tension. Her with me and me with her. We get in the house and instead of letting her walk in on her own I grab her arm and pull her into the house.

"What are you doing? I'm here already. Let go!" She screams at me.

The rage I feel basically takes over all semblance of any rational thought. I drag her into the room and toss her on the bed I quickly grab her arm again and search for the loose end of the shackles that are still connected to the bed.

"No! Why are you doing this?" She asks realizing that I'm going to cuff her again.

"Sven, calm down! Just wait for a second!" She pulls again. I can't talk to her though. This is the only way. Then I won't have to worry about her touching other men or talking to them or being looked at. I won't have to worry about people putting their fucking hands on what's mine.

"Sven!" she screams at me again. When I don't answer she pushes her face forward and captures my mouth in a kiss.

My hands release her wrists instantly and dive into her long hair. I tug hard at it as all the rage and fucking jealousy I feel pours into her. I kiss her so hard, I'm sure it bruises her face. She whimpers in pain and I rip my face and hands away from her.

I thread my fingers in my hair and tug. "Fuck!" I growl out. I turn my eyes to her and I can see how scared she is.

"Don't fucking think about getting out of that fucking bed. Do you understand me?" I yell.

She nods her head immediately and I barge out of the room slamming the door behind me.

I escape to my study and fall into one of my chairs completely undone by what had happened today. More so because of the powerful surge of fucking unwanted emotions that I feel at the thought of anyone else touching her. She's mine and it's about time she fully understands that.

20

Sven

It takes me a few minutes to stave off the rage that is coursing through my body, but even as I make my way back to the bedroom all I can think about is how incredibly intense it was for me. Feelings I have never felt before and honestly, I don't ever want to feel them again. I can't leave her in there without any type of supervision or restraint, so I know I have to go back and face her. The beast inside me is still pissed that she would put herself in that position. Despite that the logical part of me that has always been at the forefront of my mind tells me the truth, the woman has done nothing to deserve that treatment.

I open the door and once again she is just sitting on the bed, her leg bouncing up and down in frustration.

"Ema." I grit out in an effort to get her attention.

"No, you listen to me." She interrupts me, "There will never be a time when you laying your hands on me like that will be a good thing. Ever! But what happened today is so much more than just hurtful, it's baffling. What the hell did I do for you to act like that? Nothing was said out of order, I didn't try to run. I did absolutely nothing and you flipped out like a damn lunatic." She glares at me for a moment, her nostrils flaring and her face a deep red color.

"He had his hands on you." It was the simplest answer.

"What? Who?"

"Alex."

"His hand was on my shoulder, that is as platonic as it comes Sven. What? Am I going to be punished every time someone looks at me as well? You're always talking about me forcing you to treat me like an animal, but what was the cause of this? I think it's just because that is what you are used to, treating people like crap." She turns away from me and I can't help but notice that even in all her anger she didn't curse at me. She's learning.

"You're mine."

"Here we go again with this. Yes, we're married. I have no choice in that matter, but that doesn't mean that I'm not my own person. I have a mouth, I have friends from before you, a life before you. Just because we are married doesn't mean that it all goes away."

"You're right." I concede giving in slightly as she did this morning when it came to the tattoo.

"I am? I mean, yes, I am."

"Did you notice how he was looking at you?"

"Who, Alex?"

"Yes. Alex."

"That is how Alex looks at everyone, he is a charmer. There was a time when I had first turned eighteen that he thought he would press his chances, but I told him under no circumstances would anything happen between us. He accepted it and went on to my best friend. We have never been anything more than friends since then. That was more than 4 years ago, we've both gotten over it. We're just friends.

I heard what she was saying. Except I knew what I saw; that man wants what is mine.

"Hmm, I'll take you up on your word then. I admit I might have gone off the handle a bit, but I wasn't expecting that."

"What were you expecting?"

"Not to give a damn." I growl out and close my eyes at the admission. She might have been thrust into my life without my consent, but I've never had someone who has fought as hard as she has with me. Someone who I was forced to care for. Someone who is as strong as any woman I have ever admired. She was forced to give up her life for the dealings of her uncle and father, but instead of just crumbling to the ground like some might have, she fights every day.

"You give a damn?"

"I have to, remember?" I open my eyes into a squint and focus on her.

"Why?"

"I don't fucking know. I've never been in a situation like this before. I know one thing for sure. I need to get my mark on you as soon as possible, maybe then I'll feel a bit better about it." I don't want to admit the real reason why I give a damn, there is no way in the world that I would give her the upper hand. Not when I know she might be liable to use it against me.

"Fine." She huffs out and pulls herself up from the table.

"Wait, what?"

"Let's go. If that is going to stop you from acting crazy,

then we can go do this right now. I won't be subjected to that again if I don't have to." She stands in front of me, her arms crossed over her chest and clear defiance in her eyes. I should be upset that she is trying to get me to do what she wants and when she wants me to do it, but this is a win-win situation for the both of us. I can get my mark on her and the deal will be set. I'll feel better whenever she is around anyone even though they might not see it, she is signed for—all mine.

"This isn't going to be a quick and painless process."

"Does it look like I have anywhere else to go?" She rolls her eyes at me before she turns her head to the side and looks at the shower.

I grab her face, not as hard as I had earlier and turn it back to me. "I'm letting you get away with quite a few things, because of how I acted this evening. But don't push it. Remember your respect."

"I'll remember my respect when you remember yours. Let's go." She stares at me. I can't do anything besides move out of her way.

Here I thought that I was on the way to breaking her down when it looks as if she is stronger now than when she got here.

21

Ema

I'm fucking livid.

I've known Alex for years now. Sven thinks just because we are stuck in this sham of a marriage, he has a say on who my friends are? I can't stand it.

"Where are we going?" I say over my shoulder as the both of us leave the bedroom. If this dumb mark is going to get him to back off, then so fucking be it. I would split my own lip in two if he would just ease up a bit.

"This way." He steps in front of me and leads me up the stairs to the second floor of his home. My eyes take in the framed artwork that he has along the walls and the statues he had perfectly displayed in the hallway. It was exquisite.

I had yet to venture up here, but it seemed as if he kept the best stuff up here. He opened the door to what might be a small guest space—there was a large flat screen TV at least 72 inches, a small full sized day bed, a creative space with books, paints and various puzzles, and even a chair that looked like it belonged in a barber shop or salon of some sort. Except it was a bit more plush than what I have seen in salons.

"What is this room?"

"Just a guest room, sometimes Zeus likes to come over for a few days. He plays a lot of video games and he says this chair is the best. I leave it in here, because I have no use for it." He shrugs and pushes me to the chair. "There is a bar over there, get yourself a drink if you'd like. I need to get the materials for this. You're positive you want to do this now. Once we start it's best to complete it all at once."

"Yes, let's just get it over with." I walk over to the side of the room where he had indicated the alcohol was kept and poured myself a drink. I have never been a huge drinker, not when the last time I had too much I woke up with a man on top of me. At 22 there is still a lot that I haven't really gotten back into especially after everything that went down with that bastard. Drinking really fell to the bottom of the list of things I wanted to do. Though the whiskey I am drinking warms my belly perfectly, easing the butterflies that have suddenly began to flutter in my gut.

I pour myself a second glass after gulping down the first and the door opens to the room as Sven walks back in.

"Whiskey, huh?"

"Oh yeah, I guess so."

"I'll get you better whiskey if it is what you like."

I don't really have a preference. When I did drink back with Bryson it was whatever he had in the cupboard, usually it was a darker brown liquid—more syrupy, like cough medicine.

"You don't have to do that, I don't think drinking is going to become a pastime that I will be pursuing." I smile tightly at him. I see a small box in his hands along with a bottle of rubbing alcohol and gauze.

"Have you done anything like this before?"

"No, you are the only one who has ever worn my mark. Probably the only one who ever will." He says it plainly and chuckles softly before putting the case down on one of the small tables by the side of the chair.

"What's funny?" I ask, moving over to the chair that he is getting set up for me.

"I never thought that I would marry. A wife is a lot of responsibility and usually leaves a huge vulnerability. Yet I always knew that if I did marry, the person to wear my mark would be honored. I never thought I would be putting my mark on a woman who was being forced to wear it."

I had no reason to want to make him feel better about everything, but something resounded in my mind.

This shit could be a lot worse.

"Well if it helps any, I'm glad that it's you who was chosen and not someone more like my uncle. I've heard stories about what the men in my family do to the women that are supposed to be their wives. It's rarely just them being handcuffed and left dirty. They usually don't survive past the first year and I've never heard of any of the husbands guaranteeing their safety. Yes, I'm glad it's you." I meant it and even as the words came out of my mouth, I could see the change in him. His body relaxes from being extra tense to almost languid by my side. It pleased him to hear me say that.

"Thank you for that. I appreciate it." He nods once before he clears his throat and continues. "Now, like I said this isn't going to be as quick as a normal tattoo. I'll make it as small as possible while still making sure that it is legible, lucky for you I have a steady hand. All I can promise is that I won't make this any more painful than it has to be. Though you can't move around, if you squirm it'll be worse."

I nod my head and lay back on the gaming chair. He locks the chair in place and pulls the armrests down, giving him full access to me.

He grips my pants and I'm flushed with embarrassment. I've spent so much time recently without wearing any underwear, it's only now that I realize that I don't have any on.

"I have to go get some panties. Sorry I forgot."

"No, it'll only make it more difficult. Bare is better." His dark eyes cloud as he slips his hand into the waist of my pants. He pulls them down and I shiver slightly as the cold air circulating in the room blows across my naked pussy.

"Remember you have to be still." He pulls the table and a small stool closer to where I'm sitting and opens up the case. Inside were some inks, fresh needles, and then a strange looking wood holder along with a paddle of sorts. I couldn't understand what any of it was for.

I watch as he put the strange contraption together, the wood holder acting as the tattoo gun and the paddle as the energy that would be used to draw on the skin. He lays it to the side and picks up a felt pen. He leans over my abdomen, his beard tickling my stomach as he did. I shift slightly.

"You chose this location." He grumbles and presses down harder on the space. Maybe this wasn't such a good idea. I was already so sensitive in that area.

"I'm doing my best." I grit out.

"I know, don't worry. I'm going to help you." He

promises. I feel the coolness of the ink as he draws on my body.

"Ok?"

My eyebrows reach up to my hairline as I stare into his face, "You're asking me?"

"You are the one that is going to have to live with this forever. It has to be my name, but you could at least have a say on whether or not it's to your liking in size and location."

He was compromising. More and more I was finding that he was doing things like that. Asking me where I wanted to shop and driving me to Las Vegas. Even little things like letting me choose what we ate for lunch. It wasn't the big choices, but it was more than he was doing before.

I lean up and look at where he had drawn his name. It was thick and the letters were legible, but it wasn't very large or ornate. It was 2 inches across if that much.

"Yes, that's fine."

"Good, do you want the rest of your drink?" He asks as he puts some rubber gloves on and picks up the instruments to start.

"Yes, please." My voice squeaks out.

"As you wish." He walks over to the cabinet and pulls the whiskey out for me. He gives me the rest of what is in my glass before he pours me another and leaves it on the desk near his equipment. I would be able to reach out for it when I needed it—thoughtful of him.

"This is going to hurt and I'm going to have to hold you down. It's the only way." He looks into my eyes with something akin to sorrow painted on his face. He really didn't want me to be in pain, but he didn't have a choice.

"Ok, Ok. I'm ready." I blow out some air and brace myself on the chair.

I keep my eyes closed tight as he leans over me, a large portion of his body weight on my midsection as he keeps me still. He moves around a bit, I'm assuming for ink or whatever else he needs. I relax slightly as the alcohol begins to take hold, but when that first tap of the needle hits my skin, I nearly jump out the chair.

"Holy shit!" I scream out in pain. He just presses down harder and continues. The small paddle tapping like crazy on the needle holder that is pressed against my skin. After a few hundred taps I'm already wishing for it to be over.

I don't even want to ask him how much he has left to do.

"Where are your parents?" I blurt out the first thing that is on my mind. It has nothing to do with anything. Except I know that I need to do something to distract myself from what is going on here or I was going to lose my mind.

"What?" he stops tapping.

"No don't stop, I'm trying to distract myself ... just talk to me, please." I breathe again through the pain as he began to tap away.

"My parents are still in Croatia I would assume."

Assume, didn't he know. "What do you mean assume? Why don't you know?"

"My parents gave me to Marko Juric when I was just a child. He paid them to adopt me and I was his son from then on out."

"Oh, I see." I couldn't keep the sadness out of my voice. That seems so cold.

"It was for the best. My parents were able to pull themselves out of poverty and I became one of the most important people in the Juric family, it was good for everyone."

He picks up the needle, leaning over to get more ink and then brings it back to tap away some more.

"Hmm, did you play any sports?"

"Sports, no, I was home schooled mostly and didn't have time for sports."

"That sounds sad." I say through gritted teeth.

"I did like football, or soccer as they call it here, but I never was on a team or anything like that. Luka and I used to play out in the courtyard, but he was just as secluded as I was."

"Who's Luka?"

"My brother, Marko's other adopted son."

"Lots of adopted boys."

"No, just the two of us. Marko was only blessed with biological daughters and even though they all have his blood running through their veins, he will never leave the family in their hands. He probably won't even leave the family in my hands. He is waiting to see if a male grandchild pops up that he can make them his heir."

"I see, that all sounds very complicated." I'm not sure if it's the booze or the conversation, but the tapping doesn't seem to be as painful as it was before. It's almost a dull lull accompanied with moments of intense pain.

"It's not really, he wants the family to be continued by a family member with Juric blood in their veins. It's tradition."

"What about you, what do you want to do?"

"I want to be the best at what I do. That's all."

"Ok." It was hard trying to have a one-sided conversation. The next thing I was going to start talking about was pets, but I'm sure he doesn't want to talk about that. The room fills with a strange partial silence. The sound of the tapping is the only thing that I can hear along with our breathing.

"What do you want to do with your life, if you had a choice?" He speaks up, I almost sit up in surprise.

"Honestly, I thought that eventually I would take over my father's fishing ship."

"Fishing?"

"Yeah, it's not glamorous at all, but I love being on the water. It's good money and I can't say that I don't like the excitement of it all. Knowing that it's only because of your instincts and smarts that you find what you need. It's thrilling."

He laughs and the vibration rolls from him into my body. Right at the apex of my thighs. I suck in a breath in surprise.

"I don't think I have ever met any woman in the family that has ever said that they dreamed of working hard labor."

"Well, I'm not every woman." My breath was coming quicker, and it had nothing to do with the fact that he was still pressing that needle into my skin.

"Don't I know it." He replies and blows slightly on the tattoo in progress. I have to bite my tongue to keep from moaning out. What the hell is happening to me right now?

"Are you feeling more at ease now with Bryce out of the picture?"

I squirm slightly. When Sven had shown me the message from Dagger saying the job was done, I have to admit that I was a bit skeptical at first. There was just no way that it could be that easy, then I remembered who I was dealing with. He was one of the most important men in the Juric crime family. Of course, it was that easy.

"Yes, very relieved. I'll admit when I was home even

though I made sure to stay away from him the best that I could, it always felt like he was watching me. Like he was just around the corner waiting for me. Now that I know that he's gone, maybe I can breathe a bit easier." I hiss out in pain as he taps in one particular sensitive spot. Only for the pain to transform again back into a deep ache.

"What about marriage and kids?" He continues completely oblivious to the fact that I was slipping down a strange path of need.

"Marriage? Well I have never been the obedient type, I knew it was going to take a very strong man to handle me. If that happened, then I would have thought about it, but it wasn't a necessity."

His hand swipes at my thigh pulling the skin taut while his forearm lay tightly against my inner thigh. He was so close. I didn't even feel the pain anymore at least not the pain from the tattoo. Now it was a deeper pain, one that I'd only felt while watching the naughty movies that my friends would steal from their fathers. Bryce had been the only man to have me. Though that incident happened it didn't mean that I didn't have my own desires. It's been over five years since that bastard took advantage of me, I was so ready to move on with my sexual life.

"I guess meeting me was the best thing for you then." He chuckles again and I had to clench my thighs at the sensation.

"Guess so."

He picks up his hand and drags it over the bottom of my stomach making me clench up even more in need.

"Fuck." I moan out unable to keep the sound in. He stops and looks up at me slightly, but doesn't say anything to me.

He starts tapping again, the humming pain and feel of

him breathing revving my body up more with every passing second.

"What about boyfriends?"

"Hmm?"

"What about boyfriends? Did you have many boyfriends when you were home?"

"No, just dates ... A few dates." I groan out and a low moan slips out of my mouth when he rocks against me to get to a different angle. What the fuck is wrong with me? I need a drink. I bend quickly to reach it. Except his hand shoots up from where he is holding me down and presses against my chest to keep me from moving.

"I told you to be still."

"Sorry, I want my drink."

He picks it up and is about to bring it up to my lips, but he smirks slightly and brings it to his instead.

I see him take a mouthful and gulp slightly—such a fucking tease. I pout, but it doesn't last long as he leans forward into my space and grabs my face. His thumb lightly presses on my bottom lip and tugs it down. I open slightly and he neatly lets the whiskey in his mouth pour into mine. My eyes go wide at his audacity and from how intensely turned on it makes me. No one has ever done anything like that to me before and he didn't even hesitate.

I swallow it down and he smirks at me. My arms are trembling, I'm holding onto the chair so tightly.

"More?" his voice is gruff and authoritative.

"Yes." I speak and nod at the same time.

He takes another drink and repeats the process, keeping my body still, but giving me what I want, this time letting a few drops fall to the corner of my mouth.

"You've made a mess." He whispers close to my face. I have been holding my breath for a few seconds now. Only when I feel the tip of his tongue trace the outside of my mouth, I can't keep it in any longer.

"Oh fuck." My voice is low and filled with a need even I can hear in my tone. My hands release the chair and I wrap a hand around his bicep, trying to pull him down to me.

"You're distracting me." He complains, pulling away to leave me frustrated and too hot to sit still.

"That's the point." I huff out and latch my hands back onto the side of the chair.

"The point is for you to be distracted, not me. I'm not even a third of the way done." He picks up his tools and starts tapping away again.

The more he taps, the wetter I can feel myself getting. The wetter I get, the harder it becomes for me to sit still. It felt like he was purposely torturing me.

He moves to a different angle now, a large portion of his forearm pressing directly on my pussy as he pulls my skin in a different direction to continue the tattoo. My back arches slightly at the pressure. My bare pussy, the strange arousal building from either him being so close or the tattoo. This need has been lying dormant inside me for so long, now has me almost crying in need.

"*Izluđuješ me.*" He growls out before he bends down slightly and kisses the spot right above where he is placing the tattoo.

"You don't know what I feel right now. Crazy isn't the half of it." I reply in English, so he knows that I understand what he said. If I'm driving him crazy, then he's already made me insane.

He moves his arm once and it sends shock waves straight to my core. I become emboldened with my need and try to open my legs a bit more so I can better feel where he is applying pressure. He's right there. The fine hairs on his bare arm tickling the shaved parts of my cunt.

I subtly try and move my hips, but he only presses down again.

"Please." I whisper more to myself and I hear him groan out below. Did he hear me? The tapping has slowed considerably. His arm slides down slightly before it moves back up again, and a zing of electricity renders me speechless. I stay as still as I possibly can as he does it again. Over and over until my body is so tense with the need to come that my knuckles ache from the force I'm using to hold on to the chair.

"Ema. How are you feeling?" He asks me, but his arm doesn't stop its slow deliberate movements.

"Agonizing. It's agonizing."

"Hmm, maybe I should do more to distract you?" His arm flexes and moves down where I can clearly feel him between my legs.

"Oh my ... mmm." I bite down on my lips as I skyrocket to the tip of my mountain, but don't fall. I hang there on the precipice, suspended for a few seconds fearful that I'll slowly come down and not fall like I so desperately want.

"Ema, open your eyes." The command is rushed and clipped.

I do and find his. The second our eyes connect, he moves his arm one more time and I go flying off the mountain.

"Oh God! Sven!" I call out his name as I dig my hands harder into the chair and my body revolts against my demand to be still. My back arches high as contraction after contraction rolls through my body.

"Fuck, did you just come? Fuck. What are you doing to

me?" His voice is raw and primal, and I hear him drop the instrument on the table.

I think he's mad. Only when I feel him grab my legs and turn me towards him, I know it's the exact opposite. He's as turned on as I am.

He pushes my legs apart and places one over his shoulder.

"Shit, you're soaking wet. I need to taste you." There is no further conversation about the matter. He simply tears the gloves off his hands, uses his deft fingers to spread my pussy apart and laps at my slit from bottom to top.

"Wait. Oh my God. Sven. Wait." The previous orgasm still pulsing through my body.

"No." He barks out, continuing to lick and suck at me.

I moan and grip my hands in his hair. The silky strands giving me something to hold onto while he forces my body straight into another toe-curling orgasm.

"Oh, fuck that's so good. That feels so good." I want to cry from how perfectly he is hitting the right spot with every swipe of his tongue.

He moans against my mound, the vibrations and the feel of his beard tickling me in the process.

My hands grip his hair tighter as I jump back up to a sweet painful release.

"Yes, right there. Please."

Just.

One.

More.

Lick.

"Shit! My God!" I scream out as I shatter, and my thighs shake on his shoulders.

He kisses my legs before rising from between my legs, wiping my juices from his face and beard.

My body is wrung out and as he rises, I can feel his cock rub against my body straining against the cloth of his pants.

"*Želiš li me?*" He stares in my eyes, his clouded with lust and restraint.

Do I want him? It's a straightforward question, but the answer isn't that simple. I shouldn't want him. I should want to kick him in the balls for what I've been forced to do by being married to him. Yet I can't deny that I do want him. I love that he is so protective of me. I simply adore that I've been able to chip away at his control piece by piece until he shows me that he can compromise. He's not as bad as I've been trying to make him out to be. He's just as stuck as I am.

"*Da.* Yes, I want you." I pull at him thinking he is going to take me right here in the chair, but that's not what he has in mind.

"Hold on." He grabs hold of me, my legs wrap around his waist and my arms go around his neck.

I latch on just in time as he stands up and rushes out the door. My unfinished tattoo the very last thing on either one of our minds.

22

Sven

It feels like a fucking explosion.

My desire for this woman in my arms pushes me way past my peak and I don't have a choice but to give in.

I never wanted a wife, but I have one. A woman that tests me at every fucking turn and pulls things out of me that I've fought for so long to keep in check. She is pure fucking chaos and I crave every second of it.

I quickly find my way to the stairs and carefully begin my descent down them. When Ema grabs my face and starts to kiss on me, I have to stop. I press her hard against the wall and lose myself in her kiss.

When she whimpers into my mouth, I nearly rip my own pants off to slam myself into her pussy.

"Wait Ema, Fuck." I pull my face away from her, I didn't want the first time that I take her to be up against the wall. I move quicker down the stairs. I need to get to my bedroom and fast.

I push the door open and kick it shut with my foot as I rush with her to the bed. She falls down, but reaches up right away for me. She is already naked from the waist down, so I don't have to worry about getting her pants off. I push her shirt up and over her head, kissing my way up her body and over her tight nipples. Her moans urge me to keep going. I just want her to keep making those sounds. I lick and nip at those tight buds while she squirms and writhes under me.

"Sven, more." She begs and tries to pull me up.

"Don't worry, Ema. I'm going to give you all you want."

I kick out of my pants and underwear. Even the slight bobbing of my cock causes me to have a deep ache. I grip my shaft with one hand and fight the need to jerk myself. I want to save all I have for her. I pull my undershirt off. Completely naked, I crawl up the bed to her. There is no soft kisses or gentle touches—only fire and lust. Her pupils are dilated and her focus is solely on my mouth. She pulls my face down to hers in a deep kiss. Our tongues entwine and war with one another as I hitch her leg over my hip so I can get access to her cunt. I hesitate only briefly, I'm not wearing a condom. Reason is thrown out the window when one key phrase pops in my mind, she's my wife.

I press the head of my cock against her tight slit, she is soaking wet and ready for me, but she is inexperienced. I know what that bastard did to her and the last thing I want to do is hurt her or make her second experience with sex be one she regrets. I rock into her slowly going against every instinct I have to just plunge in to the hilt.

"Oh God." She moans lightly and turns her head to the side. Her eyes are closed and her eyebrows cinch in.

"Ema, look at me." I order her. I have to see her face, to make sure she's ok.

Her eyes find mine and I push in a little more. "You do things to me."

"I know."

Her simple response causes my mind to reel. She can see the changes even if she's only been here for a short while. I had thought I was changing her when in actuality she was changing me.

"You tell me what you want. You're in control." I bend down and bite the lobe of her ear slightly to get her to moan out in that sexy way I like.

She hooks her other leg on my hip and pushes against my ass so I push all the way in.

"So much. Never ... ugh." She bites down on her lip hard as she forces her body to take all of me. I know that I'm well endowed, so I didn't want to give her too much too fast. She had other plans though.

Her pussy fits like a glove one size too small. I knew she would open up for me, but I had to move slowly at first. It might be too painful for her if I go too hard at first.

I rock into her at a snail's pace, her body is stiff and clenched, she's still not used to me. I lean up and pinch her nipples hard for a few seconds before I let my hand trail down to where we are connected and play with her plump clit.

"Oh yes, I need more of that."

I rub and massage more, all the while I stare down at the motion of my cock disappearing and reappearing as I pump into her. It's hypnotic. My shaft glistens with her arousal and after a minute or so of me playing with her, her hips begin to move along with mine.

"Sven, I want to come. Again. I need it." Her hips begin to move faster, she's telling me that she can handle more.

"Yes. More." I groan and fall back down on top of her.

Gripping her hips I quicken my pace, the new speed causes her to gasp out in surprise before she grabs onto my neck and pulls me back down to her.

"You drive me crazy." I hold her down on the bed. I don't want her to move too far away after my thrusts. I want to stay as deep inside of her as I can. I want to etch myself on every one of her walls. I want my mark not only to be etched in her skin on the outside, but also on the inside.

"Sven, harder. Can you ..."

I don't even wait for her to finish her request. As her husband it's my duty to give her what she needs and if she tells me she is ready for me to go harder than that is exactly what I'll do. It's what I crave.

I pull her further down and rise up on my knees to lock my arms around her legs. I pound into her, her tits bouncing hard with every thrust and her moans from before turning into deep guttural groans.

"Let go, let me take care of you. Give in to me Ema. I'm here."

"I ... oh fuck ... it's so intense ... fuck."

The telltale shocks of my impending orgasm begin to build in the small of my back. I have to get her off. I refuse to finish without her. She needs it, so I have to give it to her.

"Fucking come Ema. Let me see you come."

She reaches back for me and I lay back down as far as I can making sure to keep her bottom half up off the bed. I kiss along her neck and up to her lips, but she grabs my face and forces my eyes to hers. I gaze deep into her lust filled needy eyes and she looks back into mine.

I wonder if she can see that she's breaking me apart.

Can she see that I've never wanted someone as bad as I want her?

"Ema, my Ema." I whisper.

"Oh… God!" Her mouth opens slightly and a deep tremble starts in her legs. She keeps her eyes locked on mine until her back arches up and I can feel her pussy clamping down harder on my cock. I'll never forget her face in that moment and right now it's the main goal of my life—to make her look like this as often as possible.

She sucks in a deep breath and her eyes slam shut. I keep fucking her through her orgasm. I pick up the pace not wanting it to end for her. Her body is mine to do with as I wish and I want to pump my seed deep inside of her.

"Fuck you're so beautiful. You're going to be the damn end of me." I growl as she racks her nails down my arms and she struggles to catch her breath.

"Sven, so … so good. Oh, fuck it's so good." She whimpers and her legs clutch at me keeping me flush against her. I roll my hips upwards. Only I must have hit something inside of her that she wasn't expecting me to, because her hand shoots out and she buffers my thrusts.

"Oh no, Ema, you can take all of me. Every part of you is meant for me. Feel me. I want you to feel me claim all of you." I reach up and grab her hands to press them to either side of her head as I race towards the finish line. I'm so fucking close. Seeing her lie under me like this, her lips puffy and bruised from our rough kisses. Her eyes completely unguarded and pleading. Her body open and accepting mine, I know as much as I had wanted to push her away that she's already starting to get under my skin. I'm not sure I'll ever be able to let her go.

"Sven. Sven. Sven." My name sounding like a prayer coming from her mouth. She completely submits to me.

"Shit, I'm going to come. Fuck." I press down on her wrists hard and she cries out in pain, but that only spurs me to thrust harder. My body clenches hard and I pump into her one final time as the most powerful orgasm I have ever had in my entire adult life bursts through me. I spurt shot after shot of my seed deep inside of her. After ten seconds the orgasm is still making its way through me. I roar in ecstasy as I wrap myself around her and keep her tightly smashed to my body. What the hell is this?

"Oh shit."

"Mmmm." She moves her head to the side so she can get some air, but I can't let go yet, my body is still spasming with its release.

Once I force myself to get a grip I pull out and she hisses out a breath.

"You ok?" I ask, but she doesn't answer. She moves her head to the side and looks away. "Ema."

"Yea." Her voice cracks, I grab her chin and turn her head back in my direction. Tears stream down her face unchecked.

"What's wrong? Are you hurt?"

"No." She tries to pull her face out of my grip, but I'm not going to let her. What could I have done to cause this?

"Tell me!" I order her.

"I feel like a goddamn traitor. I hate that I didn't have a choice in who my husband is. I hate that I have to be dependent on someone. I hate this entire fucking thing, but I loved what we just did. I've never …" She rolls her eyes and blows out a deep breath before she continues. "How can I hate everything about this situation, but need you as bad as I do?" She looks up to me, expecting an answer. I had none. I completely understood what she was talking about. She was supposed to be nothing more than a punishment. Now that I've had her, there was no way for me to see her in that light anymore. Our hands were forced and we should be fighting against it, but it feels so good to just let it happen.

I press my forehead to hers, kiss her once, and roll off her. I lay on my back mulling over what she'd just said. I drape one of my arms over my forehead. When she scoots over and nestles herself into my side, I let my other arm wrap around her. Holding her close to my body as if she were the greatest gift I've ever been given. Maybe she is.

23

Ema

"Yes Sven, oh yes."

"You're fucking perfect. I'm never going to let you go."

"I know. I'm yours."

"Until death do you part."

His soft touches turn rougher. He trails his hand up the ridges of my ribs over my breast and settles on my neck. He applies a light pressure, more and more until I can't breathe. I'm suffocating.

"Until death, Ema"

I POP UP IN BED, sweat already beading my forehead and my breath coming fast. My muscles are sore and a delicious pain dully aches through my core. It wasn't as painful as I remember the first time being, in fact it was slightly addicting. I wonder how many times Sven can make me come. I run my hands down my body the small area above my mound still very sore.

I push the sheet off my body and examine the small bit of tattoo that he was able to finish. A S, a V and an E, the tattoo would take a lot more time. I shiver slightly from the chill of the cooling system and realize that I'm still naked. No wonder I feel so discombobulated. I'm not one of those people that likes to sleep naked. I had two whole drawers full of pajamas back home. Besides I need to go wash up, my thighs are sticky.

I slip out of the bed and walk over to the bathroom. I do the best I can to wash myself, but I still don't have any of my toiletries in the house. A birdy bath it is. Once I dry myself off with the plush towel hanging on the wall, I grab one of Sven's shirts. I move as quietly as I can so I don't wake him. He seems to be sleeping soundly.

I could go back to bed, but I would really like to wear one of the pajama sets we had bought yesterday. Though I don't know where he put the bags. I walk over to the main space, but I don't see them there. He could have brought them inside and put them in another room. Except I didn't see him bring them in, maybe they are still in the car.

I look at the door, I'll just go check really quick.

I open the door and even in the dead of night the Nevada heat is oppressing. I don't know how people live here without sweating like crazy all the time. I miss the cool air of Alaska, the spray of the water, and most of all I miss my family. I sigh and shake those thoughts away. There is nothing that I can do about that now. I was stuck here with Sven for the foreseeable future. A sudden thought pops in my head. He's not the most unreasonable person I've ever been around, maybe I can convince him to go visit them. Or maybe bring them here! My sisters would get a kick out of the strip! The more I think about it the more excited I get.

I walk over to where the car is and sure enough all the bags are still in the back seat of the car. I put my hand on the handle, but just as I'm about to open it the hairs on the back of my neck stand on end.

My stomach rolls and I have the strangest feeling that someone is watching me. I look back to the front door, but it's only open a little. I don't see Sven there. I turn around slowly. If it's an animal or something I don't want to spook it.

It's so dark and my eyes haven't completely adjusted yet. I don't see anything at first, but just as I'm about to turn around a bright red ember lights up and a puff of smoke blows into the air.

Someone's there watching me.

My heart stutters for a second before it starts up again at a breakneck speed. I swear it feels like whoever is out there is moving closer. I don't want to stay around to find out. I turn away from the car and take off toward the house. I run through the door and smack straight into Sven's chest before falling on my ass.

"Where the fuck are you going?" He roars out. "I should have fucking known you can't be trusted! Goddamn it!"

I'm still trying to catch my breath when he grabs me by my arm hard and yanks me up.

"No..." Gasp, "I wasn't..." Gasp, "Damn it, Sven wait!" I try to get myself together, but he's not hearing it. All he saw was me running back into the house.

"Sven! Listen!" I scream at him and he turns his rage filled eyes back to me. Stopping in his tracks.

I suck in a deep breath and try to get my body to stop shaking, "I wasn't running."

"Then what the fuck were you doing outside?"

"I was going to get the bags, I wanted my pajamas, panties, soap." I exclaim.

He squints at me as if he were trying to see through my lies.

"Honestly, if I couldn't make it out there fully clothed, do you think I'm stupid enough to run away with just your shirt on, no panties, no shoes? I wasn't running."

He looks down at what I have on and his grasp eases up.

"Sven, there was someone outside."

"What?" His voice is sharp.

"I saw someone outside, that's why I ran back inside. They were smoking."

"Who?"

"I don't know I couldn't see them." He began pulling me again, but with less anger.

He pushes me into the room and I crawl over to the bed while he walks over to the window. It looks out to the front of the house, where I had just come from. He picks up his phone and slides his finger a few times and a flood light illuminates the night.

He scans the area for a second.

"There's nothing there."

He continues looking at his phone, swiping a few times. Finally, he shows me his phone which must be linked to the surveillance cameras attached to the house. All of them pointing in tactical directions but none showing the man that was standing there.

Impossible. I know what I saw. I hop out the bed and rush to where he was just standing by the window. "He was there." I point to the area I saw the person.

"There is no one there and it doesn't look like anyone

has been there." He turns his gaze back to me, slips his phone back into his pocket. His jaw clenched tight as he peers at me.

I lean back, "You think I'm lying?"

"I think I know you were outside. I think I know you like to fucking try to escape. I think you are either more conniving or dumber than you pretend to be."

I can't fucking believe it, feels like we go one step forward and then five steps back.

"I can't believe you, Sven. I know what I saw. Believe what you want." I storm back over to the bed and get under the covers. I don't have time to fight with him nor the energy.

24

Sven

I stay up the rest of the night. It didn't make sense for her to try to run again, but she's done dumber things. I let my guard down with her and I shouldn't have. I have to remember that she is set on getting away from me. No matter what her body was telling me last night.

My cock springs to life just thinking about her. Usually the act of fucking for me is measured, I make the girl come, I come and then I get the fuck on with my business. With Ema, I wanted to make her come over and over again. I had wanted to stay buried inside of her for as long as her body would accept me and I was even worried about her afterwards. This close contact was skewing my perspective. I need to get this shit under control.

That means no more fucking.

At 7 in the morning, I'm up in my office going through the files about the men on Filip's crew. I have to make sure that none of them have any affiliations with groups that we don't deal with or have a reason to snitch on what is going on. I need to get leverage on each of them to ensure that they go along with the plan. It's not hard. Most of them are family men, some of them are unfaithful, others are not as financially secure as they try to appear. It's much easier to break someone down then most would think.

There is a knock at the door, I look up expecting it to be Olive asking me about breakfast instead it's Ema.

Her hair is freshly washed, with her face clean and she's wearing a tank top and short set. Just that simple outfit is enough to distract the hell out of me.

"What?" I bark out at her.

"Good morning." She says taking a step further into the room and putting her hands on her hips.

"What do you want Ema? I'm busy." I look back down to the photos on the desk. I had to get this done, Luka would be looking for it later in the afternoon.

She storms over and glares down at me. I almost laugh at her expression. Is this supposed to be intimidating? I'd be more intimidated of a house cat.

"What is your problem?"

"Why do you want to know my problem? What concern is that to you? Tell me what you want and be on your way."

"I want you to stop acting like a temperamental jerk! What is wrong with you?" She huffs and I jump out of my chair. She might not have cursed at me, but she was on a thin line, "Watch your mouth. I don't like to be played for a fool. I have a feeling that is exactly what happened last night. I won't let it happen again."

She blinks in surprise looking away for a second before she looks back to me, "You think me having sex with you last night was part of some sinister plan?"

"I don't know what it was. I know I trusted you to act appropriately and woke up to you running in the house from outside. Where you're not supposed to be." I growl at her.

"You're impossible. I'm not lying! I just wanted my clothes." She screams in my face and my patience snaps. I grab her neck and push her against my desk. I move my fingers from her neck and grab her face. This gorgeous girl has the power to drag the worst parts of me out. I can't stand that she has that much of a hold over me.

"Sven, I don't want to go backwards. All this anger all the time." Her voice is soft, "I can't handle it. I don't want it. I don't deserve it."

"What do you want?" I ask again, my voice hoarse as I do my best to keep a leash on the fury inside. I wish she would just tell me so I can get on with my day.

Her eyes focus on my lips and I let out a small gasp in surprise when she tries to push her face forward. I release her and she presses her soft lips to mine.

Fire. It feels like fire starting at the top of my head rolling through my entire body. I snatch her against my body and deepen the kiss.

We pull and tear at each other, the clothes we have on in the way. I move back for a second to grab her tank top and pull it over her head. "Shit, I need this. I need you." I murmur more to myself than to her.

"Take me, please take me." She whispers right back and I smash my face back to hers. Her hands shake as she tries to get the buttons open on my shirt. After a few tries it doesn't work, just as I'm about to pull away and help her. She puts her hands on either side of the opening and rips it open. Buttons fly everywhere.

"Oh fuck." I growl. I'm desperate. If I don't get inside of

her right now it feels like I'm going to be crushed to death from the weight of my need. The shorts she had just purchased are thin and easy to pull off. She has on a thin white thong. Her pussy is completely shaved now, she must have trimmed more in the shower.

"Sven, I can't wait. Oh God." She moans and pushes her fingers into my hair tugging me toward her.

I know how she feels.

I lean my head to the side and suck at her neck, while I pull my shirt out of my pants and rip it the rest of the way off. She whimpers and rolls her neck to the side. I'm quick with my belt and pants. I push them open and pull away from her slightly.

"Are you ready for me?" My voice is gruff.

"Yes, I'm ready." She nods furiously and tries to move closer to me, but there wasn't much space on my desk.

"Shall I make sure?" I slide my hand up her leg until I reach the top of her thighs. Her slit was absolutely sopping wet. The thong she was wearing a darker color from the moisture between her legs.

"Sven, you're torturing me." She gasps out and presses her cunt down harder on my hand trying to get some relief.

"You've been torturing me from the moment I laid eyes on you." I squeeze her thighs and then wrap one arm around her back. I pick her up from the desk and walk over to my favorite chair. "Your attitude, your defiance, everything I should want nothing to do with, but I can't get enough. I can't stop." I groan out to her as I settle us into the plush piece of furniture. I pull my pants and underwear down, my cock springs up between her legs. She rises up figuring out what I'm setting her up to do. I push the crotch of her underwear to the side and she slowly impales herself on my dick. A deep growl rumbles through my chest as she lets her head fall forward and she lowers herself as far as she can. It's only about halfway down my shaft.

I need to be deeper.

"More." I grab her legs and push down slightly.

"It's so deep. It feels different." Her eyes open up and she gazes at me, her eyes pleading for release, "Is it always this intense?" Her breath was short.

"Only with you." I answer before I could think about it.

She gasps out and falls down a little more on me.

"Mmm, shit, Ema I have to move." My hips began pushing up into her and she throws her head back, a moan mixed of pain and pleasure floats into the air.

I get a good grip on her back side and let my other arm snake up her back so that I can push her forward. Her head falls down to my shoulder and her hands latch on to my arms as I pump up into her.

"Tell me what you need." I grunt into her ear and she swirls her hips slightly.

"Hold me ... Close Sven." She whispers between her gasps and moans of delight. I have no problem with that. I wrap both my arms around her small frame and crush her to my chest. She wraps her arms around my neck and her hands dive into my hair. She pushes herself further dropping all the way to the base of my dick. I feel her tense before she lets out a low keen moan. I stop moving just to soak up the sensation. At this rate I wouldn't last another five minutes.

"Sven, I feel you everywhere."

The caveman deep inside me bangs on his chest. Woman. Mine.

She begins to move, testing out a few different things

before she starts a deep grind, her cunt sliding back and forth on my lap. Her own sweet juices making the ride slippery.

"Ema. Fuck." I stretch my legs out and just let her go. To ride me for her own pleasure with no instruction, purely instinctual. The stimulation of her clit must have been just what she needed to get close. As soon as she was comfortable with my size and depth she switches up, began to bounce up and down with a slight grind at the end of every motion.

"Sven. I'm ..." Her voice leaves her as she leans back slightly to put her hands on my thighs showing me her gorgeous body. Her mouth gapes open and her stomach contracts hard.

Her pussy clamps down and releases, over and over again on my cock, milking me. "Goddamn it Ema. I pull her up so her front is back against mine. I angle myself off the chair slightly to get more range of motion. Needing it hard, I hold onto her and pound into her. The smacking of our bodies and the wails of pleasure from our mouths create a primal atmosphere. It doesn't take long after her orgasm for my balls to pull up against my body. My head falls back against the chair as the first wave of my orgasm ripples through me. I can't move, but Ema isn't done with me yet. She grinds on me and sucks on the side of my neck licking and biting at that sensitive spot.

"Mother fuck!" I howl and my body clenches as my cock completely empties itself into her womb.

When I open my eyes again, she is sucking in large gulps of air and her body is shaking slightly.

"Ema?" I push her back. I don't want her to be crying this time. It had affected me last night more than I let on.

"You're going to kill me." She pulls back, a tired smile on her face.

Happy. She's happy.

"Me ... if I remember correctly, you attacked me."

"Hmm, I don't recall." She drops her head back down on my shoulder. I relax and let the sound of her breathing against my neck lull me into a meditative state.

I should go back to working, but sleep comes quickly.

25

Sven

A knock on the door jolts me from my sleep.

"Mr. Kokot," Olive walks in. "Oh heavens!" She gasps.

My eyes focus and I try to get up, but there is something heavy on my chest. Ema is still sleeping on my lap. My cock, though not at full mast, is still nestled inside of her.

"Shit. Olive a minute please."

"Yes, certainly." She answers with her back turned to us. "Ah, just to let you know. Mr. Juric and Mr. Kasun are here for your meeting." She hurries out of the room.

Oh fuck! The background checks. They were supposed to be done for my meeting with Liam Juric and Ante. I'd fucked myself.

"Ema! Get up." I shake her and she wakes slowly. Too slow. "Ema, *sranje*, Ema wake up now!" I bark at her and she finally moves. I stand up with my pants still around my ankles and drop her into the chair not even caring that she barely gets her legs out from under her.

"What the hell!"

"I'm late. Shit. I apologize, but I have a meeting right now and I didn't finish what I was supposed to do." I rush to my desk and rummage through the papers.

"Oh, crap, can I help?"

"No, I was supposed to vet the men on your father's ship. I didn't get through all of them." I answer without looking up.

"I can help you. I know all of them. Had dinners with them." She stands on wobbly legs still completely naked and a bit of my cum running down her legs. She takes a few steps towards me, but I don't move and I'm blocking the papers. This is all top secret information. If this information got in the wrong hands it could ruin the family. Showing her meant that I trusted her enough to believe that she wouldn't go against me. Did I trust her that much? Yesterday it seemed like she was still trying to run away.

"You going to let me help or not? I know these men." Her eyes look sincere and right now I really didn't have a choice.

I move so she can see the remaining crew that I hadn't finished vetting. There was only three left. "These are the ones I have left."

"What do you need to know?"

"If they would be a good fit to keep quiet about extra activities happening on the boat. Also, what in their lives we could use as leverage if we needed to."

"Leverage? Like you would do something to hurt them?"

"If they went against us? Yes." I say it matter of factly. She has to know what she is a part of. I'm not going to lie to her and say that the information's not for that purpose. I'll have a man's wife killed right in front of him if we suspect that he is going against Marko Juric.

Her face falls and I can see that she is having second thoughts, but another knock comes to the door.

"Shit. I'm out of time." I scramble to pull together the papers on my desk.

"Wait. Him, Jamie, he isn't a citizen and he is a wanted man back where he is from. Eamon has an elderly mother in a home that he works really hard to get the best care for. This one," She pulls the last picture out of the bunch, "Slater. Don't take him with you."

"Why not?" I store everything she says in my mind.

"He's a merc. He'll go anywhere the money is better. Nothing really holding him anywhere. No family or kids. If someone offers him more money for information he'll tell." Her jaw clamps shut and she waits for me to respond.

I'd have to take her information as fact right now.

"Thank you." I swiftly kiss her and pull my tattered shirt from the ground and put it on.

"You're welcome." She replies, but the look of disappointment is still on her face. I can't deal with that right now. I have to go explain to Marko Juric's brother and the head of all the nuclear arms deals for the family that I don't have full portfolios, because I fell asleep balls deep in my wife.

∽

"SVEN. SORRY TO DISTURB YOU." Liam puts a hand out for me to shake.

"It's my oversight, *ujak*. I apologize."

"Hmm, that's a hell of an oversight." Ante laughs his

eyes roaming over my disheveled appearance before gluing themselves to my neck. I put my hand where he is looking and realize that the spot is tender. I have a fucking hickey. Fuck.

"Yeah, well you know, newlywed life."

"Ah, yes. I'm glad you've gotten a handle on that. I know Marko was worried. Ivan had said ... some things."

"I'm well aware of what was said. I have everything under control." I have to hold back my animosity. I'm higher in the family then either of these two, so they have no business asking me about my personal matters. The only thing that keeps my mouth shut is that not only is Liam my adoptive uncle, but he's Marko's older brother. He's never even been thought about to take over as head of the family, he just doesn't have what it takes to lead. Though that doesn't mean he doesn't have Marko's ear. I'm sure there have been plenty of times that he has put a bug in Marko's ear about some of the things I have done.

"Wonderful. Let's get down to business then."

"Let's." I walk them to the main sitting area. The couches are made of a plush grey fabric, with a wide coffee table nestled in the center. I lay out all the information that I've managed to gather.

"And what of these?" Ante picks up the photos of Jamie, Eamon and Slater.

"These two are clear to go, I have the leverage we need on them. This one will need to vacate the ship. I'm sure Filip can come up with an excuse."

Ante looks over everything, every once in a while nodding his head. Liam was solely here to act as support. He may be in charge of all the bratoks, but it was going to be Ante that set up the bulk of the deal here in the states.

"And the transport on the ground?" Ante looks to me.

Fuck.

Fuck!

I was supposed to have a transport set up. How had I missed it?

"I'll have that for you shortly."

"Shortly?" Ante's eyes pop up to mine. I glare at him for a second daring him to say anything to me. I was his superior. I was in the wrong, but it wasn't for him to say. "Ok then, I'll hold them off until you do. If you could call me when it's ready, then I'll come back to pick everything up?"

"Of course." I nod and stand from my seat, the both of them do the same. Ante shakes my hand and walks out, but Liam stays behind.

"*Ujak*?"

"Sven, everything ok?"

"Yes. Why do you ask?"

"Sven, I don't think I have ever seen you in such a state."

I feel like a child being reprimanded. Only I'm not a fucking child. There is nothing going on with me, but respect keeps my mouth shut.

"I'm fine." I repeat.

"Make sure you are. Women have a way of bringing out weakness in us. I won't be a fool to think I know the inner workings of Marko's mind, but I know he is watching you. You're slipping and he's not going to be there to catch you. Make sure your priorities are in the right place." He stares in my face waiting for a sign that I'm taking what he is saying to heart.

"Will that be all, *ujak*?" I deadpan.

"Yes, say hello to the little lady for me." He nods once and walks out.

I wait for the front door to shut before I curse loudly. If

my uncle was telling me that Marko was watching me then everyone knew that he was watching me. If this were simply a punishment I wouldn't have to worry, but Marko was testing me for weakness and right now I had one.

Ema.

26

Sven

I need to get my head back in the game. I know that I can't do that here. Not with Ema walking around tempting me at every turn.

"I'm going to be gone for the majority of the day." I say as I watch her shower from the doorway.

"Ok."

"You're not to leave the house." I make sure my voice is loud and clear. I don't want to hear anything about how she didn't hear me say that.

"Fine." She turns the faucet off abruptly and storms out of the shower. Ripping one of the towels off the rack to dry herself.

"Let me guess, you have another problem?" I stand behind her and watch her face through the mirror. She looks up and locks eyes with mine in the reflection.

"Yes, I have a problem with that."

"What could it possibly be?" I sigh and wait; I know

she's going to tell me. Sometimes I wonder how any married couples have communication problems, Ema sure has no problem saying what's on her mind.

"You leave me here alone with no communication to the outside world, nothing to keep my attention besides eating and sleeping. Why can't I go outside for a walk? There is nowhere for me to go out here. Yes, I tried before and I learned my lesson."

My mind goes back to the day I had to chase after her through the dirt and together we came across a sidewinder. Not the best experience for either one of us.

"Let's learn to walk before we run, you'll be here alone. Olive is gone for the day. You are free to move around the house as you deem fit. But until I finish that mark, I really wouldn't feel comfortable with you just walking around." I'm trying to be civil, when I really want to tell her that I could just lock her in the room if she doesn't like it.

"Oh please, like anyone would know who I am."

"Everyone knows who you are."

She looks off for a second. "Ok, I'll stay put. I saw some paints and clay in that guest room. Can I use that?"

"Yes, you can use anything you like. I will bring home a laptop for your own personal use when I come back as well. Though I will monitor it."

"Whatever. I just want to talk to my sisters." She shrugs and I can see her getting excited just thinking about it.

"Ema, focus." I do my best to reign her in.

"What kind of laptop do you think I can get? I would love to have one with a webcam. Oh please, please please! I would be able to face time with them. Please, that would be so great!" She claps her hands and I have to fight back a smile. Her happiness is truly a sight to see.

"I'm sure whatever laptop that we get will have a

webcam, but it doesn't change the fact that whatever goes on around here has to be kept quiet. You understand?" There was no way I could let my job become a gossip mill. I did too much for the family for any of it to be leaked out, because my wife decided to over share with her sisters.

"I know, you can trust me. I swear I wouldn't do anything like that."

"Hmm, ok. If you say so." I walk over to her and kiss her forehead before I turn and walk out the door.

"Wow."

I turn slightly and look at her, "What now?"

"That is the most domestic thing I have ever seen you do. Did you just kiss me bye?"

I did, what the fuck?

I don't bother to answer her just close the door on my way out. What the hell is happening to me?

Ema

The house is a lot larger than it would seem. I've only actually been on the second level once, when he had started the tattoo. Though after that I haven't been back up there. I'm actually a bit excited to finally be able to do a little bit of exploration. Along with the guest room that I've seen already, there are three other rooms up here. One of them is a blank room, at least that is what it looks like. Except there are metal rings on the walls, bars on the windows, and a metal toilet.

"Holy fuck." I was looking at a prison. Now, I'm a little happier that the most he has done is lock me in his bedroom. My mother's favorite motto springs to mind, things can always be worse.

I quickly close that door not wanting to know what the hell he has done in there. I've seen how he gets when someone touches my arm. I don't need to know what he would do if someone truly crossed him. My husband may be calm on the outside to most folks, but he is a dangerous man.

The next room is another guest room while the last room is a gym. Complete with treadmill, free weights, elliptical, and everything anyone would need to keep themselves in shape. I found myself wishing I had bought more work-out clothes. I love a good exercise. When I walk over to the window and look down, I'm peering out the back of the house and find the one place I know I want to spend the rest of my day. A pool! It's a nice size with a small rock slide and an attached hot tub. Gorgeous brown rocks decorate the area all around it. I can't wait to get in there.

"That's what I'm talking about!" I rush back to my room to search through the bags and bags of clothes that I have yet to put away. Finally, I pull out one of the three bathing suits that I'd bought. Honestly when I bought them, I didn't think I would be able to use them for a long time. I'd thought they were to be used on a vacation I would take at some point in my life. If I ever got out of this there was no way that I was just going to sit around any longer and let my life continue to pass me by. I wanted to live. That included lots and lots of trips to places with warm water.

I bet the pool doesn't even need to be heated! I stand up slowly my foot paining me for only a quick second, a reminder that I need to take my antibiotics. I slip into the two piece and look at myself in the mirror. Finally, the bruises are fading and I can see my skin again.

I hurry over to the side table where I keep my medication and open it with a heavy hand. When I do the contents in the back of the drawer slide forward—papers, candy, his gun. My breath catches in my throat for a second and my hand reaches down to touch it. I pull back before I do though. I know nothing about guns and the last thing I want is for it to accidently go off.

I grab my meds, pop my pill and throw the bottle back in the drawer.

I pull one of the towels and sunblock out of the bathroom and rush to the back of the house. There is a small lock on the door, but the key is still inside of it. I think back on what Sven had said about me staying in the house. Surely, he didn't mean that I couldn't go outside to the pool. That was silly.

"It's not like I'm leaving his property. I'm still in the house." I reassure myself.

I look around the area, it's so bright out, but my mind goes back to what I saw last night. The man just standing there. Sven had showed me the surveillance videos again and sure enough there was no one there. Maybe I had hallucinated it. Still it makes me a little edgy to be on my own. At least a quick swim would relax me a bit.

I take my time making sure not to aggravate my foot and slip into the warm pool. It feels like heaven. I love the water. Everything about it soothes me. I never understood how people found it strange that I want to be a fisherwoman, I've always felt at home in the water. If I could live on it, I would.

The pool starts off at a modest four feet deep, but quickly drops down until I can no longer touch the bottom. The pool takes up most of the backyard so it's quite large. I wonder how often he comes out here and uses it? Part of me thinks that it's not that often. How sad.

There is a single floatation raft on the side and I pull it in the water with me. I hop on and relax, letting the water calm me and the hot Nevada sun bake my skin.

It felt like I had been laying on the floatie for hours and I'm more than content to lay on it for a few hours more, but I'm hot. I didn't bring anything out with me to drink and this sun is no joke. When I open my eyes again the sun is directly over head—mid-day. I need to get some food and water before I dehydrate out here. I stretch out my body and then let myself roll off the floatie into the deep end of the water. I push myself swimming all the way down to the bottom, letting my hand touch the floor before I turn and swim back up.

Oh my God, what the hell is that?

A dark shadow crosses the water and when I look up to the side there is a man standing there.

I startle and blow out some of the air in my lungs. My heart kicks in my chest as it beats wildly in fear. My mouth opens in a gasp, but I'm still under water. I force myself to blow out instead of suck in and the bubbles block my vision. The figure retreats from the edge of the pool. I rush to the top, right under the floatie. I break the surface of the pool and sputter out the water that found its way into my mouth.

It must be Sven. I brush my hair out of my face and push the floatie away.

Where did he go?

"Sven?" I call out while I'm still treading water in the pool.

There is no reply.

"Sven are you there?" I call out again. When he doesn't answer the second time around, I get out of the pool and make my way inside. Maybe he's upset. It would make sense as it seems like the simplest shit would tick him off.

When I walk in the house, I don't hear anything. "Sven? Where are you? I saw you already."

Still I hear nothing. I walk around from room to room, but I can't find him anywhere. Maybe it was Olive? Though it couldn't be, that figure was a large person. Olive is tall, but very trim. Only I was underwater maybe what I saw was distorted? I make my way to her room, but it's the same way it was when she left. There was no one here.

A loud hissing sound erupts from one of the rooms and my heart picks up speed again.

"Sven? Sven is that you?" My voice shakes and the hairs on the back of my neck rise.

I open the door to the guest room with all the gaming equipment and the TV is on. Not on any channel just on one of the channels used for input.

"Sven? Olive?" I can feel the frog in my throat as I look around the room and realize that there is no one there.

How the hell did the TV come on? I quickly turn it off and then tip toe to the closet. I rip it open thinking that I'm going to find someone in there, but I don't. What the hell is going on here? I don't want to cry, but if there was a ghost or something why the hell was it choosing to scare the crap out of me now.

I make my way out of the room and all the lights in the house have mysteriously been turned off.

"Oh what the shit!" My entire body trembles as I turn around in circles trying to figure out who the hell is in the house and fucking with me right now, because there had to be a reason for this. "Who's here? Who?" I scream and my voice screeches.

I turn around in a large circle, but there is no one around. This is probably the only time I wished that Sven would have toted me along with him.

I run as fast as my foot will allow to my bedroom and like a little girl jump under the covers. I hold my breath as I listen around me, but again I don't hear anything.

Did I turn the lights on when I came back in the house? Did I turn the TV on by mistake when I went in? Was the shadow just a fucking bird flying overhead? I had been in that pool for hours with no drink or shade from the sun. Could I just be fucking imagining all this stuff going on? Maybe it's just my brain's way of telling me that I need to get some water in my system and quickly.

I chuckle and pull the cover off my head.

"Dumbass." I whisper to myself. There was nothing going on here. I was just dehydrated. I walk out the room and nothing had changed. None of the chairs were stacked on the table, no cupboards open, everything is exactly how it should be. I grab a water out of the fridge and chug it. My silly mind is just playing tricks on me after a long day in the heat.

I would have to remember next time to bring some water outside if I was going to be out there for so long. I make my way back to the room and throw myself on the bed. The pool had drained me something serious and all I want to do now is sleep. Hopefully when I wake up again, Sven will be home with the laptop. I won't feel so alone if I can at least call him when I need to.

28

Sven

Getting the information on the transport team is a lot quicker than I would have thought. Yet it took me days to do it while I was home. I was right in my original assumption that Ema was distracting the hell out of me. Marko expected a certain level of professionalism and promptness to my work and since Ema has come into my life, I hadn't been delivering that. I need to get my shit together. Once I finish gathering all the information that I need to make a solid decision. I forward it all over to Ante and he lets me know that we will be able to get the shipment within the next week. Finally, everything is going to go through as planned. Once we get these weapons, the family will be a force to be reckoned with. Besides, they will go for a pretty penny on the black market—upwards of hundreds of millions of dollars. If Marko was smart and I knew he was. He could sit on this until the buyer was willing to pay billions. If it wasn't him it would be someone. A nuclear weapon is something people always search for.

I spend the rest of the day looking up the best types of laptops that I could get for Ema. Every time I would settle on one, I would find a specification that it was missing and then I would have to search for a computer that had those specifications. I know she told me that she only wanted it to talk to her sisters, but she was my wife. My wife deserved the very best of whatever she had. I wasn't just going to get her a regular computer and that be the end of it. Her laptop should be able to do everything for her short of getting up and cooking her a five-course dinner.

There are plenty of locations near the strip where I would be able to get a good one, but I found myself in the Apple store browsing all the newest MacBook's. Even these beauties were still missing quite a few things that I thought she would need.

"Sir, honestly I don't think you will find all that you are looking for in any of the generic laptops. Not on a mac or pc in my experience."

I had been talking this guy's ear off for the past hour and a half telling him everything that I wanted the laptop to have. Still, we couldn't find one that would be suitable for what I wanted.

"Yes, it seems not." I look between the top two MacBook models trying to figure out what specification I was going to have to give up when he interrupts me again.

"Sir, I don't mean to be forward, but could I ask a question?"

"Yes."

"How much money are you willing to spend?"

I shrug my shoulders and glare at him for a second. I was going to be upset if he had some newer models in the back that he didn't want to show me, because he didn't think I would be able to afford it. I could buy this whole store three times over and not even flinch. "Money is of no object to me."

"That's what I thought. Well, there is another option if you would be open to it?"

"Tell me."

"If you want to go home with something right now, we could get you set up with one of the MacBook Airs and then in a few days we could have a custom MacBook built to your exact specifications. It's very expensive, but I believe that is the only way you would be able to get everything that you are asking for and all in one system."

I didn't think of that, of course I thought that I was going to have to make some modifications, but it didn't occur to me to ask the company itself to make a custom MacBook just for me. It makes sense and now all I wanted was that. "Yes, that is what I want."

"Great and then when we finish the custom MacBook, we will buy the separate MacBook Air back from you so you aren't stuck with two." He nods his head and leads me back towards a desk. I assume that he is going to take down the exact specifications of what I want.

"No need. I never know when a second laptop will come in handy. How long until the custom one is made?"

"Come over here and let's talk about it." The man smiles wide. I wonder how much commission he was going to make off of something like this. It made no matter to me. What mattered was that I was going to see Ema smile. I find myself liking it more and more when she is happy. This is the least that I can do.

I WALK in the house and all the lights are off. That's strange. Why would she turn all the lights off? I flick them on, and immediately I know something is off. The sofa in the main room isn't the way that it should be. It's shifted slightly and the cushions are mussed up. I drop everything in my hands down by the door and walk over to fix it, but when I get there, I can see an evident wet mark. Was she sitting here?

I lean down, but don't touch it. From what it looks like it's not something I want to put my hands on.

There is no fucking way.

I can't fucking breathe. My head pounds with the anger that is about to erupt from my ears.

That shit looks like cum.

Who was she fucking in my living room? What the fuck?

There is no way she is this fucking stupid. There is just no fucking way. I lean down further thinking maybe my eyes are deceiving me. I pull out a handkerchief that I have in my inside pocket and dab at the foul substance.

It's fucking cum.

I can't stop myself from running to my room. If she had that motherfucker in my bed right now, I would have to rip him limb from fucking limb, kill him nice and slow just so she could watch. Only after I know she is thoroughly traumatized will I make sure to rip her guts the fuck out of her midsection.

"I can't believe this shit." I don't hear anything, but that doesn't mean a thing. I kick open the door, but she is there alone in some small panties and bra set. She'd got dressed for him?

She pops up, clearly still groggy from her sleep. "Sven,

what the hell? What is your problem?" She rubs a hand over her eyes.

I can't believe I trusted her. I close the distance between us and tower over her. She leans back slightly on the bed. "Where the fuck is he?"

"What?"

I don't have time to play games. I don't think she realizes that I will blow her fucking head off and worry about the consequences later. If she was going to disrespect me so thoroughly, they couldn't hold it against me if I put her ass in the dirt. I pull the gun from my pants and press it to her forehead.

She gasps loudly and her entire body begins to shake, but she can't get any words out.

"I said where the fuck is he?"

When she doesn't answer I pull the gun away and fire a shot. She screams loudly and lunges forward pushing me back. She opens the drawer of the bedside table and pulls out the gun that is there. The same gun that I'd used on her the first night that we slept in the same bed together. She points it at me and her hands shake hard.

"What the hell are you talking about? What did I fucking do?" She screams at me.

"Pull the trigger. Pull it." I growl, daring her to do it.

"Sven. What is it? What-"

I lunge in her direction and purely in shock her finger flinches squeezing the trigger in the same second. There is a click, but no fire. Of course, there is no fire. There are no bullets in that gun. In fact, the firing pin is messed up and I haven't been able to get around to fixing it. That gun never had any bullets in it.

She gasps and throws the gun on the bed before trying to jump on the other side of the bed to get away from me, but I'm not having that. I grab her hair as it flies behind her. The motion slams her backwards, her body bouncing on the bed.

My free hand balls into a fist and even through all the anger I feel right now I still can't bring myself to punch her.

"Come on, I think you forgot to clean up your fucking mess." I growl at her and pull her off the bed using nothing but her hair.

"Sven, stop! Let go!" She kicks and tries to get up, but I don't let go. I don't slow down. I drag her to the couch.

"I'm going to ask you one more fucking time. Then I'm really going to get seriously pissed the hell off. Who the hell were you fucking in my house?"

Her eyes squint. I have to give it to her; she's got to be one of the best fucking actors I have ever seen in my life. "I don't know what you're talking about. I haven't fucked anyone, but you!" She screams up at me, the tears and snot running down her face.

"You lying bitch!" I roar at her. "Then who's is this? Huh?" I grab the back of her hair again and push her face down towards where the cum stain was. There is still a bit left on the fabric.

"What the hell? What is that?"

"You know what the fuck it is! Cum. It's not mine, and it's not yours, so who the fuck's is it?"

Her face falls, her eyes scan back and forth like she is trying to solve the greatest math problem in the world. "Oh my God. Oh my fucking God." She grabs onto my leg, wiping the tears and snot from her face as she looks up to me and babbles almost incoherently. "Sven, there was someone here. I thought I was fucking hallucinating or some shit, but if this is here that must mean that there was someone else here!"

"Do you think I'm stupid?" I snarl down at her. The alarms didn't go off. There is no one that close, all my neighbors live more than a mile in either direction. Those that do live in the homes are old geriatric couples who couldn't make it to their driveway let alone a mile down the road to jack off on my couch.

"Sven! For fuck's sake you have to believe me!"

"I don't have to believe shit!" I scream back at her. "I thought that I could trust you ... that we were moving past this shit, but it seems like you've been playing the long game all along. If you think that this is going to get you out of our marriage, you're fucking wrong."

She is shaking her head no, like everything I'm saying is wrong. "Sven, I didn't, please, just listen to what I'm telling you."

"Fuck you, I don't have to listen to any shit you have to say. If no one was here, why the fuck do you have that outfit on?"

"Outfit? Are you shitting me? This is a bathing suit, I was out in the pool for the majority of the day. I went for a swim in the pool and I was coming back up I thought I saw a shadow of a man. Maybe it's because of the antibiotic but I was so parched when I finished swimming that I worried I was dehydrated."

I had to cut her off at that one. "The same man you said was outside when you went sneaking off in the middle of the night? Tell me was it your lover out there?"

"Fuck you! I'm telling the fucking truth. Why won't you fucking believe me?" She gets up on her feet and grabs my shirt with both her fists.

"It doesn't make fucking sense!" I pull away from her.

"It's Bryce. It has to be."

Now she was just grasping at straws. I had already taken care of that fucking issue. "I told you already that he's dead. Now you are going to tell me that he came back to life and jerked off on my couch. Ema, you really have to learn to lie better."

"Ugh, I'm saying he's not dead."

"Dagger is the best fucking hitman I know. If he said he is dead, then the man is fucking dead."

"Did you see the proof? Tell him to prove it!" she screeches in my face. If I didn't know any better, I would think that she is telling me the truth.

Could it be possible that Dagger did fuck up and not get the mark? I never heard of that shit happening, but maybe today was the first time for it. I pluck my phone out of my pocket and put a call into Dagger. He picks it up on the first go.

"Dagger. Everything good?'

"Yes." He answers not understanding what I was asking.

"You have photos?"

There was a slight hesitation on the phone. My request was completely against protocol.

"That wasn't part of the desired parameters." Dagger's voice is clipped.

"Indeed, I'm aware. But the client is suggesting that the job has not been completed."

There is some muffling on the phone and then I hear things being shuffled around.

"You have time for a steam?"

He was asking me if I had time to meet him at one of the many bathhouses around. They were a great place to relax, but it was also where we could meet to talk business without all the cloak and dagger routine.

"No. Personal. I'll leave a candle burning for you." I hang up the phone, knowing he understands what I'm telling him. I need to see him face to face and at my place where there were no fucking witnesses. If he hadn't completed the job, then I would put a bullet between his fucking eyes. It was that simple.

I kick the couch away from me and go to sit down on the chair on the other side of the room. Ema sits back down on the floor, tears slowly coming down her face, but she didn't try to move. We just stare at each other while we wait for Dagger to come and show us that he had indeed killed Bryce. If I were Dagger, I would get here quickly. I'm already thinking of all the different ways that I can kill either of them. Someone here is lying to me and I'm about to find out who it is.

AN HOUR LATER, Dagger pulls up in my driveway. I hear his footsteps coming up my front steps, it's the first time that I've taken my eyes off of Ema since I'd brought her down here. She is no longer looking back at me, just looking down at the floor. I open the door and can see that he is beyond pissed off. Dagger has never been accused of not doing his job. He is the best hitman for a reason.

"This is highly irregular, Sven."

I pull the gun that I have in my pants and press it under his chin. He has no right to tell me what is regular or what isn't. I don't know when they all started to forget that unless it was Marko Juric who was asking me the fucking questions, they could all kick fucking rocks.

"Does it look like I give a shit how irregular this is? I want to see proof. My wife here seems to want me to believe that you left the man alive and therefore that man broke into my house ... and decided to relieve himself on my couch."

Dagger's eyes pop open and they cut over to where Ema was still sitting on the floor.

"Not possible."

I move the gun away from him and motion him inside the house. "Please do show us your masterpiece."

He pulls out what looks to be a burner phone, it was old and a flip phone at that. I didn't think they still made those types of phones anymore. "This is the man you told me to take out did you not?"

He shows me some photos on the phone. Several of them with the man's limbs cut off one at a time. One photo of him crying with no hand and in the next, he had no leg. After that it was an ear, so on and so on, until the final photo was of him without his body. The anger that had tried to die down as I waited for Dagger revs back up. I snatch the phone from his grasp and storm over to where Ema is sitting. I grab her by the neck and shove the phone in her face.

"How the fuck is he here, when he was fucking decapitated over in Alaska?"

She groans and tries to push the phone away so that she doesn't have to see it. "Oh, Sven, I don't know. I swear I didn't do anything. Please, you have to believe me."

I shake my head in disbelief. I did that shit before, not again. I trusted her more than I have trusted anyone who wasn't family. That was my first and last fucking mistake.

"I don't have to do shit." I grab her arm and pull her behind me. My mind doing its best to drown out all the fucking noise of her screaming and begging behind me. She was just another fucking distraction that I didn't need.

I turn and walk up the stairs.

"Where are you taking me? Sven, answer me goddamn it!" She pulls at my grip almost causing me to drop her ass down the stairs. At this point I really don't fucking care if she were to break her fucking neck. Dagger was here, he would be a witness that I didn't kill her and still upheld my side of the agreement.

"Sven!"

"Shut the fuck up! I don't want to hear your fucking lies anymore." I open the door to the room that I use for any excess prisoners. There are times that we can't keep them at the Košnica and all the rest of the locations are full. Especially if they are being moved from one place to the next. I can use this room just as a temporary holding cell. It's not to be used for long term care, except now it would be. This is where Ema would live out the remainder of her life while she was in my care.

29

Sven

It hurt. Not just mentally, but my body physically aches to be away from her. She screams all night. Even now while I lay in this king-size bed that I used to feel comfortable in I hear her crying and screaming for me. I can't shake the look of confusion in her eyes. I like to think of myself as a great judge of character and this just didn't make sense. She didn't know anyone out here, no way for her to communicate to the outside world. No one knows where I live besides allies to the family and none of them would ever come here and cross me. None of it made any fucking sense.

"Sven! I know you hear me. Please. I beg you. Please. Don't leave me here."

That was all I could take. I throw the covers off and hurry up the stairs to the room. I swing the door open and she immediately comes running to me. Her face is puffy and red from all the tears. "Sven, please listen. Please." She continues to cry. "I've never and wouldn't ever do something like this. What do I have to do to prove it to you?"

"What are you proving? That you're not the slut it appears like you are? I mean only a whore would bring a man into her husband's home and leave his spunk smeared all over the couch. Is that what you're trying to prove?"

She cringes at my vulgarity.

"Sven, I'm yours." She grabs my face and tries to force me to look at her. I don't want to though. I don't want to see the truth there and not be sure if it's just my mind playing tricks on me. "I've been yours, only yours." She leans up on her tip toes and presses a shaky kiss to my lips. Her breath coming in shudders. What if he'd kissed her? What if his lips were on what was mine? I wanted to burn them off her face. She's mine!

I growl, tearing my face away from hers before I turn her around by her neck and press her hard against the wall. She squirms and screams slightly, but there were no other sounds from her after. I rip the flimsy, wet, bathing suit off. My mind logs the fact that they are still wet, meaning she wasn't lying about being in the pool.

"Are you mine Ema? Because if you are then I can use you any way I like. Prove it to me." The words fall out of my mouth like poison. I push her chest up against the wall, smashing her face against it as well. I pull my cock out with no preamble and shove it straight up her cunt.

"Sven!" She cries out at the brutal force, but I have no desire to make her feel good. I don't care if she's not in a comfortable position. She tries to push herself back so she can enjoy what's happening as well, but I don't budge.

"Are you mine Ema?"

"Yes, I'm yours" Her voice is strained.

I'm thrusting into her at a pace faster than before. My sole motivation is to come inside of her. I want to mark her, and if there are any remnants of another man I want to erase it with my cum.

I pump hard and she slams her hand against the wall still in this fucked up position. I feel her pussy clamp down. She's going to come, but she doesn't deserve to come on my dick. I smack her hard enough on her ass to draw her attention away all the while I continue to move. It's not long before I'm coming deep inside of her. I let two spurts shoot inside of her before I pull out suddenly and she falls like a heap to the ground.

"If I find out who he is. I'll kill him. I swear to you I will find him and I'll fucking kill him." I pull my pants up and walk out of the room. Leaving her crumpled on the ground with my cum dripping out of her pussy and tears rolling down her face.

I WAKE up with her in the bed with me. Well rested.

I can't believe I caved like that for her. I don't know what to fucking believe, but I know I can't trust her. I have shit to do and now I have to bring her along with me.

I push her roughly and she startles awake.

"What?" she snaps at me.

"Get up, I have to go."

"Then go."

"Do I have to drag you out of the bed or are you just going to do what you're told?" I snarl at her, my hand ready to grab her hair and drag her behind me like a large bag. That was all she was to me right now. A large sac of bones and blood.

"No, I'm coming. I'll get dressed right now."

Within twenty minutes the both of us were ready and on the way to the Košnica. This time using an entrance through a small coffee shop.

"Sven." She tugs on my arm slightly. "Can we get a coffee before we go or something to eat?"

I didn't give her dinner last night and we had yet to have breakfast. Saying no right now would just be childish. My meeting wasn't set to start for another few minutes and I don't want her down there with me passing out from malnourishment.

"Fine. Get what you want and hurry the hell up." I sit at one of the many tables and watch as she stands in line.

She looks to me a few times, a trying smile on her face. Does she think that I'll just forget everything that happened yesterday? On one hand I can't prove it, but on the other hand there is no other explanation. I'll get to the bottom of it though.

"Good morning." A woman walks up to my table and slides into the seat across from me.

"I'm sorry ma'am, but that chair is for someone else."

"Yeah. Me." She giggles and moves her legs closer to mine under the table. "Look I know you don't know me, but I've spent the last few years holding back who I was for a husband who didn't want me. Now that I'm divorced, I told myself that I was going to go for exactly what I want. And this fine morning it's you. Nothing long term just a one time thing."

"Are you asking for payment?" She didn't seem like the streetwalker type, but I've been wrong about that before.

She bristles and sits back slightly, "No, I'm not a hooker."

"No, you're just a fucking homewrecker." Ema snarls from behind her.

"Excuse me?"

"That is my husband you're trying to sleep with."

"Oh ... I'm so sorry. I didn't realize." The woman quickly gets up out of the seat and rushes away.

Ema sits down in the chair and throws a muffin at my chest. "What the fuck was that?"

"Do you think I won't punish you here in the coffee shop? They won't call the cops on me." I lean my head to the side and wait for her response. If it has any expletives in it, I'll reach across this table and pull her to me.

"What were you doing?"

"That woman approached me and I was talking to her."

"No, you were entertaining her proposition!" She hisses.

"What is it to you?"

"I'm your wife! What do you mean what is it to me?" she raises her hand and closes her eyes as if she were trying to calm down. "Don't do that again Sven. If you need to entertain other women don't come to me, because I want nothing of it or you. I don't need anyone's sloppy seconds."

She turns in her seat and sips on the coffee that she had just bought.

She's jealous? How the hell can she be jealous with everything that happened yesterday? I'm flustered to say the least. She's not acting like someone who just got caught cheating. She acts like I'm the one in the wrong. Am I?

"Let's go." I stand up and wait for her to gather her things. When we make it downstairs there are quite a few people already milling around.

It's unusual for anyone to bring their woman with

them, but there is no way that I can leave her at home right now.

I knock on the door where I believe Marko is and the door opens.

"Ah, Sven. Come in, nice to see you." He kisses my cheeks and allows me into the room. "Oh, you've brought company." He spies Ema behind me and bends to kiss her cheeks as well.

"Yes, she needs supervision it would seem."

I hear her huff out, but she doesn't say a word. Good girl.

"No need to explain." He waves his hand in the air before he sits at the table. This being his private area the table is much smaller. Though this table is full of food except this all looks like samples of different things instead of full meals. "Sven how are things?"

"Everything is fine." I reply right away.

"I'm not so sure. I've been getting reports that you have been late on several occasions recently with vital information. The family doesn't feel like they can depend on your word right now and this saddens me. Can I not depend on you?"

I can't react. I can't show weakness. "If they want the correct information then I would think them having to wait on it wouldn't be a problem. I can rush it, but I don't think that would be the best thing for us. For you."

He nods his head and pops a small tart in his mouth, chewing a few times before he swallows. He drinks from his glass before leaning back in his chair.

"Do you know what happens to dogs who can no longer hunt?"

The tension in the room is palpable. "Da."

"Yes, so tell me. What do you do with a dog who is no longer good for what they are bred?"

"You put them down."

"I groomed you to be the best at what you do, you've never failed me before and I don't expect you to start now. What good to me are you if you are no longer able to do what I groomed you for?" Marko smiles at me—a warning. He was my father, but he would kill me.

A loud grumbling sound comes from behind me.

"Sven, how rude of you not to ensure that your wife isn't hungry. What are you doing to this beautiful snow flower? Come child have some food." Marko put his hand out to Ema.

She looks to me once before she quickly makes her way to Marko.

"Eat what you wish. Let me know how it tastes. I'm sampling a new restaurant to see if they will cater my next event. So far everything is great in my opinion." He lifts up a spoon of something and presses it to her lips.

She opens and takes it in. "What say you?"

Her eyes flutter closed and she moans slightly. "That is absolutely sublime. Where is that from?"

"Oh, a new place here on the strip, *Ryshe*. I believe a friend of yours is the investor. Alex?"

"Oh, is that where he works? Yeah, he always did have a taste for the best foods."

"It seems so." Marko laughs and wraps an arm around Ema's shoulder. "He is the one who recommended it. He's proven quite useful over the last few weeks. We are even starting on construction through one of his restaurants as another access point to here."

"That's good. He's a good man." Ema nods her head a few

times, her eyes looking off into the distance. She's probably wondering right now what her life would have been like if she would have taken him up on his advances. If she had married him instead of being given to me. Much different.

"Well, it's been nice to have a visit this morning. Thank you sweet, Ema for your opinion. I think we will be going with this restaurant after all. I'm sure Sven here has some work to get done?" He turns to look at me, "Make sure you find out what has been going on with the Varva family. I know Ilia is still upset with Dagger. Find out what we can do to smooth things over. I wouldn't want there to be any bad blood between us over your little mistake." I grit my teeth, but don't say a word. How long would he hold that over my head? Bryn Valentine didn't look anything like the illegitimate daughter I knew Ilia to have. Of course, we hadn't been updated on her whereabouts or given a new picture since her tenth birthday. However, I still didn't expect the small mousy haired girl with big glasses and buck teeth to grow up into that. Of course when I saw the picture I said I didn't recognize her, because I didn't.

"Of course Marko. Ema, come."

She takes one more bite of the food before she rushes over to me.

"Oh, one more thing." Marko calls out from the table. I turn towards him. "Ema darling, show your mark."

Fuck. Fuck fuck fuck!

"Um. I" She stutters not wanting to show him that it's not finished. This is bad.

I push her forward and shake my head. Stalling it will do nothing, but piss him off more. "Show." I whisper.

She takes another step forward and pulls down her pants slightly showing the 1/3rd of a mark.

Marko's face falls and he looks up to me. "Sven, I'm disappointed. Very disappointed."

"I know. I'll rectify it shortly."

"I've been hearing that from you a lot. You'll get to it soon. You'll rectify it shortly. Eventually." He slams his hand down on the table and a few dishes fly off. "When I give a fucking directive it's not to be done when you want to do it. It's now. You do it now and correctly. I don't need you otherwise Sven. Don't make me do this." He leans back keeping his eyes locked on mine.

"Now. I'll fix it now." I nod at him and he waves his hand, dismissing me.

I grab Ema by her arm and quickly pull her out of the room.

"Sven, you're hurting my arm. Slow down."

"No. Fucking no. I will not slow down. Since you've been here, you've been nothing but a distraction, now you're going to get me fucking killed. No, I'm not going to slow down. I tug her through the coffee shop not caring who she bumps into in the process and push her into the car. We need to get back to the house right now. I have to finish this fucking mark.

30

Ema

This is crazy. He is driving like a fucking mad man through the streets. Does he think that Marko is going to send someone after him in the next hour if this isn't done immediately? I know it's a big deal in the family, but I've only been here a little while. It takes time. Just when I thought that maybe we would be getting on good terms, something like yesterday has to happen. The problem is Sven doesn't believe me.

I know I didn't cheat, and I didn't bring anyone in the house. It means that someone was in the house when I was. Someone had broken in while I was sleeping and did that to the couch. I'd rather sit in the car with Sven while he was driving like a fucking lunatic if it meant that I wouldn't have to sit alone in the house again. Not until I can get him to believe that something is going on.

I'm not stupid, I know exactly what it looks like. If I were him and came home to someone else's sperm on the couch I would be just as upset. I had to show him that it wasn't me and if that meant that I would have to go everywhere with him than that is what I would do.

We pull up to the house and walk in to see Olive rearranging a few dozen roses.

"What the hell is this?"

"More wedding gifts it seems. I wish they would leave a return note, but there's nothing." Olive shrugs and continues arranging the flowers.

"Olive, Ema and I will be indisposed for the rest of the day. Make sure we are not disturbed unless it's Mr. Juric himself."

"As you wish."

He drags me up the stairs and into the guest room. I guess today is the day that we finish this. I knew it was coming, but this time things are so different. I'm not nervous, but there is no sexual energy or any type of energy behind this. He's doing it because he has to.

The set up is the same as before except this time he leaves my pants on and just rolls them down. There is no distracting me from the pain this time. Nothing but dead air and the tapping of the needle into my skin.

"Sven are you never going to talk to me again?"

"I have nothing to say."

"Sven, I didn't do it." I repeat for the millionth time. I'm getting sick and tired of people not fucking believing me.

"So you've said."

"There was someone here. Don't you think maybe you should look into that? Even pretend you're giving me the benefit of the doubt." I snap at him, but make sure I don't raise my voice too much. He is still tapping a needle into my skin after all.

"You're not outside on a spit being roasted to death.

That's your benefit of the doubt right there." He raises his eyes to mine briefly before he goes back to tapping.

I let my head fall back and just lay there taking the pain, every once in a while a tear falling from my eyes. I feel like I'm going crazy. I had no idea what I could do to prove to him that I wasn't lying. I had caused him to distrust me so much already that now it was going to be impossible for him to do anything else.

31

Sven

Twelve hours. It took the rest of the day to complete the tattoo. It was nicely done, but there were still a few places that could use a going over. The sight of it on her skin did nothing for me. I wasn't happy or proud. I wasn't anything besides relieved that it was over. She had my mark.

Great.

I walk into my library, but as I open the door the hairs on the back of my neck stand up. The drawer to one of my file cabinets was open. She was in here looking for information? I didn't see it yesterday in all my rage, but it makes sense for her to do that.

Now I could kill her and they wouldn't ask any questions, but first I had to find out what she knew.

I go back to my bedroom and find her laying on the bed, her head down and shoulders shaking with fake tears.

"You were in my office?"

Her head pops up to mine. "What? No, I wasn't!" She jumps up from the bed.

"My file cabinet is open, you were in there looking for information. What did you want to know?"

"Oh my fucking God. I can't take this anymore. Sven I did nothing!" She screeches.

"What was in there?"

"I don't know. I didn't look in your stupid file cabinet. I don't even go into your study unless you're there." She throws her hands up. "When did I have a chance to do that? I've been with you all day. I was in that stupid cell, then in this bed, with you. When could I have possibly done that?"

I think back on yesterday when I came home and put her in the cell. I don't remember it being open when I went to the study. I can't fucking remember though.

Shit. I can't kill her without more information. I have to be sure first, to be absolutely certain that my wife is indeed the traitor that I think she is.

"I don't trust you." I whisper.

"I didn't do it Sven. I don't know how many times I have to say it."

The answer never changes with her.

My cell phone rings. When I look down I see the number of the apple store. Shit, I was supposed to pick up her laptop today. Not that I would need it anymore, but I did give my word that I would purchase it.

I need some time away from her. I walk over and quickly pull out the handcuffs that I had left in the nightstand.

She shakes her head, but doesn't say a word when I fasten her to my headboard. She turns in the bed and just gets under the cover, at least I know she's not going anywhere.

When I walk out of the room, I see Olive pacing back and forth. There are flowers everywhere. Blood red.

"Olive?"

"Oh sir." She rushes over to me and I can see her face is quite flushed. Like she's about to cry. "I'm sorry. I just had a terrible fright."

"What is it?"

"I don't know who is sending all these flowers and none of them are coming with cards. I finally thought I would try and consolidate them. Only there were scorpions at the bottom of one of the vases. Scared the bejesus out of me. I'm alright now."

Scorpions. What the fuck!

That is one hell of a coincidence. Sure, there are scorpions all over the place and it's not unlikely for one of them to get inside the house. Except for them to come delivered in a mysterious bouquet of flowers isn't normal.

"I see." My mind begins to race, what the fuck is going on here. "I have to run to the store. Please ensure that no one comes in and my wife doesn't go out. She is upstairs secured and sleeping right now."

"Yes sir." She gives me a soft smile before she walks back over to the dining area and begins moving the flowers around.

"Olive, another thing. Throw all those flowers out. Keep none of them."

Her mouth drops into a pouty frown before she nods her head yes. If I didn't know who they were from there was no reason for them to be in my house.

∼

"Oh Mr. Kokot, I'm so happy you were able to make it. I have your custom laptop right here."

"Good, ring it up so I can go." I say, much shorter than I need to be.

"Oh, er, ok. Don't you want me to set it up, show you all the features?"

"Does it look like I want to stand here and waste fucking time with you. I'm on a schedule, ring it up and let me leave." I was getting more and more agitated the longer I left Ema home without me. There is nowhere for her to go since she's cuffed to the bed though.

"Yes sir." He moves quickly, the polite conversation he was trying to include me in moments ago gone. I feel like a jerk, but I can't focus on that. I just want to get back home. My total is close to four thousand dollars. I don't even blink as I hand him my American express card. When he hands me over the receipt, I shove it in my pocket and take out five hundred dollars for him. It's not his fault I feel like my life is going to shit.

"Thank you. Good work." I outstretch my hand to him.

He smiles at the sight of the large tip and shakes my hand.

I'm out of the store quicker than I thought possible. It's only been about two hours. Surely, she couldn't have done anything in two hours.

I don't stop for anything on the way back. I can see all the flowers outside in the trash bin. When I open up the door, I don't see anything out of the ordinary. I hear Olive moving around upstairs. I make my way into the room and can see Ema still sleeping in the same position. Instantly I feel better and also drained. I've been tense since I walked out of the house.

I kick off my shoes and shrug off my shirt, and walk to

my side of the bed. When I pull the sheets back, my mind goes completely blank.

In her free hand she's clutching a rose. My side of the bed looks like it's still made except the edge isn't tucked in like it usually is. Like she had tried to make the bed and forgot that one spot.

"Wake the fuck up!"

Did she really have the nerve to fuck someone in my bed?

"Hmm?" Ema raises her head off the pillow.

"You want to die?"

"What? "She looks down to her hand and a gasp leaves her mouth as she drops the rose to the bed. "Oh my God. He came back." She cries and tries to jump out of bed. She turns over awkwardly, because her other hand is still cuffed to the headboard.

"Ema. Stop it now."

She puts her hand through her hair to pull it out of her face and suddenly her hysterics stop. A look of disgust crosses her face. "Oh, what the fuck! What is that?" her voice is only a whisper.

She pulls her hand away from her head so both of us can see. Her fingers are laced with an off white, slimy substance.

Cum.

She gags hard before the panic starts again. "Let me out. He's here. Out. Out. Out." She falls down to the floor and tries to rip her own hand out of the bind. The metal already cutting into her skin as she screams and heaves in hysterics.

This isn't an act. It can't be.

"Stop!" I rush over to her side of the bed and try to pull her up so she's not putting so much strain on her wrist.

She sobs worse than I've ever seen her cry, "Please, you said you were going to keep me safe. Please, don't leave me here again. Let me out. Please. Please. Please." She begs, her entire body shaking in fear.

My heart drops to the bottom of my gut.

I grab her face, and force her eyes on me. "Ema, did you let someone in here?" I need to see it one more time.

"No! No! I didn't. I don't understand. I didn't do it!"

I believe her. Fuck, someone has been in here terrorizing my wife and I'd thought she was cheating on me.

"Please let me out."

I quickly undo her cuff and she takes off to the bathroom. She presses a few buttons on the display and the hot water turns on before she comes back in the room. She throws the clothes that she was wearing out the window. It seems excessive to me, but I couldn't say anything about it.

She rushes back into the bathroom, but skids to a stop.

"Sven!" She screams out my name.

I rush over to her just as she crumbles to the floor in a heap and wraps her arms around her legs.

I look in the bathroom, the steam of the water has started to fill up the large area. My eyes widen as I look at every available glass surface, the word mine written over and over again—on the glass, on the mirror.

That's all the proof I need. Someone was here and they were here for my wife.

32

Sven

I pull Ema up and push her into the bathroom. I stand there with her as she washes that foul substance out of her hair.

"Ema, did you notice anyone following you when we were outside?"

Her eyes dart to mine, anger clear as day.

"Oh now you want to fucking believe me? Now you have questions?" Her voice cracks as she continues to rigorously wash her hair.

"Ema, do you want to argue, or do you want to catch the bastard who has been sneaking in here?"

She blows out a breath. "You didn't believe me." Her voice is low and she starts crying all over again.

I kick my shoes off and shrug out of my suit jacket before I step into the shower with her. I never want her to feel alone again. I should have listened, I know that now, but at the time I couldn't see past my own jealousy.

"Ema, I'm so sorry. I should have listened to you and I wouldn't feel so much guilt over it now. If something would have happened to you, I don't know what I would have done. I'm sorry." I caress her face and she stares up at me with those large dark brown doe eyes.

"You think I'm just going to forgive you like that?"

"No, from what I know there is going to be a bit of groveling involved on my part. I'm man enough to admit that I need to do that."

"A lot." She turns her head to the side, but I can see that sneaky smile trying to break across her face.

"Ema, please. Help me here. I'm going crazy thinking someone is going to hurt you. Work with me." I feel like a pussy.

I don't think I have ever been the type of person to grovel, but if it meant that she would be open to letting me back into her life I would. I didn't want to be just a part of her life. I wanted her to be happy here with me, for her to be safe. I wanted her to be glad that she had my mark.

"Just don't leave me alone, ok?"

"Never. I'll never leave you alone again if it makes you feel better."

She doesn't kiss me, but she leans her forehead against my chest and lets me take care of her. I continue to wash her hair, over and over until she is satisfied that she is clean. I make sure to take all the weapons I can out of the room before I grab a few pieces of clothing for her to put on.

I give Olive the rest of the week off and instruct her that she isn't to come back in the house for any reason until I give her the say so. I didn't want to scare her more than I needed to, but I told her that we had some unwanted guests and hoped that she would get the hint.

Ema stays glued to my side the entire time. Usually something like that would be annoying, but now I couldn't get any fucking closer to her.

"Take your laptop." I point to the bag on the floor.

"You can't buy me Sven." She crosses her arms over her chest.

"I'm not trying to buy you, but there is a chance that all of my electronics are compromised. Your laptop is the only piece of equipment that I know no one has touched."

She quickly grabs it up and comes back to my side.

"Do you have any idea who it might be?" I ask her.

"Bryce." She shrugs her shoulders.

"Ema, I showed you the pictures. He is very dead."

"The only time I've ever felt like this was when I was home. But I knew he would never do anything to me. Now I'm not so sure."

"Wait, things like this have happened to you before?"

"Yeah, but I thought it was him. I never said anything to my mother, because I knew she didn't believe me anyway ... No one ever fucking believes me."

Another dig at me. "I'm sorry, I don't know how many times I can say it, but I'm telling you now it won't be many more. I should've believed you, but even you have to admit its very fucking hard to believe."

She rolls her eyes, nodding.

"If this was happening before maybe we need to be looking into someone who was also with you back home."

Suddenly it struck me that maybe someone in the Sever family was trying to get me to believe that she was cheating on me so that I would harm her. If I were to kill her in the first year or something bad happens to her then the deal between Ivan and Marko would be void. The nuke was on its way to the states already. If the deal was void, Ivan could demand that Marko give him back his property. We would basically be doing all the dirty work for him. It was a genius plan. One I had to dig deeper into to find out. It didn't matter though. I would do whatever I had to do to make sure that Ema was safe.

33

Ema

I can't believe it took him this long to realize that what I've been saying all along is the truth. I do agree with him that it's a hard thing to believe. Despite that I hate that it took him this long to believe me in the first place. The bastard whoever he is, jerked off in my hair. How the fuck did I not realize that shit? I mean I was tired, but jeez.

Sven sends Olive on her way and we take off in the car. He does his best to drive at a normal speed, probably because he knew that I had problems when he drove fast. When we pull into the driveway of the house where I was forced to take my nuptials, the disgust rises in my throat. What the hell are we even doing here?

"Sven? Why did you bring me back here?'

"I have to talk to Marko, if there is something going on I don't want to wait until he is at the Košnica. I need to get this settled right now. Your father's ship is already on its journey. If it's your Uncle trying to pull this off than whatever is going down will happen sooner than later."

Fear blossoms in my chest and I grab hold of Sven's leg. "Do you think he is going to do something to Tata? Is my father in danger?"

He grabs hold of my hand and kisses my knuckles. "I don't know Ema, If I had to guess, with your uncle there is a strong possibility that he is. We are going to find out together."

I nod and grip his hand tightly. Finally, he was seeing me not as just his prisoner, but as a partner—his wife. I don't even know why that makes me so happy, but it does.

We get out of the car and can see that even though the lights are on in the house all looks quiet. Well, it was quiet for a moment before a loud screech of laughter filters through the house—

a child's laughter.

What the hell?

Sven knocks on the door and a guard peers through the window. His face scrunching up in confusion.

"Mr. Kokot?"

"Da, I need to see Marko."

The door opens and I step in with him. The place is just as huge as I remember and part of me is upset that I didn't get a chance to explore it back when I was getting married. The home is really magnificent. I hear the laughter again and my mind immediately searches for it.

"Is there a kid here?" I turn to Sven and he looks around for a second maybe a bit confused about what I'm talking about. Before high-pitched laughter floats through the air.

"Ahh, yes. Lily."

"Lily? Who is that?" When I think about Marko Juric, I don't picture him with children running around. The fact that there is a child here is a bit scary to me, but she's laughing so maybe it's not as bad as I'm thinking it is.

A woman with dark hair runs very slowly while a small child, maybe about six years old, laughs and chases behind her. It seems so normal. So domestic.

When the older woman sees me, she stops and grabs for the child running behind her.

"Keeley, it's ok. No trouble. This is my wife, Ema."

"Ema, I'd like you to meet Keeley, my sister."

The woman he'd just called Keeley, her eyes open wide before she looks from me to Sven and then back again.

"You got married Sven?"

"It wasn't a planned event."

"I would hope not, because I didn't receive an invitation to that."

"If it makes you feel any better, I didn't receive an invitation either. They pulled a bag off my head and poof here I am." I give a sarcastic smile and the woman glares at me for a second before she bursts out laughing. Laughter, now that I didn't expect.

"Oh yes, this is going to be perfect. I can't wait to see how great you two are going to be together." Keeley walks over to me and pulls me into a hug. It was nice, not at all cold and uncomfortable like I thought it would be. When she pulls back her eyes twinkle with love. Love of me? Probably not, more likely love of her family.

"Ah, actually, I need to speak with Marko quite urgently. Keeley maybe you and Ema can catch up a bit?"

"Of course." Keeley looks at me.

I nod my head. I may have just met this woman, but something about her makes me want to make sure she's happy. I don't want to disappoint her and I've only known her for all of two minutes. I watch as Sven bounds up the stairs not bothering to leave me with any threat about escaping or embarrassing him. His mind is completely focused on the task at hand, trying to figure out who is terrorizing my entire fucking life.

"Come let's go sit. Looks like you need to take a load off." She grabs my hand, and we walk to the kitchen. I say kitchen only because it has a stove in it. Except in reality this must be a whole fucking restaurant. There are enough burners in here to cook for five hundred people. There is a massive island, light wood cabinets, and two refrigerators. Not to mention all the pots and pans hanging around. Truly it was the biggest kitchen I have ever seen in my life.

"Wow, I don't think I have ever seen a kitchen like this." I marvel as Keeley directs me to one of the stools at the island.

"Yeah, my father loves to eat so he makes sure that the cooks have everything they need to make whatever he would want. I guess growing up poor in Croatia where there was not much to eat makes him feel like he needs to make up for it now. The cravings that man gets is off the wall." She laughs and comes back to the island with a small cup of water for me and one for herself.

"Momma, what about me? Can I have some milk?" The small child that has yet to detach herself from her mother's arm speaks up.

"Yes, baby, but I want to talk to Ms. Ema for a few minutes. Grown up talk. Can you go play with your dolls in your room?"

"Oh mom!"

"Lily!" Keeley raises her voice slightly and turns her head towards her child.

The little girl doesn't say another word just steps loudly

to the fridge, pulls out a Yoo-hoo, and stomps even more dramatically out of the kitchen.

I have to chuckle at the whole scene. Lily's antics make me miss my youngest sister, Mila. She's only seven.

"She's precious." I say to break my mind away from the sad road that I'm going down.

"She's my everything." Keeley sighs looking over my shoulder for a second before focusing back on me. "So, Ema, I see you were roped into my family. I'm sorry that happened to you."

"Yeah, I can't lie it was really bad in the beginning, but Sven isn't as bad as I had wanted him to be. I guess that's a horrible thing to say."

Keeley reaches out and grabs my hand, "No, it's not a horrible thing at all. It's supposed to be our hearts decision who we fall in love with. Not some calculated, planned deal between two people that have nothing to do with you. Of course you thought Sven was the worst thing to ever walk the face of the earth. It makes perfect sense."

"Did you have to marry someone you didn't love?"

"No." Her face breaks into a wistful smile, "No, I love my husband." A tear threatens to fall from her face, but she swipes it away. "We're not together right now."

"Oh, I'm sorry. That must be hard."

"It's agonizing, but it's the best thing for my family right now. Love should never overtake safety. Until my family is safe, our love will have to wait"

That had to be the most profound thing I think I had ever heard any woman say.

"I hear that."

"So what about you, now that you've realized that Sven isn't the boogey man, how do you feel about him?"

It seems like quite the loaded question, "I don't know. He's still a lot to handle."

"Yeah, that I can believe, but who he is, is just that, who he is. I don't think he is going to change very much."

"But he has." I admit.

"How so?"

"Just small things. The control mostly. He is letting loose, relaxing a bit with some of his control. He is including me more in decisions. He asks my opinion. It's only recently that we've hit a snag." I blow out my breath and take a sip of water.

"Snag?"

I look over to her, not knowing if I should divulge everything that is going on.

"You don't have to say anything, but I may be able to give you some insight. Sven and I were raised completely different. I'm Marko's biological daughter. He's tough on me, but he's also not as tough as he could be. Sven and Luka are a different breed all together. My father was tougher on them thus making them tougher on everyone else."

"He thought I was lying. He thought that I was cheating on him when I didn't. He gets so mad. I don't know what he is going to do when he gets that angry. It's scary."

"Did you cheat on him?" Keeley asks, but her voice doesn't change in the slightest. Part of me thinks that if I were to say yes either she would completely dismiss it or she would rip my face off. Her poker face is amazing.

"No! Not at all. Someone has been breaking in and leaving little disgusting things around the house. It's only now that he believes me. I wouldn't do that to Sven." I shake my head like it's the most abhorrent thing to even think about.

"Why not? I mean you were forced here against your will. Marked, I'm assuming and kept from your family. Why wouldn't you want to find someone else?"

It felt like she was trying to get me to want to be with someone else. What kind of fucked up sister would do something like that? I don't know how Sven feels about Keeley, but I would never betray him like that, "Sven has given me everything that he's promised. He doesn't lie to me. He does his best to keep me safe. He makes me feel more than any man has ever made me feel. I would never ..." Keeley's mouth is set in a huge smile, "What's so funny?"

"You. I thought you said you didn't know how you felt. Seems to me that you know exactly how you feel. I think that maybe you are fighting it just for the sake of fighting it. Sven is a good man. You both may not have come into this relationship the way that either of you wanted, but I don't think there will be a better match for either of you."

My mouth drops open in shock, she played me. Laughter bubbles up out of my throat as I think back on what I just said. I can't think of one lie in the whole spiel. I care for Sven more than I thought I did. Day by day, piece by piece, that man has wormed his way into my heart. Now I can't see myself without him.

"Hmm, do you do that often?" Finally, I am able to say something.

"What's that?"

"Being right."

Keeley laughs and takes another sip of her water. "Not always, but most of the time."

A man comes up behind me and waits in the doorway for our attention.

"Yes?" Keeley is the one to respond.

"We need Mrs. Kokot upstairs right away."

A frog jumps up in my throat. I hope everything is going the way it should be, but with this family you can never be sure.

Keeley gives me an encouraging smile before she lets my hand go and I follow the guard up the stairs. I have to be strong not just for me, but for Sven as well.

34

Sven

When I get upstairs, Marko has already laid down to bed in his night clothes. He grabs a robe off the side chair when I step in the room. "Sven whatever this is about, I'm sure it can wait until tomorrow."

"No. I don't think so. I believe we have a problem."

Marko walks over to the table in his room and takes a seat. I don't move from where I'm standing. When he is ready for me to join him, he will tell me. Until then I will wait.

"Come, sit. Tell me what brings you here to disturb me."

I sit right away and steel myself for the conversation that we are about to have. My adoptive father isn't someone who relies heavily on gut. Right now, I have no proof that it's someone in the Sever family that has been doing this to Ema, but it's really the only thing that makes sense. I can only hope that he sees this as a problem and does what he can to cut the ties between us and the Sever family. We don't need enemies that disguise themselves as friends.

"I believe that Ivan Sever is trying to force my hand with the deal that was made. He is trying to get me to get rid of my wife so that we will have to renounce ownership of the nuke."

"Impossible, the weapon is already on its way."

"Indeed, so wouldn't it be beneficial for him to make sure I harm Ema now. Then once the shipment has reached American soil, he can just take it. No hard work done on his behalf. It's us that rebuilt Filip's ship. Us that vetted the people that made the moves to get the ordinance. It was us who are keeping the coast guard busy. We are doing all the work. He would be able to swoop in and demand that the nuke be given to him if I were to harm Ema."

Marko squints his eyes at me for a second before he rubs his hand over his face.

"Well, all of that is possible, but there is one variable that shouldn't change. Don't kill your wife. I don't understand how that can be so hard."

"Marko, he is testing my honor. He has someone coming into my house and terrorizing my wife. Someone leaving cum and God knows what else around so it would appear as if Ema is cheating on me."

His eyes open wide, disrespect can't be tolerated. If Ema was truly cheating, Marko wouldn't bat an eye if I killed her. Ivan would though.

"And you are sure she isn't indeed going behind your back with another man?"

"I'd bet my life on it."

"Hmm, I see. Well let's find out for sure shall we." He

smiles at me. "Bring your bride up to see me. I would like to talk to her."

I turn and send one of the guards down to retrieve her. I hope Keeley was able to put her a bit at ease. Ema is still so on edge with everything going on. I don't blame her I would be on edge too if an intruder was in the bedroom while I was sleeping.

After a minute, there is a knock on the door and Ema steps in.

"Ah, Ema. It's so nice to see you again. Come." Marko lays on the charm thick as he pulls her into a hug and kisses her cheeks.

"Thank you for having me."

"Of course. Unfortunately, the circumstances are not the best from what I hear."

"No sir." Her voice is measured, respectful.

"Well let's get down to it then, Sven here tells me that someone has broken into your house and made it appear as if you are cheating on him. We seem to believe that it's just a lover of yours."

A sharp gasp leaves Ema's mouth as she turns her eyes in my direction. I know what's going on here, but she doesn't. I do my best not to lock on to her gaze. I don't want to give it away.

"No!" Ema backs up.

"Ema, darling. I understand. We both do. You're forced to be in this marriage with Sven. Honestly as long as the title and the mark are intact what you do on the side is of no matter to us, if you wanted to be with someone else there are allowances that can be made. We just need to know for certain, so we are not running around killing everyone, because of false information."

"No!" She barks.

"I'm sorry, sweet Ema, I need a bit more information than that."

She turns in my direction and I can see the tears falling down her face. She thinks I don't believe her again.

"Are we back to this? I thought we went over this shit already!" She screams at me and I have to stop myself from reacting to the profanity she's spewing in my direction.

"Dear. It only makes sense." Marko says from behind her.

"No, it doesn't make sense. None of this makes fucking sense. What do I have to do Sven? Tell me what I have to do to prove that you're the only one I want. You are the only one I want touching me. The only one who I trust to keep me safe. The only one I want to be standing next to." My eyes focus in on hers. I wasn't expecting this, for her true feelings to mirror exactly what mine are. I don't interrupt her though. "I would never do something like that to you. Even if my life depended on it, I wouldn't betray you. I don't know what you want me to do."

"That." Marko says from behind her.

Her eyelids flutter for a second before she turns to look at Marko. "What?" It's nothing like letting your mark believe that they are in the clear to get them to tell you how they really feel. If she would have admitted to wanting to be with someone else there would have been nothing else for me to do. That's not what she would do though. She fought. She went against the easy way to prove that she was loyal to me.

"What is he talking about?" She turns back to me.

I can't keep my composure anymore; this woman does things to me that no one ever has. Now that I know for certain how she feels I know there is no way I will ever give her up. Year be damned she is going to be my woman until the end of time. I shove my hands into her hair and smash my mouth to hers. She squeals in shock and smacks at my arms a few times before she melts into my punishing kiss. Her moans push me to go further, and her arms wrap around my neck giving me permission to do so.

"Children." Marko's voice rings out behind us.

I reluctantly pull back. I don't want to stop, but there are more important things going on right now. "You see, she's loyal. She's telling the truth." I grab Ema's hand and tug her into my side.

She huffs out a breath, finally understanding that it was all a test.

"I agree, so tell me what proof do you have that it's her uncle?" Marko goes to sit back down at his small table.

"It has to be. Ema said that certain things used to happen before. But she believed it was another man that had wronged her. That man has been dealt with already, yet these things continue to happen. Her uncle is the only person from her past that would stand to benefit from us falling out."

"Where is the proof Sven?" Marko asks again.

I force a breath from my lungs. "I don't have any solid proof."

"Ah well, I don't see what I can do to help here then."

"Marko, I just think-"

"No! You know as well as I that I cannot just forfeit an alliance based on a hunch. Furthermore, the Sven of old would have never even suggested such a thing. Go get me the proof and then we will talk more about it."

There is no reason to argue any further. There is nothing that I can say that will make him change his mind. I need proof. "As you wish." I snap my mouth shut and turn to walk out of the room.

"Son."

I stop in my tracks.

"I'm glad you found your someone. You deserve to have some happiness."

I don't turn back or say thank you. I wouldn't want to ruin the moment. It was the very first time that Marko admitted truthfully that he was happy for me. Not because it was going to get him further or because I had done something that could help him. It was the first time as a father, he was happy for me as his son.

35

Sven

I couldn't find anything. The more I searched for anything that would link Ivan to being here, the more I was coming up with blanks or perfectly good alibis. He didn't leave the states as he claimed he was going to do. Instead, he was down in lower California, mostly getting shit faced and messing around with strippers. How could he be there and here at the same time? I already know that Bryce is dead and I don't know of any of Ivan's sons coming back in the states. I've exhausted all of my pull with Interpol and the FBI, but I can't see any type of connection. I log into the cloud to view my home surveillance videos of the last time we were at the house but whoever it is stayed to the very edges of the cameras range of sight, I can see a shadow but nothing I can used to identify them.

I slam the laptop shut and pinch the bridge of my nose. When I open my eyes again, a glass of vodka is placed on the table in front of me and Ema is standing there in one of the hotel robes with a concerned look on her face.

"I feel like a fucking failure. I don't understand why I can't find it. I don't understand why I've let someone kick me out of my own fucking home and into a hotel, because I can't find the damn link!" I slam my hand down on the table before I run it through my hair. I'm the man who finds all the information. I make sure every job and every deal that the entire Juric family makes goes over without a fucking hitch, but I can't find out who is stalking my wife. It's frustrating as hell.

"We'll figure it out." She rubs the back of my neck, a balm.

My hand latches on to hers and I pull her so she is standing next to me. I tug on her thigh, so she puts her leg over my lap and straddles me.

"You mad?"

"I don't think I have the energy to be mad. This past month must have taken at least thirty years off my life. I'm exhausted. Physically and mentally."

I nod understanding her. I feel the same way, like everything I thought I had a firm handle on in my life is being torn apart by a fucking tornado. My control feels almost nonexistent. "I'm sorry that I've put you in this position. That I'm not able to just rip this out of your life so you no longer have to worry about it. I'm sorry I didn't keep you safe."

"Hey ..." She lifts my head and peers into my eyes. "You couldn't have known that something like this was going to happen. I mean really, who goes around knowing that their new wife has a stalker?" She laughs slightly and the vibration of it bounces through my own chest.

There is an ache inside of me that I didn't realize was there, I need her. I push my hands into her hair, and tug her down to my face. She hesitates though.

"Ema, I need you. Please." It's the most vulnerable that I've ever been with anyone before in my life, but I let her see. I need her to know that it's not just her who has these feelings. She gasps, pressing her mouth down to mine, kissing me deeply and full of all the emotions that are swirling in her body.

I push open the robe that she has on and am happy to see that there is nothing stopping me from enjoying my woman. I stand up from the chair that I'm sitting in, making sure that she wraps her legs around my waist, and walk her to the bed. Her mouth never stopping from worshiping mine. My hands grip onto her plump bottom tightly as I put her down on the bed. She opens the robe fully letting me see her naked body in all its glory. My mark is still healing, a stark contrast against her pale skin.

It's a small thing, but now that I know she is truly all mine, I feel so much fucking pride seeing it. I drop down to my knees and tug her to the edge of the bed. I kiss around the tattoo and massage her legs with my hands.

"Oh Jesus, Sven, you're driving me up the wall." She moves her hips, so her beautiful pussy is closer to my face. Whatever she wants I'm willing to give her. I kiss down the side of her stomach, making the muscles clench and roll before I make my way to her mound. Arousal already causing her pussy to turn to a deeper pink color. I let the very tip of my tongue snake out of my mouth and flick the tight nub at the apex of her slit.

"Mmm, yes Sven." Her back arches slightly just at that one contact. Now it's time to really play.

I hold her legs open, locking my elbows against the edge of the bed so she can't pull away. Then I press my face into her juicy cunt. I lap and lick at her until she is writhing and trying to pull away from all the sensations.

"Oh Fuck. Sven." She half moans half screams. "I'm coming. I'm going to fucking come." She sucks in a deep breath and her midsection begins to tremble as my name leaves her mouth in a long moan. I'm not through with her yet though. I keep her legs open making sure that I pay more attention to the actually opening itself, sticking my tongue in and out as far as I can, hooking the end so I can taste more of her. I want all of her. When I feel her body start to calm a little more, I go to suck her clit again and pull her back up to another orgasm. She deserves to orgasm until she can no longer walk. I don't know if that is more for me or her, but either way I'm sure we are both going to have fun doing it.

"Shit! Oh my fucking God!" She cries out as another orgasm rolls through her. I can't take it anymore. I was trying to make this all about her. Except the more I hear her breaking apart above me the more desperate I become to get inside of her. I have to let go of her legs to get my clothes off. The second I do she clamps her legs shut and tries to push away from me. I quickly undo my pants and pull them off while I'm still kneeling between her legs. Once I successfully get rid of my clothes, I pull her back to my mouth.

"Sven, God ... What are you doing to me?" Her head whips from side to side as I continue to lick at her. I flatten my tongue and lick from the bottom to the top lapping up every drop she has to offer. "Shit." She moans out and covers her face with her hands, clearly spent.

I stand up from where I am kneeling in front of her,

"I've told you time and time again to watch your fucking mouth. Maybe we need to try a different method."

Her eyes pop open and she focuses on me. My hard cock is completely engorged and leaking drops of precum. She sits up quickly. I watch her bite her lip and look up to me before she looks back down to my cock. She wraps a hand around the shaft very softly.

"Ema?" Usually, she is as excited to do things with me as I am with her, but I'm not used to seeing her so uneasy.

"I've never ... uh, I don't know how." She admits and the red blush of her embarrassment floods her cheeks. I understand now.

"First, do you want to? I don't want you to do something you don't want to do." I brush a few strands of hair out of her face and tip her head back so she is looking at me.

"Yes, I want to do it, but I don't want it to be bad."

"I promise there is nothing that you can do that would be bad. I'm here. I'll guide you until you get comfortable and then you do what you want. Ok?" I wipe my thumb over her bottom lip as she nods her head.

"Ok, I've seen porn. I can do this."

I didn't want to laugh and her get self-conscious, but I really hope she doesn't do what she saw in pornos. All that shit is over the top and fake. "Just do what feels right to you."

"Ok." She scoots a little closer to the edge of the bed and wraps her hand around my shaft tighter. She presses her lips together and presses a soft kiss to the slit of my cock. My eyes shut at the feel of it. Shit this was going to be mind-blowing I can tell already. She does this a few more times and I have to fight myself not to move. I want to be inside her mouth so fucking bad right now.

Finally, she opens her mouth as wide as she can and sucks in the tip of my dick. The warm heat followed by the feel of her tongue on the underside of my cock has my knees almost going weak.

"Oh shit." I moan out and fist my hands in my own hair.

"It's ok?" she pulls back slightly and mumbles at the head of my cock.

"Fuck yes. Keep going. Fuck."

She opens her mouth again this time taking me deeper in her mouth. She bobs her head up and down. Her tongue pushing and swiping against my dick. Every time she pushes forward, she takes a little bit more of me. My hands drop down to my neck. I want to ram myself down her throat, but I know she needs to be in control of this. I don't want her to not like it.

I look down at her and the second I do, I know that I shouldn't have. Her wide brown eyes are staring up at me. Her long hair tumbling down her back and half of my cock is disappearing between her plump lips. The sight of it will forever be seared into my brain.

"Oh, damn it!" I drop my hand to her head, but don't squeeze. The restraint is the biggest test of my will that I have ever faced in my life. She moans and takes me deeper swerving her neck slightly so she can cause a different sensation.

When she opens her mouth wide, she pushes forward until I can feel the very back of her throat and the last thread of my will power snaps.

I bury my hands in her hair, sliding my cock in and out of her mouth at a much quicker pace than she was just doing. She grabs onto my thighs and matches my speed. The moans from her getting louder.

"Oh shit, Ema. It's perfect. So good." I praise her. Her eyes flutter closed for a second before they open again slightly. She moves her hands from my thighs and lets me fuck her face while she works just her mouth on me. Her hands snake down her own body until they get to her cunt. When I see one finger disappear, I know that she is fucking herself while I'm fucking her mouth. I want to cry it's such a beautiful sight. When the second hand moves between my legs and she starts to play softly with my balls I roar in fucking pleasure. Though I have to snatch myself out of her mouth and she falls forward slightly.

"What's wrong? Come back? I won't do that anymore if you don't like it. Please come back." She reaches for me, but it's not that she was bad at it, it was too fucking good. I don't want to come in her throat.

"Ema, you better be fucking ready for me." I stroke my own dick. The pace is hard, but I clench up trying my best not to nut before I even get inside of her. My voice is raw and I can hear the animalistic grit in my words. Her mouth pouts slightly, but before she can say anything else, I push her back on the bed. I tug her legs so she is stretched out, then lift her thighs so they are resting on my forearms, bend them back towards her chest and slam my aching cock into her.

She screams out and her nails claw at my back to get some purchase.

I crawl on the bed, still buried deep inside of her and every attempt that she makes to get some space for herself I negate.

"Wait, fuck wait Sven."

I don't want to though. I want to move, to feel her walls sucking and milking me, but I do. I wait, holding my breath and focusing on every pulse rocketing through my body.

"God you're so deep. You're so deep this way." She swirls her hips once and I have to bite my lip to keep from fucking whimpering like a baby.

"Ema." I growl out.

She swirls her hips again. Just as I'm about to break down and start begging her, she pulls my face closer to hers and nips at my lip. "Now Sven, take me."

It feels like every bind, every restraint, every piece of me that I have had to force myself to be evaporates. All that is left is Ema, me, and my need to mark what is mine. I thrust into her, quick and with enough force to knock the headboard against the wall hard. If I cared I would be worried that the hotel neighbors would call the cops.

She moves her face away from mine to moan loudly as her body clamps down on mine and another orgasm rolls through her. She cries, but this time they aren't tears of sadness it's complete pleasure. Her head presses back and I take that opportunity to drop my head to her neck and suck hard on that one spot I know she goes crazy for. She gulps in breaths and groans out my name. I lift up slightly, my breath coming fast, the pressure of my impending release building to an unbearable level at the lower part of my back and the base of my abdomen. Sparks and flames lick at the inside of my body as I stare down into the eyes of the woman who was put here as a punishment for me, but has turned into one of the greatest gifts I could have ever been given in my life. Her eyes lock onto mine again and a sweet smile blossoms on her lips as she softly mouths the words, I love you.

My world crashes as every part of me entwines with

her. My soul feeling like it physically attached itself to hers. How is this possible?

"Ema, shit, I love you too." I kiss her one final time before my body jerks hard and I shake with the force of my orgasm. My cum shoots deep inside of her, and I feel absolutely complete. If I could lay deep inside of her like this for the rest of my fucking life I would.

She is my wife, so maybe I'll do just that.

36

Ema

I open my eyes and feel Sven's arms wrapped tightly around my waist.

He loves me?

Oh fuck.

I love him too. I know I shouldn't, but I can't help that I fell for him. I move slightly and his head pops up.

"Where do you think you're going?" His mouth curls up into a small smile.

"Well to get the heck out of bed. We need to go relax and I've heard that downstairs is one of the best places to do it."

I was seriously getting stir crazy. Sven had booked us into one of the hotels on the strip. He said that the stalker wouldn't know where we would go. Even if he did find me there are so many people around here that there is no way he would just be able to take me. We are on the lookout for my uncle or any of my cousins. It's so sad that my family is this fucked up. I mean, who would do this to their own family?

"Hmm, I never heard that. In fact gambling is one of the most stressful activities in the world." He leans back and threads his hands behind his head.

"I wouldn't know, I've never done it."

There are very few places people can gamble in Alaska. There is no way that I'm going to be staying in a casino hotel and not actually go downstairs to try it. It was a life experience I needed even if it meant that I lost all the money I played.

"Fine, let's go." He says with feigned annoyance.

I clap my hands once bouncing on the bed. I lean over and give him a kiss before I rush of the bed to get ready. Wrong move. My legs give out the second my feet touch the floor.

"Oh shit, Ema. Are you ok?" Sven races to the side of the bed and helps me up.

His eyebrows crunch in as he realizes I was laughing.

"You broke my legs with your dick." I say between breaths and he tries to hold it in, but it's only seconds before he is laughing right along with me.

This Sven I can get used to.

THE ENTIRE PLACE is buzzing with activity. There's so much to do I can't just concentrate on one thing. Every few seconds I want to try something else. Instead of Sven getting upset that I don't just make up my mind, he simply grabs hold of my hand and walks me over to the game that I want to play. I did play one hand of Texas Hold'em and end up winning over a thousand dollars. Sven said it was beginner's luck. Despite that, he then called me crazy, because I cashed out immediately and went to play something else. I could play cards anywhere. What I really wanted to play was one of those old timey slot machines. The ones where you could still put the coins in.

Apparently, they were all being phased out and the new ones had a slot for a key card. Those were nice, but it didn't feel authentic.

After bouncing around for what seemed like hours, I find one of the only ones in the entire casino. There is a slot for change and a slot for the card. I basically run to the machine, barreling over anyone who would think to go for it.

"Yay!" I jump up and down on the seat. My heart's thrumming excitedly in my chest.

"I don't think anyone was going for this one." Sven remarks after catching up with me.

"I couldn't take the chance." I sit there when I realize one important fact. I spent all this time looking for a machine that took change, but didn't have any change.

"Come on, let's go get you some more money." Sven puts his hand out and I recoil away from it like it was a snake. Did he really think I was going to give up my seat now?

"Um, I'm not moving my butt from this chair. You go. I'll be right here when you get back." I bounce a little more looking at the authentic look of the reels, the heavy steel handle. Even how the paint on the machine itself was fading.

All of it was amazing to me.

"I'll be back in a minute." Sven pulls out his phone and kisses the top of my head.

The shrill of the machines around me takes over all my

senses. I could see how people could get addicted to something like this.

"Ema! Oh thank God, Ema!"

I nearly jump out of my skin at the sound of my name being called from the side.

"Alex?" The fear on his face was incredible. "Oh, what's happened?" I turn and look for Sven. Maybe something happened to him?

"Where have you been, we've been looking all over for you. We got in contact with your housekeeper, Olive and she told us that you guys were in one of the casino hotels. We have to move right now."

"What? Why? What's going on?" Oh God, something happened at home. That's the only reason they would be looking for me.

"Your sister. She was hurt. She ran away to come find you, but she got hurt. She's at the hospital now, but it doesn't look good. Something happened to a man back in your village. Something about him watching over you guys. I don't know exactly what happened, but I know if she dies and you're not there that you'll never rest. Your father sent your uncle and your cousins to come look for you. They even asked me to help as well. I'm so happy I found you. We have to go right now though."

Oh God no. Why would she do this? I had told her that I would be back. I feel like such a horrible person. I spent so long trying to fight Sven when I should have been figuring out a way to get in contact with my sisters. They depend on me so much that it makes sense for them to be upset that I was ripped from their lives. Mika is headstrong. She's only fifteen, but I know there is nothing that she wouldn't do. Especially for me.

"I'm surprised Sven didn't tell you. She's been missing

for the past two days. How could he keep something like that from you?"

He knew? How could he know and not tell me? He said he loved me, if that was the truth then he would have told me that my sister was fucking missing.

Alex picks up his phone and his face goes pale. "The car is outside. We have to get there now."

"Ok, ok. I'm coming." I jump out of the seat and follow Alex. He moves so quickly. God, I hope I'm not too late. My hands shake with adrenaline.

"What the hell did she do to herself?"

"She was trying to hitchhike, they found her on the side of the road. She was close though." He says from in front of me.

"Oh my God." My heart seizes in my chest and I have to remind myself to breathe. What did they do to her?

Alex opens a door and I follow behind him. The silence is the first thing I notice. I can't hear the casino anymore or anyone walking. Actually, I don't hear anything, but the heavy boots Alex is wearing and the sound of my own breathing.

The hairs on the back of my neck stand up, this feels off.

"Alex, what are you doing here?"

"What? I just told you." He says over his shoulder.

"No, I mean, did you fly all the way here from Alaska to find me?"

"Of course not. I told you I'm back and forth a lot. My business is really booming." He huffs out and my mind begins to play back all the conversations I've had with him.

He's someone from my town that knows my family. He was always close to my uncle, doing whatever he could to get on my uncle's good side. He was at the wedding. He was there on the strip the first time Sven showed me around. How could he have found me at the very second that Sven walks away from me? It's not possible unless he never lost me to begin with. Unless he's the one who's been following me all along.

I stop short and look back at the door I had just come through. It's a fire door and won't open back up. Fuck.

"Ema, what are you doing?"

"I was just thinking I have to let Sven know where I'm going or he's going to flip out. It'll take one second and then he can come with us. I'm sure he's going to want to be there as well." I take a step away from Alex trying to keep my mind calm. I didn't want to alert him that I knew what was going on.

"He knows. They've already told him, I'm sure he is on his way there now."

"Who? Who told him?"

"Well ..." He looks off to the side for a second. "Well shit, you got me, didn't you?" The fear that was just on his face transforms into a sinister grin. His eyes focusing on mine.

"Shit! Help!" I scream as loud as my lungs will let me and I try to run. He runs behind me and quickly catches me around my waist. "Help!" I scream again.

Alex just laughs, "You can scream all you want. There is no one here to help you. Don't fight me, Ema. It'll be so much easier if you don't fight me."

Did he not know who I was? All I did was fucking fight. I kick and claw while he drags me towards a car that I assume is his.

He tosses me in the front seat and pulls a knife to press at my throat. "Stop the shit now, I don't want to have to hurt you Ema."

I do what he says, I can tell he isn't as sane as I had thought he was. I've known this man for years. I just don't understand why he would do some shit like this to me. He keeps the knife pointed at me through the wind shield as he quickly runs around to the driver's side.

"Alex, what are you doing? Do you know who Marko Juric is? Sven? Do you know the people you are going up against right now?"

He buckles himself in and takes off. It's an underground parking facility.

"Yes, I know who he is. I don't care. When they induct me I'll be a made man. This has to show them that I deserve to be a part of their ranks." His voice is forceful, but I don't think it's meant towards me. He is trying to convince himself.

"What are you talking about? You think the Juric family will take you in after this?"

"No, fuck them. The Sever family will! I have done everything that they have wanted, but still they do not deem me fit to join them. But if I'm married to a direct family member than they have to open their eyes and see. I'm worth millions. I have been helping them launder their funds for the longest time now. I can even help them find locations for all the supplies they want to bring in from overseas. The Sever family is going to be the next leader of all the Croatian families. I deserve to be a part of that and you are going to help me. I claimed you the second you turned eighteen, just waited for the right time to truly show the world how great we can be together." He nods his head before he takes his hand off the steering wheel for a second and tries to caress my face. I cringe away.

He sneers in my direction for a second before he takes that same hand and slaps me hard across the face. My lip splits on impact, the blood dripping down my chin onto my clothes.

"You're not a fucking Juric. I refuse to leave you with that scum. No. You're mine Ema. You're all mine now." He rubs my head softly. I can't do anything besides sit there quietly and pray that Sven has noticed that I'm not there anymore.

A tear pops at the thought, even if he does, he'll never find me. No one would think to be suspicious of Alex. I'm going to have to fight my way out of this on my own.

37

Sven

The line to get change is abnormally long. There is only one so I can't even go to another. I get her two hundred dollars worth of change. I would let her play until her heart was content, if something as simple as this would keep that smile on her face than I had no problem doing it.

There was a bounce to my step as I make my way back to the area where I'd left her.

Dread fills the lightness in my step as I look over to where she was before and didn't see her. I pick up the pace and then at the final leg of it I run. When I get there the machine is still vacant, but she is nowhere to be found. Did she run off again? It hadn't been so long ago that she tried to run away from me. I shake my head. No, she wouldn't do that. I trust her, she said that she was going to stay right there so that is what I knew she would do.

There was no one in the area that I knew or even seemed to be someone that would have some information.

I couldn't go running around blindly trying to find her. By the time I did that whoever it was could have already done something to her. No, I need to find her and I need to do so now.

I pick up the phone and dial the one person I've never wanted to reach out to when I was in a bad way. Marko never overlooked a weakness and right now I was weak. Without Ema I was nothing but a fucking liability.

"Da." The line picked up.

"Marko. I need help." I got straight to it.

There was a silence on the line. The last time I had called him for help he'd left me to fend for myself, told me it was a learning experience. I have no doubt that he will do the same again this time. I don't expect him to come and rescue me, but I need his permission to go against the family. Our ties with the Sever family may be strained after what I'm about to do.

"What can I do to help you son?" His voice is clipped.

"I know you told me not to pursue this line of action with Ivan until we have more proof, but I'm out of time. They took Ema."

"She bears your mark, no? They will return her." The nonchalance in his voice annoys the hell out of me.

"But only after they do God knows what! Marko, I can't wait for that to happen. I need to speak with Ivan directly. I need to find out what he knows about this." I grip the phone hard enough to hear the plastic creaking in my hand.

"What makes you think he has anything to do with this?"

"There is no other option, he never wanted this marriage to hold. I don't think he has ever wanted to hand over the nuke to you. It's the only option." It is the only option that I can think of. I just don't have any proof of it right now.

"Fine, Sven. If you are sure that this is the path that you are going to go down. I will allow it. But know that if what you are suggesting proves to be false, I will have nothing to do with it." His way of telling me that if I fuck up and am wrong, then he is going to disown me. I could lose it all if they aren't a part of this like I think.

"I understand."

He hangs up not letting me say another word. I reset the phone and dial another number. Kaja.

"Sven?"

"Yes, Kaja, I need you like yesterday and anyone you can get in contact with that can roll out with me. Immediately."

"Tell me where and I'm there." Kaja answers immediately. He is already a made man. However, if we get through this and I'm right in my assumption, I would have to talk to Marko about giving Kaja more responsibilities. He is more than loyal to our family and it's time that he is rewarded. I explain to him what is going on as quickly as I can and tell him to meet me at the casino.

I make my way to the security office of the casino. When I knock on the door a heavyset rent a cop opens the door. He is clearly not prepared for someone like me to be stepping up to him.

"What do you want?" he spits out, but is looking over his shoulder to one of the CCTV's. Looking for a threat that is right in front of him. I quickly punch him hard in his solar plexus before I pull my gun on the other security guard in the room. The guard that opened the door falls down to his knees and tries to shuffle over to the silent alarm. I press my gun to his head.

"No, no, don't do that. I'm not here to steal from you or kill you. I just need you to relax."

"What do you want then?" The second security guard says, his voice shaking in fear.

"Someone kidnapped my wife. I need to see your video of about ten minutes ago, to see who it was."

"Kidnapped. Impossible, there would have been a ruckus." The man on the ground says as he stands up in front of me. I move the gun from his head and keep it down by my side. If they weren't going to give me any trouble, then I wasn't' going to give them any trouble.

"It's possible that it's someone she knows or someone who has a weapon so she wouldn't scream. Either way I have to see who she went off with." This shit was taking way too fucking long. They could be in a different state by now.

"Fine. Come on. Where do you want to see?" The second guard says. I rush over to where he is and watch as he rewinds the video of the area that Ema was in. Ten minutes ago I can see her there at the slot machine, fidgeting slightly with excitement. For a few seconds there is nothing and then I see her jump in surprise and talk to someone on the side.

"Who is she talking to? Who is over there?" I ask agitated that the angle of the camera doesn't show me what I need to see.

"Shit, I don't know. Wait. Let me try to get this camera over here." The second guard works on a different screen and rewinds that tape. This one shows a man standing in front of her, but I can't see his face. I'm still at a fucking loss.

"Motherfucker!" I curse and slam my hand down on the table. I move around the guard and go to the second tape, where I can only see the man's back. I can also see her face. She is very animated, her hands moving quickly and her eyes darting from side to side.

I focus in on her face, zoom in.

"What are you doing?" The guard asks from the side of me, but I don't answer. I zoom in again, getting as focused on her face as I can. I rewind it again, over and over trying to see what she is saying.

Then like a fucking light switch I can understand what she is saying.

Alex, what's happened?

It's fucking Alex!

KAJA IS WAITING for me in his car when I run out of the casino. "Sven? What's going on?"

"Alex kidnapped Ema." I bark out and close the car door.

"What, which Alex? You mean the restauranteur? Why?"

"What the fuck! Does it look like I understand the inner workings of that man's mind? I don't fucking know, but I know he has had a thing for her since before she came to me. This is a long standing obsession. I think it was Ivan Sever that put fire under his ass though. It's the only way I can see him getting so brave all of a sudden."

Kaja's eyes dart from me to the street and back again.

"Are you saying that we are about to accuse the head of an allied crime family of sabotaging a deal? Because that is means for a war. You know that right?" He looks uneasy. I know exactly what it means. It's the reason Marko is so reluctant to go with what I'm saying. It's not like we would lose, but we would be less one ally.

"I know it." I pull out my phone again and dial another number that I didn't think I would ever have to dial again.

Ivan Sever.

There is loud music when he picks up the phone. "Yes. Speak in a hurry, yeah." His thick Croatian accent coming out with every word.

"Mr. Sever, I hate to disturb you, but there is a matter that I need to speak with you about right away. One that requires a bit of privacy on your behalf. Immediately." I do what I can to not sound too fucking disrespectful. This is what I'm good at. Getting the information, being a hundred precent sure. Pushing people into a corner until they fucking break. That's what I'm good at and it is what I'm going to have to use to get Ema out of trouble. The music dies down and I can hear a door close through the line.

"Sven, that you?"

"Yes. Ivan it has come to my attention that you have someone, either an associate or someone directly related to your family, who is trying to force me to go back on the deal that was brokered between our two families."

He chuckles slightly. "Impossible, I can't make you do anything that you don't want to do. Ema is all yours to do with as you please."

"Indeed, except there have been several instances over the past few days where someone has broken into my home and made it appear like Ema was cheating on me. A man of lesser will power would have killed her on sight, but that's not me. I didn't kill her and soon found out that it was all a big ruse."

"What exactly are you accusing me of right now?" Ivan speaks through what sounds like a clenched mouth.

"I'm accusing you of nothing. I know that you would never go against, Mr. Juric. That you would never risk your fledgling family for something as small as one shipment, especially when there will be countless more that you will benefit from. I am just asking if you know of anyone that would be dumb enough to go against us in this matter. I would like to get my wife back without starting a war. The Juric family, the Varva family, the Deluca family, not to mention all the various connections that we have already made in the states would be happy to assist us if that were the case." I had just painted a very bleak picture for Ivan. It wasn't just the Juric family he was going after right now, it was us and everyone that we were allies with.

"I don't know anything." He says again.

I exhale forcefully and was just about to hang up the phone when I hear him start to speak again. "I don't know anything, but there is talk of one of our associates moving precious cargo quite suddenly. He only put in the flight plan about five minutes ago at a private airfield. I can send you the location. Maybe they know something about Ema." He doesn't say anything else just hangs up the phone. A second later the address to a private airfield pops up on my phone.

"Kaja, airport now." I order, showing him the address and he takes off in the direction I'm hoping to find my wife. The bastard better not have done anything to her. Either way he was going to die, but if he touched her, he was going to die so much slower.

38

Ema

I keep myself calm until I see him turn onto what looks to be an abandoned tarmac. We were going on a plane. There was no way that anyone would be able to find me if he flew me out of the fucking state. I had to do something now if I was going to get out of here.

"There is nowhere for you to go. Even if you do end up being brought into the family. I'm a marked woman. I belong to Sven, there is nothing that you can do about that. Do you think the Juric family is just going to let something like that go?"

"What are you talking about now?" Alex looks over to me in complete confusion.

I lift up my shirt slightly to show him the tattoo of Sven's name on my skin. His eyes widen and he lets out a small gasp. "It doesn't matter. They won't see you. I can keep you hidden."

"See this is how I know you don't know what the fuck

you are doing. If you are able to get me away from Sven, they are going to want you to show it off as a victory. What proof will you have if you have to keep me hidden?"

"I ... You ... I ... shut up. I don't have to think about that right now. I can figure something out later. Ivan promised me that if I was able to get you away, he would bring me in. I would be one of them. I would have you and be one of them. My dream ... It's my dream."

"Your dream isn't going to come true. There is no way that you come out of this alive. You stole a marked woman from another family. They will see me and just send me right back." I snarl at him, "The task, I'm sure, was to get Sven to give me up. You almost did it too. Except you don't know how tenacious I can be or how headstrong he can be. There is nowhere he won't go to find me. Your days are numbered Alex." I laugh for a few seconds before he grabs me by my hair and pulls me out of the car.

I scream out in agony as he drags me along the pavement. My fight doesn't stop there though. I turn my head to the side and bite down on any piece of flesh I can reach. He screams out and let's go of my hair. I move quickly and hop back into the car that he'd left running. He isn't far behind me. He jumps in the car on the passenger side and begins to punch at my midsection and face, but I don't stop or move away. I put the car in drive and put my foot on the gas.

"What the fuck are you doing? What the fuck!" He yells at me and starts hitting me harder to get me to stop.

It only takes a few seconds for the car to hit the small jet. There wasn't even much speed, but the impact had enough force to bend the landing gear.

"Shit!" He screams and pulls at his on hair. He knows what I know, the plane can't take off like that.

"You stupid bitch! Do you realize what you've done? I love you Ema! We need to be together. Why can't you see that?" He grabs my face hard.

I just shake my head no. How did I never see how fucking crazy he was?

A speeding car catches our attention.

"Fuck! You better make sure I can make it out of here in one piece. I just need to get out of here, Ivan will help me when I do."

He was so dumb, if he truly believed that my uncle would do anything to help him, he was as good as dead already.

He pulls me out of the car, this time through the passenger side and holds me close to his body—a human shield.

I can't help but smile as the car skids to a stop a few feet from where we are and my husband steps out. His ice cold eyes shooting daggers at the man behind me.

39

Sven

"Ema. *Jesi li dobro?*"

"Yes, I'm ok." I reply loudly as Alex pulls me closer to his body.

"Alex you need to let her go. She belongs to the Juric family now. She belongs to me. Whatever deal you made with Ivan needs to be handled a different way." I want to keep him calm. I don't know if he has any weapons, but I don't want to chance him hurting her.

"You don't fucking deserve her! She's mine!" Alex screams back from behind her.

"What the fuck, no I'm not." Ema spits out.

"Ema!" I reprimand her. This isn't the time for her smart mouth.

"What?" She screams back. Ugh, this woman.

"I don't have a shot." Kaja says from the side of me, "but there may be someone else who does."

Fucking Kaja for the win.

"Is he here already?"

"Yeah, he just texted me that he's in position."

"Tell him when I give the signal to take the shot, but not to kill him."

"You got it." Kaja steps behind me to shield his hands from Alex's gaze.

"What did you think this was going to accomplish? Did you think that by kidnapping my wife I would just let you live? That I wouldn't hunt you down to the ends of the earth to find her?"

"I'd be protected. There is nothing that you would be able to do to me. You'll see. I'm protected!" He screams back.

Protected? Did he really think that Ivan Sever had his back?

"This isn't how it's done kid. It's a shame you had to find out this way."

Alex starts to move away to the side, dragging Ema along with him.

"Ema, my love, you trust me?"

"With everything I am."

"I know it."

I put my hand up and a lone shot rings out. The sound only echoing once before the bullet explodes through Alex's legs.

Blood and muscle splatter against Ema, she cringes in shock. Alex collapses to the ground, his mouth open in a silent scream before the sound could escape his mouth. He lets loose a loud wail as he reaches down for his legs which are now mangled by the large caliber bullet Dagger had just shot through him.

Dagger is the fucking best.

Ema runs over to me and I wrap my arms around her. I don't think anything has ever felt so good.

Kaja, Dagger, and I manage to get Alex into the car. Dagger fashions a tourniquet on each leg to stop the bleeding. I don't want to kill him here. Even though everything inside of me is screaming for me to just end this little fuck's life. He could have ruined everything by believing the wrong fucking person. Alex wasn't part of the Sever family, but he was an associate. Plus, he's claimed that Ivan will come to his aid. I wonder what Mr. Sever will have to say about that.

IT'S hard work keeping him alive long enough for Ivan to show up, but I do my best. Now that I know the threat is handled, I let Ema go back home where she can relax. Just to think a month earlier I would have never sent her home on her own. I trust that woman with all that I am now.

I call a meeting with Marko, Luka, Ivan Sever, and Pieter Sever with Dagger and Kaja as witnesses. For this to go over without a hitch I would need to prove to Marko that my hunch was right. Even if Ivan didn't admit to it. Marko would see it for himself.

I have Alex set up in one of the abandoned warehouses we own on the outskirts of the strip.

Marko and Luka are the first ones to arrive, neither of them look very happy with me right now. Next to show up is Ivan and his son Pieter.

"What the hell did you call me here for?" Ivan spits out when he gets inside the open space.

"It seems there was a misunderstanding. So I thought I

would get it cleared up." I smile at Ivan before walking over to where Alex was tied down and pull the bag off his head.

"Sven what is the meaning of this?" Marko barks at me.

"Marko, I'm trying to find out myself, because what this man says can't be true."

"What does the man say?" My adopted brother asks, moving a bit closer.

Ivan and his son glare at Alex. Probably mentally screaming at him not to fucking snitch. It's too bad, he already did.

I pull the gag off Alex's mouth. "Tell us what the deal is."

"Ivan, help me. Please. You need me."

"We don't need you. You forget your place." Pieter is the one to speak up.

"You said ... " Alex stares at the Sever men dumbfounded.

"What was the deal?" Marko asks.

Alex looks from Ivan to me then finally to Marko, "He said that she would be mine. He said that if I was able to get her away from Sven that she would finally be mine and he would carve out a place for me in the Sever family. It's all I've ever wanted, Ema by my side and the power of a family behind me."

"That right there is why you would never be welcome in our family." Pieter hocks up some mucus and spits it directly into Alex's face.

Marko and Luka turn their gaze on Ivan. If he had really told Alex this it would be in direct violation of the deal that we made. The agreement that said as long as I kept Ema safe and marked her as my wife, we would be allies. It also ensured a smooth transfer of the nuclear weapon from Ivan's connection to our safe house.

"Marko surely you can't believe such a thing. Our bond is too strong for someone like this to break us apart with lies."

"Lies you say? Well, if that is the case, tell me what you do with someone who lies in your family, because it's not tolerated in mine." Marko looks over at Ivan, wondering what he was going to do.

"Da, kill him."

"What! No. You can't ... you promised! You gave me your word!" Alex screams out. I grab the large bucket of pine tar I had Dagger go out and find for me. I pour it on him, making sure that it was heated to just the right temperature. Pine tar is special, because it has a much lower melting temperature, but it's just as sticky as black tar. Also, it's just as flammable. I let the sticky goo drip from the top of his head down his body.

"You gave me your word!" He cries out one more time for good measure. Only Ivan says nothing to stop me. Obviously, a word of honor means less to the Sever family then it did to us.

"You condemn him to death then?" I ask Ivan, giving him one last chance to save his associate.

"Da, he means nothing to me. Kill him. Let us go back and have a meal together. We have so much to celebrate." Ivan turns his back to speak with Marko as I walk up to Alex with a book of matches in my hand.

"They are forcing deals. I don't know with who or what, but they are going to try and force Marko Juric out. They are not your allies." Alex stares at me the best that he can. His last words a warning that we are in bed with snakes.

Tell me something I didn't already know.

I nod my head once and strike the match before I toss it on his lap. I back up to where my family is watching as Alex screams out in pain. The smell of his cooking flesh saturating the air long after he is dead and gone.

EPILOGUE

Sven

I don't know why I agreed to this shit.

A loud screeching sound echoes through the house as Ema's baby sister runs away from her.

When Ema catches my gaze, she smiles brightly at me. I know exactly why agreed to this, for that right there. Her family makes my girl happy and I would do anything to keep her happy.

After Alex was out of the picture things went back to normal. The nuke was delivered without any problems. Ivan made very little fuss about the cut that he was getting from the deal and Marko didn't say anything about what could have gone down if I was wrong about my information. He may have smiled in Ivan's face after Alex died, but that brief confession is more than enough for Marko to keep a very close eye on Ivan Sever and his family.

With all that taken care of I finally had a chance to get to know my woman better. One of the first things she asked for was for her family to come for a visit. Within a week I had them all on a plane and here at the house.

All of them, running around my place of peace. It was a fucking mad house in here.

Filip walks by and picks up his smallest child as Ema makes her way over to where I am.

"You seem tense." She says and wraps her arms around my neck.

"Tense? No. Maybe I'm cringing, because my eardrums are about to explode with all the screaming." I say gruffly.

She has the nerve to chuckle at me, "Sorry, we can get a bit loud. I'll get them to quiet down."

I hold her close to me, "No, it's ok. I can always lock myself in the back room or stuff my ears with everything that I can find. I'm just not used to all the noise."

"Well if I were you, I guess I would get used to the noise. It won't be long before we have our own personal noise maker." Her eyes peer into mine.

"Noise makers? I don't want any fucking noise makers. What are you planning on getting now?"

She rips her arms from my neck, "Well if you didn't want any noise makers maybe you should have put on a fucking condom!" She rolls her eyes and storms off.

Condom? What? What does a condom have to do with a noise maker? I'm so fucking confused.

"You put a baby in her belly!" The little girl squeals out as Filip totes her over his shoulder.

"Nyla! Hush!" He reprimands her.

Baby?

Oh shit!

I take off in the direction Ema just went and I nearly tackle her when I reach her.

"What the hell!" She turns around in my grasp. Slightly wobbling from the force of me running into her.

"Pregnant? *Jesi li trudna?*"

She laughs again, "Well, what did you think I was talking about?"

I fall to my knees and just stare at her flat belly, "When? How? Pregnant?" I can't even form the words I'm so fucking excited.

"How? Well, I didn't think I would need to explain that part to you, but when a man and a woman ..." I stand to my full height stopping her before she can continue. "You're ok Sven?"

"No, I'm so much more than ok. Thank you, Ema. Fuck, you've given me everything. I don't know what I did to deserve you."

Her eyes water as she leans up to kiss me. "I love you Sven."

"I love you too, and this little one as well." I press a hand to her belly and pray that the child nestled in there knows that it was born out of love even if it was a forced love we both fought with every cell of our beings.

THE END

Do you want to know more about Josip and his forbidden love? Make sure you pick up Josip's Secret here!

NEXT UP IN THE JURIC CRIME FAMILY

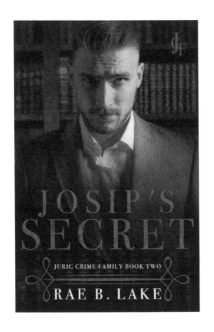

Josip

The first moment I laid my eyes on her I knew I had to have her. I crave everything about her but I know she's untouchable. The illegitimate daughter of a mob boss, a pariah in her own family, a mistake they try to bury.

But Orabella DeLuca is the only one who has ever been able to captivate me. Her purity, optimism and beauty are my undoing.

When several important people go missing including my Bella I know I will stop at nothing until I find her. Fighting has never been my go-to but it seems as if I'm the only one who will fight for her.

If they want to force the killer out of me, I'm willing to show them my true face.

I will tear through every wall that keeps me from her. Destroy everyone who dare get in my way and in the end when all the secrets are out, I will make her mine.

is what camera's the community has brought for themselves.

It isn't much.

I take my final steps toward her and put my hands up and wrap them over her mouth. The chloroform rag already in my hand. She tries to scream and claw at my hand, but I'm wearing gloves, and they are protected. The last thing I need is for her to get any of my DNA under her fingernails. Not that it would matter. She won't have them when I'm finished with her.

"Stop fucking fighting. Sleep, pretty girl." I whisper in her ear as she begins to blackout, the chemical working its way into her system. She falls limp in my arms, and I quickly pull her into my car and put her into the backseat. I bind her arms together and lay her down. She will be out for a while. I still need to get the evidence planted. I'll take her back to my hideout and keep her there until it is time to kill her. The client made it clear I'm to keep her for at least three days and fill her with fear. I don't usually do that sort of thing. I'm a trigger puller, not a fucking babysitter, but he offered to throw in another fifty thousand dollars. Torturing her isn't required by my client, thankfully. I'm not a complete animal, you know. He simply wants her as scared as possible for three days before I kill her.

I transport her to my safe house on the edge of fucking nowhere. No neighbors, no cops, no mailmen, nothing but me and an old run-down building.

She wakes right as I have her secured to the chair.

She screams and tries to kick out, but there's nothing she can do to break the binds. She tries to talk to me, but I won't fall for that. Not when I have so much other work to do. I take my knife and cut a small knick in her arm, only needing a tiny amount of blood. I tear off her shirt leaving her in nothing but her bra.

Fuck she is sexy. Her breasts heave up and down with her increasingly erratic breathing. There's a splattering of freckles across her chest, and before I can stop myself, I'm thinking about how it would feel if I could run my tongue from spot to spot. Fuck she's sexy, but she is also a dead woman. Not exactly my cup of tea. I take the shirt and smear a few drops of her blood across the fabric. I'll leave this in the back alley belonging to one of the scapegoats supplied. When they do go looking for the woman, the police will stumble across this shirt with her blood on it, and it'll be a clear indication that there was foul play. Of course, I don't want to leave it all up to the local police department. It would take months for them to find anything like this. Unfortunately, the department is not known for its quick and speedy turnaround time.

"Mmm, mm. Mmm, mm. Mmmmm."

I don't bother to stare at her anymore. Since she's been awake and discovered she isn't going to be getting out of the restraints, she's been trying to talk to me. It's not the first time someone has tried to entice me into taking the gag off, and it won't be the last.

I take the knife I used to cut her arm, and I break the chain from around her neck. I will need to plant this as well. Then finally, I reach my hand up into her hair and pull.

"MMMMMM!" She screams at the pain. The dramatics are getting old. I've pulled more strands out of a woman's head when I was fucking her from behind. I roll my eyes and put the few strands of her long brown hair into a clear Ziploc bag, ready to move on with the second part of the plan, framing someone who isn't my client.

I grab my coat and my phone, take a photo of her chained and gagged to the chair and send it off to my client through secure channels. He asks me if I've raped her, and if I do and cum inside of her, he will double my pay. I'm tempted to tell him to find someone else to do this as I won't be completing the hit. I do not fucking rape women. Kill them, sure, but rape is such an emotional crime. There's no fucking discipline, and what fun is it if the woman isn't clawing and begging you for more?

That just isn't my deal at all. I inform my client that he's shit out of luck and to never mention that to me again. The warning is taken seriously, and we make arrangements for the next step. I make my way to the location as directed by my client. The area is much nicer than where I picked up Bryn, but still, it isn't the best. I just can't understand how my client can be involved with someone of such meager means and yet can afford my services. As long as he completes his part of the deal and the money is in my account, I'm not going to ask any further questions. That's enough for me.

I make quick work of opening one of the side windows using the fire escape. It's the dead of night, and people are sleeping soundly. I listen for an animal; most times, it's the dog who almost blows my cover. Luckily, there's no dog to be seen. I drop the shirt under the radiator cover. I know people who go years without ever opening the radiator cover unless trying to hide something. The police know that trick too. It's where they find most of the drugs and firearms they confiscate from these apartments. They will have no problem finding the shirt.

I hold on to the necklace and hair, and when I have a better chance to get into the house, I will plant it. The shirt will be more than enough for now.

When I make it back to my spot, the woman is still trying to get me to talk to her. It seems like she isn't going to stop. I'm tempted to knock her out again, but I don't want to waste the supplies. I can just deal with it.

"Mmm, mm, mmmm."

All night long, the woman talks through her gag. What's strange about the whole thing is she isn't screaming, just talking. She doesn't even seem panicked, as if she's talking to a long-lost friend. The other strange thing is she never once looks away from me. She blinks when she needs, but she keeps her eyes trained on me. It's strange. Why would she do that? What is she trying to say?

For most of the next day, I keep myself busy working out and training. When I'm not doing that, I'm reading. They didn't pay me to feed her or let her go to the bathroom, so I don't. She can piss on herself for all I care. I have dealt with urine before. Shit as well. Nothing could come out of her orifices that I haven't had either sprayed on me or cleaned up. I listen as her voice starts to crack from the lack of water. She must be so dehydrated, but she never stops talking. By the second day, she is successfully driving me insane. I've had people torture me and be less effective than her.

My first rule is to never take the fucking gag off. Never talk to the mark, but right now, I will do anything to make sure she stops. I've run out of chloroform but do have a sedative I can give her, the problem is, it will stay in her system longer. A loose end that might cause the officials to start looking into other avenues than what the client wants. No, I can't use it. I don't want to risk it when I'm sure she's going to pass out soon anyway. If she doesn't, she will strip my sanity mumble by mumble.

Just wait her out. Just wait it out; she will be knocked out soon. I tell myself, and I swear I hear her answer through the gag.

It sounds like she said when she wakes up, she'll keep on talking.

"What do you want? Food? Water?" I stand in front of her, and she doesn't nod her head; she just keeps on talking.

"You know there's nothing you can say that's going to make me let you go. You know there is no one here to hear you scream." She doesn't nod her head; she just keeps talking.

"This is fucking futile, and you know it. There is nothing you can do to get out of this. Stop fucking mumbling." My voice raises slightly. I'm losing my grip on my self-control. I breathe out and look at the woman. Her eyes are glued to mine. Those same eyes that told me before there is more to her than I know. They are telling me now to take the gag off, that there's something she's saying I want to hear. Of course, that could be my psyche trying to protect me from the torture I'm going through.

At this point, I wish I hadn't already taken the money offered to keep her the extra three days. If I'd just killed her, then I wouldn't have to deal with this shit now.

I try to look away, but I can't. Fuck, I want to know what she's hiding behind those gorgeous big brown eyes. I feel my hand moving, and I force it back down to my side. I can't believe I'm even actually thinking about this. I've never broken this damn rule, and now some woman I don't know with pretty eyes and a pair of tits to die for is going to break that streak. How fucking weak is that?

My hands go up again, and instead of her getting

excited or looking toward my moving appendages, she keeps her eyes locked on mine.

Fuck it. No one will know. I have to figure out what the hell she is saying. I have to discover what secrets she's hiding behind those gorgeous eyes.

I rip the tape and ball gag out of her mouth. She closes her mouth for a second to stifle the burn of having the duct tape ripped off her skin

She looks back at me, and I get ready for the scream. I'm sure will come.

"You're being played. You just started a war, and they will kill you first."

MORE FROM RAE B. LAKE

Wings of Diablo MC
Wire
Archer
Clean
Cherry
Prez
Ryder
Ink
Roth
Mack
Storm
Dillon
Pope

Wings Of Diablo MC - New Orleans
Jameson
Yang

Spawns of Chaos MC

Shepard
Tex
Maino

Juric Crime Family
Sven's Mark

Eve's Fury MC
Becoming Vexx
Free
Riot

The Shop Series Books
His Georgia Peach
To Protect and Serve Donut Holes
On The Edge of Ecstasy
His Peach Sparkle

Royal Bastards MC
Death & Paradise

Standalones
Drunk Love
Saving Valentine

FOLLOW RAE EVERYWHERE!

FACEBOOK
READER GROUP
TWITTER
INSTAGRAM
GOODREADS
AMAZON
WEBSITE
BOOKBUB
NEWSLETTER

Made in the USA
Columbia, SC
29 April 2022